Also, by Marlene Morgan

FICTION

Sleeping with a Wall Street Banker
(Jake Logan, book 1)

COMING SOON

All Enemies Foreign and Domestic
(Jake Logan, book 3)

REVENGE I WILL HAVE

JAKE LOGAN # 2

MARLENE MORGAN

Copyright © 2023 Marlene Morgan.

All rights reserved. No part of this book may be used or reproduced by any means, graphic, electronic, or mechanical, including photocopying, recording, taping or by any information storage retrieval system without the written permission of the author except in the case of brief quotations embodied in critical articles and reviews.

This is a work of fiction. All of the characters, names, incidents, organizations, and dialogue in this novel are either the products of the author's imagination or are used fictitiously.

Archway Publishing books may be ordered through booksellers or by contacting:

Archway Publishing
1663 Liberty Drive
Bloomington, IN 47403
www.archwaypublishing.com
844-669-3957

Because of the dynamic nature of the Internet, any web addresses or links contained in this book may have changed since publication and may no longer be valid. The views expressed in this work are solely those of the author and do not necessarily reflect the views of the publisher, and the publisher hereby disclaims any responsibility for them.

Any people depicted in stock imagery provided by Getty Images are models, and such images are being used for illustrative purposes only.
Certain stock imagery © Getty Images.

ISBN: 978-1-6657-4290-0 (sc)
ISBN: 978-1-6657-4291-7 (hc)
ISBN: 978-1-6657-4292-4 (e)

Library of Congress Control Number: 2023907523

Print information available on the last page.

Archway Publishing rev. date: 06/27/2023

Life is a journey, and along the way, we lose those most precious to us. In loving memory of my father and sister. To Mom, I will always be thankful for your life and the life you gave me. To Daniel, the most important mark I will leave in this world is you. And to my husband, Michael, thank you for the story.

"Today is only one day in all the days that will ever be. But what will happen in all the other days that ever come can depend on what you do today. It's been that way all this year. It's been that way so many times. All of war is that way."

—*Ernest Hemingway*

CONTENTS

Prologue xiii

1 1
2 6
3 10
4 14
5 21
6 30
7 46
8 51
9 58
10 62
11 70
12 78
13 84
14 88
15 93
16 98
17 101
18 106
19 112
20 120
21 122
22 127
23 131

24	135
25	139
26	144
27	148
28	152
29	156
30	159
31	162
32	168
33	172
34	176
35	179
36	187
37	194
38	198
39	204
40	208
41	210
42	214
43	219
44	222
45	225
46	230
47	235
48	242
49	247
50	252
51	258
52	264
53	269

54	279
55	284
56	290
57	295

PROLOGUE

Greenwich, Connecticut

Alice walked the tree-lined pathway that followed the river through the heart of the park. The park was turning brown. An autumn gust blew, chilling the air and blowing the clouds and the trees. She was not cold; drawing close to the man sitting on the park bench sent warmth radiating through her body and her heart. "Dad!"

He reached out and held her hand. "Alice." The grass was crisp under their feet. She smiled and looked up at the clear blue sky. The trees towered over the park. Scurrying squirrels searched for food under bristles of wispy moss. Hand in hand, she and her father walked in and out of shady glades. "Alice, it's time to go." The peace of the morning was soothing. All around them, the leaves blew away in a final flight, dead yet beautiful as they danced.

She pulled her hand away. "Dad, not now. I must go back." She turned. Far in the distance, she heard her mother calling. When she turned back, her father was gone. She heard strange voices commingled with the dulcet tones of her mother's calls but could not understand what they were saying. Blurred images of faces peered down at her and then moved away, followed by darkness.

Throughout the past twenty-four hours and following emergency surgery to stem internal bleeding, her consciousness had faded momentarily, returning with scattered memories of her lifeless body being moved around on a bed. Every exhalation caused pain. Then she was left alone. She lay there trying to comprehend what was going on. "My name is

Alice … Alice Francis. Where am I? How did I get here? What's wrong with me? Why am I tied down?" Her mouth moved, but she could not hear a sound.

"Alice, can you hear me? You're in Greenwich Hospital. You have a knife wound."

Unable to raise her voice, Alice lay motionless as another nurse checked her IV drips, which seemed to be stuck into every vein. She was more aware during these periods of consciousness, but her clarity was met with a new pain. Her eyes watered.

Jessica! The knife! Pain! How long have I been lying here? Focus! I might hear something. The nurse, she tried to talk to me. Why is there so much commotion? Alice tried to raise her hand. *What's wrapped around me? Are the straps preventing me from moving? Why are my hands strapped to the sides of the bed? Jessica attacked me! Is it to keep me from getting out? This is crazy! I did nothing wrong! Hear me, please!* She willed her mouth to move, but no sound emerged.

I remember Jessica—or was it, Jess? She said she didn't plan to stab me. Yes! That's what Jess said. She told me she and Jessica wanted me to leave Jake of my own accord and that she hadn't come to Jake's house to harm me. She came to talk. She said I needed to learn a lesson, and that was why she stabbed me. She told me the lesson was simple. If a situation was explained to me, and a person made a simple request, I shouldn't disregard that request. Then she smiled at me. She didn't give me a chance to tell her I was leaving, that the car taking me to the airport was outside the house.

Concerned that Alice was becoming agitated, the nurse reached out to calm her. She stroked and gently squeezed her hand. "We had to put restraints in place while you were unconscious to prevent you from tearing out the tubes and IV drips." She looked up at the nurse administering medication via intravenous therapy. "Pauline, when you're finished, please page Dr. Milner, and tell him she's conscious. Alice, I'm Nurse Isabel. Can you hear me?"

Alice's eyes followed Dr. Milner as he entered the room without acknowledging the people sitting around the bed. He was followed by a second doctor. Her gaze was broken, and she raised her head slightly when her mother leaned over Annabel's ear.

"I'm guessing the doctor was napping in the next room to have appeared so quickly," her mother said, not bothering to whisper. "I hope his medical skills are better than his manners."

Alice's head dropped and turned toward the scratching sound the chair made when her mother pulled it so close it touched the bed. "Alice, Alice, talk to me, darling. Annabel and Jake are here."

"Please, Mrs. Francis, let us do our job," Dr. Milner said.

"Alice." She felt the warm touch of her mother's hand before her mother moved back to give the medical team access.

The doctor bent over Alice. "I'm Dr. Milner, and this is Dr. Kirk-Brown. Do you know your name?" She blinked when he shone a small flashlight into her eyes to check for autonomic responses.

Alice watched him as he reached for her chart. *I'm here*, she thought as the doctor discussed her case.

"Her tachycardia, diminished blood pressure, is a result of the hypovolemia, and the hypovolemia is more than likely a symptom of hemorrhaging," Dr. Milner said.

"We need to go back in and surgically repair the site of the hemorrhaging," Dr. Kirk-Brown replied. "Increasing the contractility of her heart muscle may buy her time."

"Isabel, introduce dopamine and noradrenaline to her IV drip," Dr. Milner said. "Pauline, I believe OR 1 and its team are ready to go. Notify them that we have an inbound patient."

Alice watched as other medical personnel entered the room. "Please?

What's happening? Where are you taking me?" her voice was barely audible.

Dr. Milner placed his hand on her shoulder. "You're bleeding internally, and we need to take you back to the OR."

Alice's mother, joined by Annabel, moved back to her bedside. Alice held her mother's hand, like she had done as a child. She looked at her mother and then at Annabel. "I'm sorry," she said, her voice quivering.

"You're sorry? For what?" Annabel asked.

"Please … let me finish. The time I lost with my family. I saw Dad. He's happy … and … waiting for me."

"We have to take Alice to the OR," Nurse Isabel said, stepping forward. "Nurse Pauline, please take the family to the waiting room."

Medics surrounded Alice's gurney as it emerged into the corridor. Jake looked at them holding the IV drips and then at Alice. "Honey!" He reached out to touch her hand. The orderlies kept moving, Jake's fingers barely reaching her arm. He followed her to the doors of OR 1.

"Sorry, sir," one of the orderlies said. The doors were closing.

Jake turned to leave but quickly turned back when he heard the doctor yell. "She's unresponsive! Crash team!"

Seconds later, the crash team pushed the doors open. Jake put his face against the shoulder-high glass windows.

"She's defibrillating!" the monitoring medic said. "Clear!"

Jake watched the medic move in with a defibrillator. Once the electric shock was delivered, the room fell silent, everyone waiting for a heartbeat.

"Clear!" More seconds passed. Another jolt. "Clear! I'm calling it. Time?"

A tear rolled down Jake's cheek as he turned and walked away.

Jake's thoughts turned to Alice's letter. It had been returned to him after the police questioned him. Yes, after its contents had been revealed to Alice's sister, Annabel. Idiots! They didn't need to cause further hurt to a grieving family, and I didn't need to read that shit. When did Alice write it? I guess when she was packing her bags to leave.

Having memorized every word, he reread the letter in his head, his thoughts focusing on one sentence. "You unleashed your psychotic ex-girlfriend on me."

Jake did not know what had been harder, facing Alice's family and explaining her death or facing the media and their ever-growing presence. On the eve of the funeral, he stood outside the funeral home for hours. The sun was setting, the days were getting shorter, and a fall breeze permeated the air. No matter how hard he tried, he couldn't summon the courage to go inside, not while the family was there and viewing was going on. Alice's family and friends loved her dearly. He was the outsider, and right or wrong he felt that they blamed him for her death. Alice was gone, and he was still there. He sensed in their face-to-face meetings that it had to be a failing on his part. If only she had not immigrated to America.

When the parking lot was empty, he moved his finger down the contacts in his phone until he reached the funeral director. Minutes later, the director let him inside. He removed thirty crisp fifty-pound notes from his wallet and slipped them to the funeral director's pocket. Jake was paying the man's overtime and for his private viewing.

The funeral parlor had done an awesome job. Alice looked beautiful. He moved closer to her casket and placed his hand atop hers. For twenty minutes, he stood at her side, emotion swelling in him. Tears rolled down his cheeks. Feeling his legs tremble, he pulled up a chair and put his hand back atop hers. She was the woman he was going to spend the rest of his life with. After procrastinating for so long, he had given her a ring, the promise of eternal love, only to have her pillaged from him. *It's all gone.* His eyes filled with unending liquid. Alice was intelligent as well as beautiful. She had stood by him when most women would have been long gone. Squeezing her hand, he cried, "I love you so much. I miss you. But most of all, I'm sorry you're gone—that I did not protect you." He let it all out. And as he did, his door to the dark opened. Jake rested his head on the casket, exhausted. He fell asleep.

Jake awoke in the earlier hours of the morning to the voice of the funeral director. "Sir, it's time to go."

Looking at his watch, he saw that he would have barely enough time to make it back to his hotel to change before the funeral.

The service was heart-wrenching. Jake was disliked and seen as the man who's convinced Alice to leave her family and move to the United States of America. In their mind, he was the reason Alice was dead. They were ignorant of the facts, and that fueled his anger. But bottom line, they were right. It was his fault she was gone. No matter how long he lived, he would never be able to escape that fact. It was another link in the heavy chain of guilt he carried over the women in his past.

Jake did not speak at the service. He sat quietly alone. He was completely empty and was relieved when the service ended. Jake retreated alone to his town car. The journey to Alice's final resting place. *And then,* he vowed, *the reckoning will begin.*

1

Naples, Florida

Jake Logan took a deep breath and looked around as he drove north on Route 41. "Gotta keep moving," he muttered. Sweat rolled down his brow. "Time-out. Clear my head and regroup. It's not safe to stay at my condo or any place for too long. Think, Jake!"

Exhausted from lack of sleep and from driving around in circles for the last two hours, he turned toward Imperial Square Plaza. He steered his black Ford F-150 into the parking lot adjacent to Jack's Bait Shack. He looked up at the red neon sign before glancing over his shoulder. A few cars were in the parking lot, as was a janitor, who appeared to have finished his shift. Otherwise, nothing looked out of place.

At the door to the restaurant, he glanced around again to make sure he had not missed anything. Then he entered the dark world of Jack's. The chairs were upside down on the tables, waiting for someone to clean the floors. The booths along the sides were empty.

"Jake, how can I help you?" asked the man behind the long, well-polished wooden counter.

"Hey, Murphy. Is the joint open?"

"Was the door locked?" Murphy asked, as he dried a beer mug.

Jake, a regular at the restaurant when he was in Naples, walked slowly to the bar. He looked up. "I guess not."

Jack's Bait Shack was a casual restaurant and, some would argue, *the* place to find the freshest seafood in Naples. Jake's fondness was for the thirty-five-inch, flat-screen televisions throughout the place, which played live football, baseball, basketball, and golf. However, the silence that surrounded him at seven in the morning informed him that all the TVs were off. He took a seat at the bar and studied the rows of liquor bottles in front of him, as well as the aquarium filled with water-dwelling plants and aquatic reptiles. Beer taps and glasses flanked the fish tank. Murphy had arranged everything perfectly.

"Dude, you look like shit!" Murphy said. "Coffee?"

Jake just stared at Murphy, thoughts churning in his head. *My fiancée, Alice, is dead. A dead man was found in the apartment of my ex-girlfriend, Jessica. And don't forget, Jessica murdered Alice. And the explosion. What the fuck was that about?* Instead of saying any of those things, Jake placed his order. "Make it a bourbon, neat."

Murphy placed a tumbler on the counter and reached for the bourbon bottle. Jake considered moving to one of the empty booths along the right, but he held his ground. Murphy was a veteran bartender who had seen and heard it all. If no reply was forthcoming, Jake could count on him to shut the fuck up.

A moment later, Jake pushed his empty glass to the side and stepped down from the stool. *Stop! Don't surrender.* The floor beneath him felt like it was seesawing. He rubbed his sleep-deprived eyes, stepped back, and grabbed the bar for support. His hand collided with the glass. It slid off the bar, plunking pitifully at his feet.

In front of him, the floor opened to a set of stairs that led to the basement. He turned to his right and saw an ascending set of stairs. His eyes moved farther right and followed an escalator that led to a black hole. He clung to the bar for a few moments, hallucinating. Then he ambled to one of the empty booths.

He turned back toward Murphy. "On second thought, I'll take that coffee. Black and keep it coming!" He slid into his seat, mumbling, "JessicaputafuckingknifeinAlice." The words fell from his mouth, the syllables indistinguishable.

Minutes later, Murphy put a pot of coffee on the table. "Sleep is what you need, Jake, not coffee."

Thank you, Captain Obvious. He raised the mug to his lips and sipped the hot coffee. Twenty minutes passed, and the caffeine had the desired result. He would and could not sleep. Whomever was responsible for the explosion at the cemetery had not in all likelihood had Alice's remains as the sole target. The coffee had cooled, and he had almost finished the pot when he heard vehicles enter the parking lot. He recognized the distinctive sound of a GMC Suburban and followed its murmur as it drove around back. His thoughts flashed back to three that morning. He had entered the ten-by-ten rental room at Naples Storage Units where he kept $1 million in cash, a med kit, several passports, prepaid cell phones, three SIG Sauer P226s, two AR-15s, three M4A1s, ten boxes of ammo, and several Daniel Winkler knives. He had removed a P226, an AR-15, a knife, and $50,000.

Jake had cradled the frame of the black, hard-anodized aluminum pistol, which sat in a holster at his lower back. The P226 had been designed for the US Army and was carried by Navy SEALs, Texas Rangers, and many other elite military and law enforcement professionals. It had earned its place among the highest-regarded production pistols. Jake moved his hand to its black polymer grip. He had boarded a flight to Florida the night of the funeral, and since then, he had been looking over his shoulder. What had made him think he would find sanctuary in Naples? The place had too many memories. He had taken what was necessary for survival from the storage unit. It was time to move the fuck on. Jake's attention was laser focused on a hushed conversation.

"Yes, a man fitting that description is in the restaurant." Murphy's voice was low but audible. He glimpsed into the entrance of the kitchen. The backside of Murphy was visible, and he could see the tip of a man's jacket. Murphy's body was obstructing a full view of the man. Jake heard a second voice. He assumed the men had entered through the back door and now occupied the kitchen area.

Jake put down his coffee cup and slid out of the booth. He turned to face the restaurant's front windows. His eyes swept the parking lot, before looking down at the running shoes he was wearing. He thought of the LALO Shadow tactical boots in his truck. "Fuck," he whispered, wishing he had changed into them. They would have given him the comfort of a stealthy approach. His running shoes would make noise on the parking lot's gravel. *I'll have to get my head in gear if I'm going to survive.*

He surveyed the parking lot a second time. *All clear,* Jake darted ahead, eyeing the kitchen doorway on his right. He slipped through the door. Standing outside Jack's front door, he took off his running shoes and lifted the P226 from its holster. He passed the first and second cars at an even pace and then ducked behind a Honda SUV, before sprinting to the fourth vehicle. He had counted five vehicles when he arrived that morning. His cover was scant, and there was quite a distance between the fourth and fifth cars. In a crouch, he moved between the randomly parked cars to reach his truck.

Again, his eyes swept the parking lot. Nothing. *Paranoid. Stop!* He glanced at the bulge in his pocket and pulled out his keys.

Climbing into his truck, his fingers found the ignition key. He searched the parking lot's entrance for an ambush. His eyes had darted back to the rearview mirror when a black Suburban pulled in behind him. He recognized the government license plates. Jake didn't move as he watched two discreetly armed men climb out of the SUV and approach, one on each side of his vehicle.

He tucked his P226 under his right thigh and kept his left hand in plain sight, careful not to make any sudden moves. The man on the left reached him, and he gently hit the window button with his elbow.

"What can I do for you?" Jake asked.

"Jake, the boys want me to bring you to JSOC for a meeting."

Jake slowly put his gun away. "BLT," he said, looking at Rob Dempsey. "You want me to follow you?"

"Ours if you don't mind."

Jake didn't talk to the men during the 174.4-mile drive to MacDill Air Force Base. He and BLT had a lot to catch up on, but he didn't know the other man, who was driving the Suburban. *These men have their orders to escort me to JSOC.* He adjusted his head's position on the headrest. His fight was not with Joint Services Operations Command (JSOC) or the two men. He touched his P226 and smiled. *Do they realize I let them take me? Lead the way, BLT. This is going to be an interesting meeting.* Jake closed his eyes for some much-needed rest.

2

Paris, France

"Jessica, stop fucking partying," Jess said to the voice in her head. "The drumming is hurting my head. Fuck! Who starts partying at seven in the morning? Are you crazy? Stop! What did you swallow last night? I can't see."

"Madam, are you OK?" the flight attendant asked.

"I'm not ... I can't spend the rest of my life incarcerated. Fuck you, Jessica. Stop! I must get a grip. Someone will recognize me," Jess muttered under her breath. Without turning to face the flight attendant, she said, "I'm good. Still waking up." When she thought the flight attendant had moved away, Jess tried to open her eyes, but the sunlight piercing the airplane windows forced them closed again. Easing herself up and out of her seat, she used the rows of seats as a guide as she made her way off the airplane.

Out of direct sunlight, her vision was blurred. The air was heavy and smelled like the sea of random faces that flowed down the hallways to their destinations. "I need help. No, think! I need to be careful, not risk drawing attention," Jess said, lowering her voice. "Follow the crowd."

"Next!" the immigration officer shouted.

Passport in hand, Jess slowly put one foot in front of the other. She held her head straight and followed the sound of his young voice. "Hello," she said, handing the immigration officer her passport. "Sir, can a partially sighted girl ask for your patience?" She ran her fingers through her short, dark hair and subtly set her lips into a pout. Minutes later, Jess cleared immigration and walked toward the baggage claim.

In the airport lounge, a cacophony of noises hit her. She heard the voices of the young and old. Their tones were either subdued with the anticipation of separation or excited to be going on a journey. She heard suitcases being dropped onto conveyer belts and happy greetings from the ground staff. In the background, she heard music and the tinkle of sculptured water features. The sound of airplanes taking off and landing on the tarmac outside periodically punctuated the commotion.

"Fuck, this place looks more like a shopping mall than anything even I could have imagined," Jess said.

The woman to her right gave her a look and then turned away.

As Jess's headache subsided, her vision gradually became clear. She gazed up at the clock and the two glass elevators leading to an upper floor, which appeared to be a food court. In the middle of several large open areas were green fabric-covered seats. The air was cool, permeated with the faint aroma of food wafting in from the restaurants. The floor tiles gleamed a silvery color, and people were milling around everywhere. She continued forward, carrying her purse but claimed no luggage. Her steps on those sleek, silvery tiles were trembling, but she had to move forward; there was no turning back.

Where are we going? Jessica asked.

"We?" Jess replied to the voice in her head. "Let's be clear. Your therapist, Bitch Beth, said I was an alter ego you created to cope with some trauma you experienced in early childhood. Fuck her! I'm no alter ego, but we both know what you did to your little sister, Gemma."

Stop blaming me. Gemma was an accident. How many times do I have to say I'm sorry? You blamed me, but it wasn't my fault.

"Why would I care?" Jess asked. "I used Gemma's image and identity to leave New York undetected and then let you nuke her so you could keep your dirty secret. Gemma asked too many fucking questions. Bitch Beth didn't meet Gemma, which is a shame. So many of her questions would have been answered."

Please be fair, Jess!

"Shut the fuck up. Bitch Beth said you and I have our own way of viewing and relating to the world. That was the only truth that came out of that bitch's mouth. Did you say something, Jessica? I haven't forgotten you were working with Bitch Beth to nuke me. I'm in charge. Fuck your soft ass. We're not taking a limo. I won't risk going to the state penitentiary. We'll mingle, get lost in the crowd. Until I say otherwise, we're taking public transit."

Jess hastened to the queue for the Roissybus. The sign on the post stated that buses ran from Charles de Gaulle Airport to the center of Paris. She noted the tickets cost 11.25€ one way and that she could buy them on the bus. She reached into her purse for some euros. "How long will it take to reach Paris?" she asked the bus driver.

"Up to an hour," he replied with a strong Parisian accent. "We terminate in the Opéra area, Mademoiselle."

"Merci beaucoup," Jess said, smiling as she stepped onto the bus.

The Roissybus traveled adjacent to the Seine River in the north of the country toward the center of Paris. The city's skyline was visible for miles in all directions. Jess beamed like a child when the bus passed the Eiffel Tower. "It's fucking amazing! Look, Jessica, that's Notre Dame Cathedral, and there's the Sainte-Chapelle. Fucking amazing!" She lowered her voice when she noticed a little girl staring at her.

The bus eventually arrived at the terminal in the Opéra area and parked in the assigned slot for arrivals from Charles de Gaulle Airport.

"Welcome to Paris," the driver said over the loudspeaker. "Please wait outside the bus for your stowed luggage." He repeated the message in French.

Jess stood up quickly when she heard the door release with a soft hiss. She was the second person to descend the steps. Despite having visited Paris many times, she was absorbed by the gorgeous monument of the Palais Garnier Opéra House and the surrounding area, with its cafés, luxury boutiques, theaters, and restaurants.

Her smile turned to a scowl. "Jessica spent the entire fucking time in the Louvre. That selfish bitch prevented me from basking in the majesty of Paris. Hooray! Jessica's fucking phony art career is done. Fuck! We almost starved to death because she couldn't let it go," she muttered.

Jess turned to face the Ritz Hotel. The man who'd brought her to Paris and was paying the bill for the Ritz would not have helped her, and they would not be meeting if he didn't covet what she could deliver. She wouldn't keep him waiting any longer. Jess walked toward the Ritz. All she had were the clothes on her back and the $30,000 in her purse. Her eyes moved down to her gray Ralph Lauren (RL) pullover, her blue color-blocked RL jersey leggings, and the RL sneakers she had worn when she left New York. *Not for much longer. My luck is about to change.*

3

New York

"Bourbon?" asked Milton, offering his guest a drink. "I don't drink," replied the man, his dark eyebrows accentuating his oval face and nomadic nose. "I thought you'd know that."

Milton smiled as he poured himself three fingers of bourbon. Ha! Abdel, for all intents and purposes, you're a ghost, an assassin—a man who travels wherever he wants, whenever he wants. Let's talk about why you're here."

"You know why I'm here."

"Of course, I do—at the behest of Asyd Omar Batdadi.

Abdel nodded his head.

"I told your superior that Jessica would take the flight to Paris. Trust me—a meeting is scheduled at the Ritz, Paris. I don't see the justification for you to be here. All you need to do is hold up your end of the bargain."

Milton's thoughts turned to that night, decades ago at the art gallery. He had been a guest, and Jessica Brooks had been the host. Her presence had filled the room as she meandered from guest to guest. When he looked

Jessica's way, her blue eyes with flecks of silver would beg you to engage. Milton had been warned she was a gold digger. *So, what?* The people in the room could hardly be described as philanthropists.

He whispered, "I'll owe her forever for the wealth she has brought me." Milton sighed.

To this day Milton did not know why she had befriended him. It certainly wasn't for sex. Twenty pounds overweight and fifteen years her senior, he combed his fingers through his head of thick, graying hair. The years had not been kind to him. When he looked in the mirror, he thought, *I'm getting too old for this*. Nothing but the promises he had made mattered now. Two days ago, he had expertly altered Jessica's passport and driver's license.

Milton had made a substantial living for himself dealing in the purchase, sale, and trade of forged art. He was cutthroat in business acumen and had an appetite for the best of everything. He made his living by duplicity.

"I have learned that, in my line of work, there can be no loose ends and there's no substitute for meeting face-to-face," said Abdel.

"That said"—Milton gulped the remainder of his bourbon—"you can't come to my home uninvited. "An uneasiness creeped over him, but he was determined to exude confidence.

"The circumstances of this arrangement are, if you don't mind me saying, quite unusual."

"Be that as it may, Asyd Omar Batdadi, is the only reason I agreed to meet you—because of our long-standing business relationship. So, unless you have something else to say, please confirm your assets are in place and leave."

"I'd like you to tell me what and how the woman, Jessica, will deliver."

"Like I said, my relationship is with your superior."

"He would like to go over the small details."

"He would? Have him reach out to me. We have much to discuss once he has held up his side of the bargain."

Milton poured three more fingers of bourbon, emptying the bottle. He took a long sip of bourbon. He could not play this man. All he could do was stick to the plan and pray Jessica delivered. If she did, he would have his revenge and become a very wealthy man. "Now if there is nothing else?"

"Actually, there is," said the assassin. His hand moved toward the inside of his Jacket.

Milton felt the warm wetness between his crossed legs. "All I want to know is that your team is in place and ready to go."

Abdel held his hand toward Milton. "Ten million, on top of which you'll be paid three times your normal fee and a bonus of twenty million once the operation has been successfully completed."

Milton smiled. "If you are successful, the Americans will leave no stone unturned and … well, there's no place they can't reach."

"You have your offer. Take it. But accept the consequences if you don't deliver." Abdel smiled as he turned and left Milton's Upper Eastside apartment.

Milton had dreamed about an opportunity like this for years. He opened another bottle of bourbon. Forgery, make-believe, that was where Milton excelled in his profession. It was astounding, especially for someone whose prospects in life had been dire. His single-parent father had abandoned him as a boy to a New York orphanage. There he was, starved, beaten, and made to perform inconceivable sexual acts. It was there Milton had learned his trade and the value of information, in the houses of the powerful men who invited him in under the guise of charity.

Milton's break had come when he'd traded a doctored passport he'd worked on for weeks for money the likes of which he had never seen. Thereafter, he'd made money creating and selling counterfeit driver licenses. Then he'd added fake electric bills, phone bills, and other paperwork that documented a person's life. Milton was good at it too—a master. His specialty wasn't just creating the documents; he made them look worn. For a price he'd create a new identity.

His first real client had been an old pal from junior high school, an art dealer who had accidentally damaged a painting. Milton had swept in and created an undetectable copy. Suffice it to say, he retained the original and sold it on the black market for a million plus. From then, Milton found a real market for his talents in the art world.

After Abdel had left, he thought, *I underestimated Asyd Omar Batdadi.* But for now, that did not matter. What mattered was that the president of Corporate Finance, HK Bank, Clint Morris had come into his just desserts. The fact that the Wall Street "fat cat" had forced appalling acts on Milton decades earlier made his reason for killing the man and partnering with a terrorist all too personal. He'd followed him for years and finally was in a position to seek his revenge.

4

FORT BRAGG, NORTH CAROLINA

Six hours after Jake left Jack's, he sat in the conference room on the seventh floor of JSOC headquarters in Fort Bragg. Facing him across the table were the Navy SEALs he had worked with on his last mission—Daniel "Dan" Benjamin; Dale Emmert, aka "Em-Dog"; and BLT. Dan, formerly an extreme athlete, had completed ultramarathons on every continent in record time. Em-Dog was six foot six and as lanky as a former Division 1 basketball player but as strong as a bison. He had a great sense of humor and a big smile that hid an astute, cold, calculating operator. BLT had been so named because, during dinner one night, a man wielding a knife had broken into his house on Chicago's South Side. When BLT asked him to put the knife down and leave if he valued his life, the man drew a gun and attempted to pull the trigger. BLT shot the man in the chest while biting into his BLT sandwich.

"Enjoying your retirement?" Em-Dog asked.

"Until six hours ago," Jake said, "when I spotted BLT in my rearview."

"Bullshit!" BLT said.

Alex Roigin, the senior enlisted advisor, intervened in the tense reunion when he entered the room, pulled off his jacket, and draped it over the chair at the head of the table. A small man of slender build and mouse brown hair, he blew out a long sigh. "Gentlemen," he said, taking a moment to adjust his tie, "we would all like to extend our condolences."

Jake nodded. "Thank you."

"We understand your ex-girlfriend, Jessica Brooks—"

"Some would say girlfriend," BLT said, interrupting Alex.

"What the fuck?" Jake said, turning to him. "You have no idea. Fuck you, asshole!" "BLT!" Alex raised his hand. "Jessica Brooks is a fugitive and, as of yesterday, is on JSOC's most-wanted list."

"And what?" Jake asked. "Why is JSOC concerned with Jessica? Is ISIS not tasking enough? What do you want from me?"

"Well," Alex replied, "now you have a decision to make."

"And what's that?"

"Simple—work for us or not."

"Why and how exactly would I work for you?"

Alex glanced at the other men around the table before continuing. "Doing exactly what you want to do, what you were trained to do—eliminate terror."

Jake pushed his chair back as Alex's words sank in. Whatever they believed he'd done or not done, they all wanted the same outcome. *Eliminate all enemies foreign and domestic.* His thoughts returned to Alice's letter.

Jake looked up to see the others around the table staring at him. "Alice wrote a letter, the contents of which are not important for this meeting," he said. "Suffice it to say, Alice's family's perception of me, right or wrong, ended in a standoff. I did not sit with Alice's family in the Lincoln Town Car that traveled behind the hearse. I was traveling in the third car."

"Who were the passengers in other cars?" Em-Dog asked.

"The first car was carrying Alice's mother, her younger sister, Annabel, and her husband. In the second car, Alice's older sister, Charlotte,

Charlotte's husband, and their children. From her house in Langley Park, England—"

"Alice's house," Em-Dog said.

"Yes!" Jake replied, his impatience with Em-Dog seeping out. "St. George's Church, where the funeral service was held, is a few minutes' walk from her house. The funeral procession drove by and stopped for two minutes as a mark of respect. The cars turned onto Langley High Street and then turned left at the cemetery five minutes later. The hearse and the two lead cars pulled to a stop in front of the church adjacent to the caretaker's cottage. I had my driver stop about nine feet back. We'd been stationary for less than a minute when a white van with 'Langley Park Cemetery Caretaker' on its side pulled in next to where the hearse was parked."

"Why stop nine feet back?" Dan asked.

Jake cast his eyes to the table and squeezed his thighs with his hands. The sound of irritable breathing was the only noise in the otherwise silent room. He looked up, straightening his shoulders. "I decided to keep my distance to avoid any discomfort to the family. A brown-skinned man with short, curly black hair appeared briefly in my line of sight." Jake shook his head. "Those eyes, that piercing stare—not a cemetery caretaker. They were the eyes of death! I've seen that look before in Iraq, Afghanistan, and Libya.

"I kicked open the car door, leapt out, and sprinted to the family cars. 'Get out of the car!' I yelled. 'Get out of the fucking car! Bomb!' I grabbed the children, turned, and ran for cover.

"The ground moved violently and whipsawed under my feet. The concussive force of the explosion propelled the children and me into the air. We hit the dirt thirty feet away. I didn't know whether the people in the family cars were alive or dead or whether we would all die there. I placed my body on top of the children to protect them from flying debris. The white van was obliterated, and the hearse and the family cars exploded. There was nothing I could do for the other family members.

"What was left of the man inside the van, Alice's body, Alice's mother, her sister, Annabel, and Annabel's husband was no longer recognizable. The bodies of her sister, Charlotte, and her husband were lying outside the caretaker's cottage, bloody, battered, and unconscious. The drivers of the Town Cars didn't wake up. They were just doing their job."

"We understand that Jessica is mentally ill," said Alex.

Jake nodded. "That's an understatement. She was diagnosed with dissociative identity disorder or DID. Her psychiatrist, Bethany A. Jones, said it was a mental illness that involved her experiencing at least two clear identities. The other identity is called Jess. Jones may have discovered a third identity, Gemma. Jones was working with another therapist, Steve Dunhill, to achieve a more peaceful coexistence between Jessica and Jess."

"Dunhill is the man found dead in Jessica's apartment, right?" Dan asked.

"Yes. Jess was becoming stronger and taking over Jessica. Jess is probably the controlling force now. I can see how Jessica's mental illness could have resulted in Dunhill's murder."

"From what I understand, he was frustrated that Jessica was not his patient and went to Jessica's apartment uninvited," said Alex. "Dunhill was not impressed that Jones was looking for an expert in DID to treat Jessica. His plan was to finagle his way to fame and higher pay. He didn't want to give up the case."

Jake nodded. "Yes, Jess would have felt threatened by his presence. Alice's murder was the result of pure jealousy and an attempt to get Alice out of the way to rekindle her relationship with me. However, the explosion at the cemetery was not mental illness at play."

"I agree. And that's where we come in," said Alex. "Our intelligence confirmed the explosion was a terrorist act and that, in all likelihood, you were the target. We have motive. The lingering question is, why now?"

A gnawing feeling radiated from his guts. Jake pivoted and directly faced Alex as he opened a file and tossed a photo across the table. "Do you recognize this man?"

Jake leaned forward and peered at the photo. "The Bat was responsible for the Langley Park Cemetery bomb?"

"Yes, but there's more. We intercepted several communications between the Bat, Jessica, and a third party."

"Don't you mean Jess? Jessica isn't a terrorist."

"Jess, Jessica, who gives a fuck? The forensic evidence team confirmed the bomb was the work of the Bat, and we need to know why and how they are connected."

Jake put his hand on his left shoulder and thought about the scar beneath his sweatshirt. The vision of Kandahar came roaring back. He had joined the Navy SEALs straight out of college. He had taken time out in his fourth year of service to heal, not physically but psychologically, from a bullet that should have taken his life. As he rubbed his shoulder, his thoughts drifted back to the members of his Navy SEAL team and the two marines who had been killed that day in Afghanistan.

Relatively speaking, the op should have been straightforward. When the target exited the building, they were to pursue and take him alive.

Jake had thumbed his approval at Mac's words. "Let's catch and cage the Bat." He was sitting in an armored Humvee with Dan, Mac, BLT, Em-Dog, and Grace, a CIA operative. She had been assigned to the team for the op. She was not her usual focused self. Instead, she was distracted and talking about how her eighteen-month career with the CIA had stagnated.

Mac was irritated by the conversation and told her to concentrate on the task at hand. Jake was not sure how he could deliver, but he promised to discuss her participating in fieldwork later. She was always complaining that equality didn't apply to women in combat positions. Distracted or not, he thought she understood her role in the op. Grace's task was to identify the target, Asyd Omar Batdadi, aka "the Bat," and keep an eye out for enemy combatants. She had seen the Bat's "new" face in person. He had undergone plastic surgery recently, rendering the photographs in the CIA database unreliable. It did not sound like she appreciated the vitality of her role.

Jake left her in the Humvee and took up his position. He heard her mumble in his earpiece that she was done serving as the team's personal assistant. Then she stopped complaining and signaled that the Bat was on the move. At that point, they all adopted radio silence.

When they caught and neutralized the Bat but couldn't contact Grace, alarm bells sounded. Her response eventually came through their earpieces in the form of screams of torture. Using the tracking device attached to her person, they located and, ultimately, paid a high price to rescue Grace from her captors. Mac, a Navy SEAL, and two marines were killed.

Grace had been instructed to hold her location until the team made contact. Her part in the op ended when she identified the Bat.

She had no means to inform us that she had identified a decoy. But still, what the fuck was she doing pursuing the Bat? She had her orders. Fuck! She wanted to join the team in the field, so fuck her.

At a subsequent investigation, Grace conceded that, had she been focused, she would not have mistaken the decoy for the Bat. She didn't defend herself because her capabilities, training, and firm instructions were against her following the Bat.

Navy SEALs are heroes, and heroes are tough, Jake thought. But his lingering memories, his personal conflict, tormented him. Deep inside his core, he felt the loss of Mac and the marines, and he cried internally.

I planned to marry Grace. Fuckin' bitch! When the CIA terminated her, she terminated me while I was lying in a hospital bed. The Navy SEALs psychologist had tried to help him work through the lingering issues. But Jake had chosen to the leave SEALs for a career as a Wall Street banker and bury his pain instead.

He thought about his relationship with Jessica. *Why? Why didn't I go for a clean break? Any sane man would've gotten the fuck out. Now Alice is dead because of me. I'm screwed up. But if I walk away from JSOC again, Jessica's wrongdoing, like most bad acts, goes unpunished. This isn't one of those times ... No! Revenge I'll have.*

"Jake! Jake!" Alex said, yanking him back to the present. "We need to evaluate you and get you back in the field."

5

Paris

Jessica stared at her short brunette hair. She looked nothing like her former self. "Jess! She made me look like Gemma to escape the manhunt for her." Her voice quivered, and tears swelled in her eyes. *Jess is scared and won't tolerate any margin for error,* she thought.

She diverted her eyes from the mirror and wiped the tears falling down her cheeks. She had always been a blue-eyed, blond babe. She was scared Jake would not want her now. Panic rushed through Jessica. She had to explain everything to him. She had not killed Alice or Steve. Jess was responsible, not her. She had blackouts and had no memory of Jess's crazy acts. She would make Jake understand. She had to.

She turned to the computer sitting on the desk in the corner of the hotel room. "I'll email Jake. If I do it now, Jess won't know," she whispered as she sat down. "I think she has memory loss. I'll be OK. He'll fix this problem."

She pulled her hands away from the keyboard when the doorbell rang. She got up and opened the door. Two waiters stood in the hall with food trolleys. She stepped to one side so they could wheel them into the room and watched as they put a crisp, white tablecloth on the table and set it for breakfast. "Thank you," she said as the waiters left. When the door closed, she hastened over to the table.

"Jess has ordered everything on the menu," she said as she stared at the table, her eyes gleaming at the yogurts, seasonal fruit, and oatmeal cooked with milk and served with berries. She lifted a domed silver cover to reveal smoked salmon and scrambled eggs. Under another dome was fried eggs, and under another was eggs Benedict. She moved down the table and lifted another dome, her nose twitching at the aromas of bacon and grilled tomatoes. From the end of the table, the aroma of freshly baked bread, toast, and percolated coffee intermingled with the smell of bacon.

Jessica sat at the breakfast table and poured a glass of freshly squeezed orange juice. She pulled a plate with pancakes oozing with butter toward her. She closed her eyes, her mouth watering as she poured hot maple syrup over them. Jessica ate slowly, luxuriating over each item. She finished the last bite of toast and bacon and had another cup of coffee.

"Fuck!" She put the cup down. "I didn't email Jake."

She moved from the breakfast table to the computer, but she was distracted once again when she saw all the news stories related to Jess's escape from New York. *Jess was lucky, that's for sure.* The news reports were full of facts but included no real details on the hunt, beyond the painfully obvious—checkpoints, house-to-house searches, watching airports and bus and train stations, and asking the public for help. Pictures of her as a blond were all over the web. Jessica thought that, if she survived this mess, if Jake rescued her, she'd do something about her aging, wrinkled face. She'd been in denial for too long about those cracks, her makeup no longer able to cover them. A facelift, a pin and tuck here and there. She pulled at her neck and turned sideways to assess her belly fat. She pouted. "Yes, I'll make myself young and fresh for Jake."

Also posted all over the web was her history, how she had dreamed of owning an art gallery and how, in addition to selling art made by others, she had produced a few pieces of her own. She smiled until she read a paragraph that said her life and career had been going well until she had persuaded a colleague to let her hold an exhibition that exclusively carried art by Luke Epstein, an up-and-coming artist and her ex-lover. The article noted that her career had pivoted when a critic and several reviewers had made comments on Luke's artwork that she did not like and that she had not been objective.

Too late now, she thought. She should've been mature and accepted that was the way the art world worked. She'd wanted to show her support for Luke. *I was stupid to remove anyone who had spoken unfavorably about Luke's work from my mailing list*, she thought, tears forming in her eyes. *I can see that now.*

She wiped her face and continued reading. The reporter had written that one of the reviewers, Luke's ex-girlfriend, had argued with her, criticizing her lack of objectivity. The argument had become heated, and Jessica had informed the woman she was no longer welcome in her gallery. *Fucking bitch!*

The article finished by stating that Jessica had not realized her error in judgment until the next morning's reviews. Not only were Luke's reviews poor, but one of the reviewers had also accused Jessica of attempting to control her own press. The article said she had forgotten the most basic rule—the press always had the last word. Jessica thought about how Luke's bitch ex-girlfriend had spread the word to other critics. She had underestimated their influence. They had the power to destroy her, and they had done just that, leaving her broke, pregnant, and alone. "Fucking Luke didn't stay around to help me pick up the pieces," she said, tears rolling down her face.

Another article said she suffered from dissociative identity disorder (previously known as multiple personality disorder). The article stated the

DID stemmed from a trauma experienced in her childhood. The dissociative aspect was a coping mechanism she used to dissociate herself from a situation that was too traumatic or painful to assimilate with her conscious self. She found the article interesting and continued reading. She thought Jess was right about their split identities. The article explained how Jess continually had power over her behavior, and highly distinct memory variations fluctuated with her split personality. The article concluded by stating that, when Jess's personality revealed itself and controlled her behavior and thoughts, it was called "switching," and the switch could take anywhere from seconds to minutes to *days*. Beth had not explained her condition in simple terms like the article had.

She looked to see who had written it. Perhaps she could have a therapy session with the author. She saw the name Edward Bernstein of the *Wall Street Journal*. "Everybody knows. Fuck you, Jake. You told them about our private shit. I have no chance of owning an art gallery now, no chance. I'm finished."

One shock piled atop another when Jessica read that the enormous machinery of the United States military intelligence, the CIA, and the NSA was searching for her. She had made it onto their most-wanted list. Her face turned white, and a wave of nausea washed over her. "Jake, please come. I need you." Tears rolled down her cheeks as her fingers moved to the keyboard of her MacBook.

> Jake,
> I'm sorry about Alice. She could never be my friend, but I did not want her dead, and I didn't kill her. Jess murdered Alice because she would not leave. She also murdered Steve because he was working with Beth to help me control Jess. You must help me. If Jess finds out I'm emailing you, she'll kill what's left of me.

Holy cow! I saw the breaking news. There was an explosion at Alice's funeral. I don't know how it happened! I swear to God it had nothing to do with me. Jess doesn't have the power to do that. No, she can't do that! You can't blame us for that mess. Wait! Fuck! Did she do that? Jess has new friends. You must believe me. I didn't know. Give me a chance. I'll talk to Jess. I promise! But understand she keeps her cards close to her chest. I'll try. OMG! Are you even still alive? Who will take care of me?

I'm not that cute blond you fell in love with. Jess made me look like Gemma. At times, you were a total waste of space, but we don't need to argue. Jess has new friends, and they are taking care of me far better than you ever did, but we know that's because you can't ever make an effort. Babies, a nice house, and a generous allowance were all I wanted and all I still want. You were so mean, but that is in the past now. Jess has shown her reach if you are not nice to me. We're staying at the Ritz in Paris, and you should have seen the breakfast Jess ordered. Amazing!

Later today we're meeting Jess's friend. I'm excited because he's bringing a whole wardrobe of clothes and accessories. I still have feelings for you and have not forgotten my frozen eggs. We still have a future once you explain to the police that I'm not responsible for Jess's actions.

I need your help. Will you come? I have chest pains and can't control Jess by myself. Will you come?
All my love,
Jessica

What the fuck did you do? Jess demanded after Jessica sent the email.

"Nothing!"

Stupid bitch! What did you do?

Jessica jumped when the phone rang.

Don't pick up! We must get the fuck out.

Jessica grabbed her wallet and walked out of the room.

Stupid, you can't take the elevator. Take the stairs.

When Jessica emerged in the lobby, she glanced at the woman standing at the reception desk dressed in a long black dress and a blue silk burka that covered her head and chest and fell to her knees. She was facing Jessica but appeared to be looking for something in her purse. "My purse—I forgot my purse," said Jessica.

Fuck the purse. Get the fuck out.

As Jessica walked through the door, the woman placed her bag over her shoulder and followed Jessica out of the hotel.

Jessica smiled at the tattooed, beanie-wearing man, who warmly welcomed her when she entered a Bohemian café. The narrow entrance at the front gave way to a sober and elegant back room dominated by a big leather sofa and a pinball machine. Her eyes dropped to the star-patterned tiled floor as she settled herself into one of the painted white booths.

Is this the best you can do? Jess asked.

Jessica hated Jess's nagging voice in her head. "Please go away. You'll draw attention to me. I can't keep running like this. I'm tired, and I want to go home."

Fuck you! We were staying at the Ritz, but you couldn't simply enjoy it or say thank you. I don't care what you want. You'll extend me some courtesy, and you can start by telling me what you did on that computer.

"Jess, please! You're hurting my head. I swear I didn't do anything! You overreacted. Please go away. I can take it from here. I'll find somewhere safe for us to stay. This isn't a good place to make a scene. Where did you put the phone?"

Jessica looked around the café, her head finally moving down to the menu. "Don't these people drink anything other than coffee?" She moaned. She needed something to steady her nerves. If she stayed calm, Jess would think she was coping and would remain dormant. "What about the email I sent to Jake?" she whispered fearfully. She gripped her tummy when she thought about the backlash Jess would unleash. She turned the menu over in search of alcohol.

When the waiter approached, she ordered a half bottle of red wine without looking up. Minutes later, the waiter returned with it, and Jessica thanked him. She poured her glass half full and set the remainder of the bottle on the table. The first and second sips hit her in the far reaches of her inner being, in places she thought were long dead. She thought about Bernstein's article. It referred to a trauma suffered in early childhood. "Gemma," she whispered. "I'm sorry, Gemma, so sorry."

In her imagination, Jessica's outstretched arm touched her baby sister. "You were only seven years old. I should have protected you, told Mom. It's all my fault." Jessica pulled a tissue from her pocket and wiped the tears falling from her eyes. She sipped the wine, allowing the intoxication to pull her back in time.

Dad, why are you climbing into Gemma's bed? Why are your hands touching and cuddling her?

"You're special," he says to her. He smiles, and she is at ease. I'm not sleeping. Why am I not special? Naked, he doesn't look like Dad. I don't think I should see Dad naked. Mom always closed the bedroom door, but I got used to his naked body and Gemma giggling. Gemma and Dad in bed doesn't seem right to me.

Jessica poured the remainder of the wine into her glass. She closed her eyes. *The river is calm. Gemma sits with me. We like playing in the river. The sky is blue, and I feel the warm summer sun on my skin. Today is the day I decided to ask Gemma what she and Dad do when he's in her bed. She says it's their secret. I threatened to tell Mom. She pushes me, and I push her back. Gemma falls into the water.*

"It was an accident! I didn't mean for her to fall. Please, Mom, please! It's the truth. I'm sorry!"

Eyes still closed; Jessica drank the remainder of the wine. She wiped her tears with the back of her hand, thinking back to the night after Gemma drowned.

Dad gently moves the duvet and slides his naked body into my bed. He says he doesn't blame me for Gemma. I'm approaching my ninth birthday, two days to go. He explores and fondles my body. "We're playing," he says. It hurts when his toy plays with mine. I don't remember Gemma crying when he played with her, but I cry. Dad said he would never speak to me again if I did not let him play inside me.

Jessica reached for the wine bottle and realized it was empty. She wiped her tears and caught the waiter's attention, ordering another half bottle.

Would that trauma be enough for you, Bernstein? My dad sexually abused me until I went to high school. I was always uncomfortable with his idea of playing, but he said he loved me and that he and Mom loved Gemma. By playing together, he meant sexually abusing me. Really! That was the only way we could make right what had happened to Gemma. Mom! I wanted to tell you, but you wouldn't listen. You didn't want to know Dad's secret. Yes! My secret. No! It was Dad's secret, your secret.

"Fuck you, and fuck Jake."

She thought about how happy the house was after her parents divorced. Then her dad called and said he missed their sexual relations. She told her mom. At first, she had called Jessica a liar. Then she'd asked why Jessica hadn't told her when it was happening. From then on, their relationship was strained. Jessica didn't understand. She tried but could not make sense of the abuse or her mom's reaction. Her dad said it was Jessica's fault. Jessica pulled another tissue from her pocket and tried to control the tears falling down her face.

The woman wearing the blue burka entered the café and approached her table. "Is anybody siting here?" the woman asked. "Don't look up. You were told to wait at the Ritz."

Jessica froze.

6

Jake winced as he held an ice pack to his jaw. He had taken two punches to the face. He knew the blows had been delivered purposely, and BLT walking over to assess the damage did not improve the mood in the one-way-mirrored training room. The blond-haired, blue-eyed thirty-six-old had been his friend for over ten years.

"Sorry, Jake," BLT said, patting him on the back. "You're doing well. Didn't think you would last this long. Just doing my job."

"Really? Why do I find that hard to believe?" Jake forced a smile. He recognized BLT's strategy and thought it was a painful way to keep him on his toes. "Fuck! When you're done with me, I won't be fit for the field." He suppressed an urge to express his anger further.

Though BLT was the one throwing the punches, he was not the only man in the room. Jake's body ached, but this assessment was geared to one purpose—to see if he still had the discipline over his mind and body to react to unpredictable threats. He thought he was overthinking the assessment, allowing his old relationship with BLT to lead him to expect a fair fight. There was no such thing as a fair fight. His training was flooding back. If he fought fair, the fight would end because the dirty fuck would always win.

Jake was trained in muay Thai, a combat sport from Thailand that used stand-up striking along with various clinching techniques. His mind focused on his physical and mental discipline, which included combat on his shins, known as "the art of eight limbs," because it was characterized by the combined use of fists, elbows, knees, and shins. When associated with good physical preparation, it made him very efficient as a full-contact fighter.

Jake sensed movement on his left and spun away from it, ducking under the tire iron BLT swung toward his chest. As he continued his rotation, he brought up his right arm and knocked BLT's hand away, grabbing his wrist with his left hand and then lunging forward into BLT's chest. The force sent BLT backward toward the floor. BLT pushed his leg and brought Jake down with him as he thrust a knife at his chest. Jake blocked with his right arm. In the time it took BLT to recover, Jake pulled out his gun and pointed it at BLT's head. "Bang!"

The door to the training room opened. "Sir, phone call for Jake Logan," a marine said.

Jake's body tensed. His whereabouts were unknown. Who could be calling him?

The answer was quick in coming. "It's Alex Roigin, sir," the marine said.

Jake's amped-up body relaxed. He smirked. He would have totally waylaid BLT, but it was not lost on him that he'd come seconds from getting his ass handed to him. Jake wiped a bit of blood from his nose with the back of his hand and then walked toward the office.

"Logan," Jake said when he picked up the phone.

"Jake."

"Hi, Alex."

"Situation in Paris. A C-40 is fueling up at Pope Airfield as we speak. There are gear bags on board, a folder on the table with your documents, some credit cards, cash, and an updated brief. Dan and Em-Dog will meet you onboard. You and BLT get there as quickly as you can."

Jake observed BLT standing in the doorway. Jake kept his face deadpan, though he wondered whether he was ready emotionally and physically to be back in the field. "Right."

"I've asked Chris to call you on the way and walk you through some equipment that will be on board.

"We're on the way." Jake handed the phone to the marine.

Sitting in the back of a black Suburban, Jake and BLT drank coffee while the vehicle headed toward the Boeing C-40 Clipper. Jake switched on his phone and waited for his email to load. He scanned the mail with his left hand and then stopped and tapped the screen.

"Something wrong?" BLT asked.

"Not sure," Jake said, his eyes on his phone. "Jessica is in Paris."

"Where and doing what?"

Jake let the words he was reading register. "Jess has shown her reach if you're not nice to me. We're staying at the Ritz in Paris, and you should have seen the breakfast Jess ordered. Amazing! Later today we're meeting Jess's friend."

"The Ritz. She was there when she sent this email." Jake jumped out of the Suburban, which had stopped adjacent to the aircraft stairs. Alex had said further instructions would be onboard the plane. Maybe Alex was onto Jessica. Jake could speculate, but that might cost lives. He wanted to give BLT as full an answer as possible after he read the updated brief.

Jake and BLT joined Dan and Em-Dog onboard the Boeing C-40 Clipper. The plane was a military version of the Boeing 737, designed to offer mission flexibility. The versatile C-40 "convo" aircraft was optimized to transport passengers and/or cargo around the globe. This one had been configured to carry a combination of both. Jake, BLT, Dan, and Em-Dog were the only passengers. The four crew members consisted of two pilots, Captain James Green and Captain Norman Peters, First Officer Karen Birch, and Staff Sergeant Rickson, who was functioning as the flight attendant.

Jake read the brief that had been left for him, his laptop open in front of him. The documents provided the latest intelligence on the Bat and included the most recent photographs and all intercepted text conversations between a third party and Jessica, which had found their way to the Bat. A communication from the day before had placed the Bat in Paris. There was no mention of Jessica. She had fallen off the radar after she'd left New York.

"Gentlemen, I have an incoming call from Senior Chief Alex Roigin," First Officer Birch said. "Please, can you all assemble in the conference area?"

As the jet raced on a route that would take it across the Atlantic to the European continent, the team quickly seated themselves in front of a flat-screen television. Staff Sergeant Rickson followed close behind, handing out cups of coffee.

Alex appeared on the screen via a satellite link. "Gentlemen, let's get right to the op." He rifled through the papers in front of him as he talked. "You have three suites at the Ritz. We've reserved the suite right above the Bat's and the suites to the right and left of his. We'll hit him hard and fast from multiple entry points. The French are working with us on this. They're going to kill the security cameras at the Ritz as you come through the door. Any questions?"

Jake sensed they were all looking at him. He noted the serious look on Alex's face.

"BLT and Em-Dog will detail how this capture will go down, but first there's a significant complication we need to address," Alex continued. "Jake has received a communication from Jessica, aka Jess, that places her at the Ritz at approximately eleven hundred hours today. Our people are working on her room and movements and will provide updates."

Dan and Em-Dog sat up straighter, pivoting toward Jake as Alex addressed him personally. "This one could get rough, Jake." Alex said.

"What are you implying?" Jake asked.

"If you feel emotionally compromised, there's no embarrassment in stepping away."

"Thank you for the vote of confidence. But if you guys didn't think I could do the job, why the fuck did you call on me?"

Jake's eyes followed BLT as he raised his hand. "Nobody is questioning your fitness, Jake." He stood and faced the room, taking over the meeting. "DGSI, French internal security, has been tailing the Bat since he arrived from Turkey in the early hours of this morning. The surveillance team completed their tail to the Ritz, and now a DCRI static surveillance team is set up in front and behind the Ritz. They have a room with line of sight on the Bat's suite, and there's a bug in place."

"I'm concerned that we're relying on French surveillance," Alex said.

"We've worked with this team several times in the past," Jake replied. "They're the equivalent of the FBI, and they're good."

Dan and Em-Dog nodded in agreement.

"OK, I'll leave you boys to work out the details," Alex said, and then the TV went blank.

Jake moved over to a window seat, pulled down the blind, and adjusted his seat. He wasn't in the mood to talk. What's more, his body still desperately needed rest. He turned to his side and closed his eyes. Two weeks before she'd died, Jake and Alice had planned to marry. They had found a quaint Catholic church to do the ceremony on Sanibel Island. Death was never comfortable. It was agonizing and complicated even on the good days. On the bad days. It was unfair, ugly, and heartbreaking. He could not sleep, but his eyes remained closed, pretending to be. That was until the tears swelled in eyes, and he opened them to see if anyone had noticed. Across the aisle adjacent to his, BLT was observing him.

"What?" said Jake.

Without being invited BLT moved over to the aisle seat next to Jake. "All things considered, you are coping better than we could've imagined. Bud, there's no shame to breaking down after what you been through."

Jake remained silent. What could he say? This was BLT way of saying we've got your back.

BLT continued. "We go way back, and I know the boys will support me when I say your brothers are here for you."

"Thank you," Jake said without raising his head. Jake's concern was not functioning. No, his disquiet ran deeper, to something more visceral— that place in every man that was dark and without emotion. He kept that compartment locked behind an iron door. Now that the iron door was open, only one thing that could close it—revenge for Alice.

At 5:03 a.m., Captain Green locked onto the final approach to Orly Airport, ten miles outside of Paris. Jake moved over to a window seat and raised the blind as the C-40's nose tuned toward runway one. He pushed

his body back into the seat when, minutes later, the C-40 touched down and then taxied toward the designated customs area.

After the plane's engines shut down, First Officer Birch opened the aircraft door and greeted a DGSI officer and a French internal security and customs officer. Both men boarded. The customs officer quickly checked their passports and luggage. Jake and the others had assembled in the galley. When the customs officer turned to the captain to look over the aircraft's information, the DGSI officer introduced himself to Jake and the others as Jean Paul Gaul. He had arranged for the customs officer to be waiting for the flight to hasten their clearance. Five minutes later, the customs officer stamped the last passport, bid them all adieu, and then left the aircraft.

After BLT and his team disembarked, they loaded their gear into the back of an Audi Q7. First Officer Birch watched as the men seated themselves. Then she turned and walked toward the lounge to arrange for the aircraft to be refueled. She had not been given a time or a date when they would leave, but she and the crew would be ready.

Gaul drove off the airport grounds. At that time in the morning, it was only a forty-minute drive from Orly Airport to the Ritz. Like the atmosphere in the vehicle, the streets of Paris were silent. Jake had checked his phone several times, hoping for another message from Jessica but had received none. *What am I missing?* He opened and read the last communication from her. *What's her end game?*

His train of thought was broken when Gaul parked the Audi behind the safe house. He handed the keys to BLT; nodded; and, as instructed, got out of the vehicle and walked away.

Inside the safe house BLT said, "Let's go over the op again. I agree with Alex; our best chance is to hit hard from multiple points, taking advantage of the room we have above the Bat's room."

Jake's heart was thumping. He looked at the others and wondered what they were feeling. *Do they trust me?* He opened his mouth to ask why they had taken this risk. Why not let the French take out the Bat?

"The four of us have the best chance to stop the Bat's reign of terror," BLT said, answering Jake's unspoken question. "We need him alive and in our custody."

"Have we figured out what his plan is?" Dan asked.

BLT shook his head. "Nope. What's more baffling is Jessica's connection." He looked down at his tablet and studied the digital maps. "We'll need eyes on the street. Em-Dog, you stay in the vehicle. If the Bat's exit from the Ritz is not in a body bag, put his lights out. Any questions?"

The other men remained quiet. BLT directed his attention to Jake. "Jake, you and I will enter the room above the Bat's suite and attach three ropes to an anchor." BLT explained that he and Jake would attach themselves to two of the ropes and lead the remaining rope to the balcony of the room next to the Bat's suite, where Dan would be waiting. A fifth man, Chuck Rogers, would be joining the team and would arrive shortly. He would enter the hotel after giving the order to disable the cameras and then head to the hallway outside the Bat's door. When all the pieces were in place, Dan, attached to a nylon harness, would swing over to the suite's bedroom window and attempt entry there. He would be armed with a suppressed Glock 23. The plan was to take the Bat alive by administering a self-contained, propellant-powered injector of anesthesia that would knock him out. When Dan was in position, BLT and Jake would rappel down to the balcony of the Bat's living room. They would use their suppressed MP7A1 short-barreled submachine guns to take down the Bat's men. Chuck would hit at the same time from the front door.

"What about Jessica?" Jake asked. "There's a possibility she'll be in the room."

"You and Chuck will also have a CO2 injector of anesthesia as a backup to Dan and to knock Jessica out cold, but the Bat is our priority."

"Em-Dog? Your role—are you clear?"

"Yes, wheel man—eyes for any signs of the police. Eliminate the target if he exits the building."

The operation was set, and if it went down as planned, they would be wheels up at Orly Airport in ninety minutes. BLT looked at the men. "Any questions? Concerns?" He nodded at Jake as he raised his hand.

"If DCRI is watching, aren't you concerned they'll see this op and/or recognize us?"

BLT shook his head. "No. The French have been instructed to stand down after they kill the security cameras. That said …" He reached into his backpack and laid five small pieces of rubber on the seat next to him.

Jake had heard about such technology but had yet to use it. He reached over and retrieved one of the packs, squeezing the rubber like a stress ball. Then he awkwardly teased it into the shape of a mask and placed it over his face. It completely transformed his appearance. The creases around his eyes filled in, his angular nose flattened and appeared smaller, his cheeks became chubby, like a cherub, and his square jaw took on a round appearance.

"Jesus, DCRI will think aliens have invaded," Em-Dog said, his eyes locked on Jake's freaky features.

"We used these masks on an op last year," BLT said. "They prevent facial recognition. We can't risk an eyewitness identifying any of us and bringing responsibility for this op back to the CIA's door." He handed out the remaining masks to the other men. "Are we good?"

The answer to his question was communicated by their actions as the men organized their gear. Jake checked his .40-caliber Glock pistol and suppressor. Chuck, who had joined them in the safe house, handed him a submachine gun. Together they carried out checks and screwed silencers onto the gun barrels. Jake reached down to his side and picked up the bag that contained encrypted mobile phones with voice-activated Bluetooth headsets, rappelling ropes, and small charges to breach doors or create entrances. Jake's eyes locked onto BLT's. His intense stare was reciprocated.

Jake agreed that taking out the Bat would be tough, but taking him alive made the danger go up exponentially. He looked away and continued checking his equipment.

Jake looked up when he heard metal chink against the glass dining table. He glanced toward Em-Dog, where the sound had come from. Something was troubling him. BLT, Chuck, and Dan were also focused on Em-Dog. "I was …" Em-Dog bent over and picked up the mask and his shades.

"Yes?" BLT said.

"Do we have the option to use ski masks or shades?"

"No, it's the latest technology. We'll have ski masks as a backup and if quick action is required. but if we're forced into an unplanned exit, we can't risk facial recognition after the fact," BLT said. "Gatorz sunglasses are also effective, and we will use them going into the hotel. Most facial-recognition algorithms use the distance between the eyes as a key identity measurement. That said, they don't have the advantage of confusion in relation to eyewitnesses."

Em-Dog was not alone in craving routine and what had worked for him in the past. Jake felt the same way. BLT's statement about using them on a previous op had not included Jake and Em-Dog. Em-Dog put the mask on as BLT spoke. "Speak now or forever hold your piece."

He paused as he fiddled with the mask. "It's a bad idea using them in the field without doing a test run first."

Anticipating further objections, BLT said. "I recommend you continue to get familiar with the masks. They can be tricky to put on, but they don't affect our ability to communicate verbally."

Em-Dog nodded as he put the mask on and then pulled it off a second time before stowing it in his backpack.

At four in the morning, the Ritz's rear parking lot was quiet. Seated in the back of the Audi, the team waited in silence. The vehicle was facing away from the hotel, though its mirrors were positioned to cover the front entrance, the street, and the sidewalks approaching the entrance. They were all wearing Gatorz eyewear and black ski masks high on their heads, so they could pull them over their face in a moment, if necessary.

Two minutes later, the team exited the vehicle, unloaded items from their backpacks, and carried them toward the service entrance. It was a bright, clear morning, so their dark sunglasses were less conspicuous than the ski masks. Nonetheless they looked no more out of place than a group of men returning from a hiking expedition.

BLT and Jake entered the fire door north of Dan and Chuck's location. They all wore a mobile earpiece linked to an encrypted mobile phone in their right-front pocket. The system was set to a voice-activated mode that allowed them to transmit without pressing a button. By pressing buttons on the mobile phone, they could speak to only one member of the team or broadcast on all channels.

In the pocket of his Kevlar vest, Jake carried a propellant-powered injector that contained enough ketamine to render an adult male unconscious in seconds. In a small leather holster secreted in the waistband of his combat pants was a Sig Sauer P226 and a Compact SAS .45-caliber pistol. The P226 possessed a threaded barrel that allowed for the addition of a suppressor, which he carried in his right back pocket.

"Chuck for BLT," Chuck said.

"Go, Chuck."

"In sight of the Bat's suite."

"Good. Jake and I are in the suite above the Bat's. No trouble getting in. We'll be ready in six minutes."

"Dan for BLT."

"Go, Dan."

"I'm in position in the room next to the target. I'll hook up once Jake swings the rope down."

"Roger."

"Em-Dog for BLT."

"Go, Em-Dog."

When Em-Dog's voice did not transmit, Jake glanced out the sixteenth-floor window down to the street, where the Audi was parked. A white police car slowed as it approached the Audi. He raised his scope to his right eye and scanned the street. Nothing was out of place, and they expected police would patrol the area as a matter of course. Jake tracked the police car until it disappeared from view.

Seconds later, Em-Dog responded. "Clear for now. Negative police on the sidewalk or patrol cars in the street. We're looking good."

"OK," BLT said.

Jake checked the time, 5:00 a.m., and scanned the street and the surrounding alleys again. If all went well, they'd be on route to Orly Airport by 5:30 a.m. Still, he'd sat where Em-Dog was enough times to know that, for him, the next ten minutes would feel like an eternity.

Jake listened to the transmissions between the other team members as he continued to scan the street below for any police on the sidewalk approaching the hotel. It was all clear. Chuck had confirmed that the hotel's security cameras were down.

"Two minutes," BLT said. "All units check in at sixty seconds."

Jake checked the rappelling ropes and small charges yet again.

"Sixty seconds," BLT said. Then the other operators began checking in.

"Dan is in position. I'll swing out over to the balcony in ten."

"Jake is in position." His reply was not strictly true. He had been distracted by activity on the ground and delayed calling in his observation because he did not want to shut down the op. He watched as two dark-haired men with dark complexions entered the service entrance. *Shit. Maybe they're OK. Early morning workers. Hmm ... only if the hour was approaching six.*

"BLT is in position. You with us, Chuck?"

"Uh ... yes. Chuck is in position."

"Forty seconds." BLT said.

Jake dropped his rope and then hooked the metal carabiners fixed to one end of it onto the balcony's heavy iron railing. He started to climb over the balcony but then stopped with one leg on the railing.

Fuck ... Alice. One of the faces was entrenched in his mind. *The cemetery.* His lips tightened, masking the horror he feared could be unleashed. He pulled his mobile from his jacket pocket and changed the channel, so his words would go only to BLT.

"Thirty seconds," BLT said on the open channel.

Any minute now, they'd be in the hallway outside the Bat's room. "BLT!"

"Yeah?"

"Trouble!"

"Where?"

"Two men, service entrance."

"Extra security for the Bat?"

"I ... I don't know," Jake replied. He did not have time to think about it, to analyze the situation, or to relive the explosion at the cemetery. "One of them was at the cemetery two weeks ago."

BLT did not hesitate to broadcast the development on all channels. "Jake has eyes on two men possibly heading to the seventh floor, the Bat's room."

Chuck only heard men and asked, "How many new mutts?"

When Jake spoke, his voice was strained. He was hanging from a harness sixteen stories over the courtyard of the Ritz, some ten feet away from his balcony. "Two," he said as he lowered himself on the right corner of the balcony outside the Bat's room. He paused, allowing BLT to position himself on the left corner of the balcony. Jake pulled out his silenced P226.

"Chuck for BLT." In the background, Jake heard what he believed was the crack of a door opening. "I have eyes on the hallway," Chuck whispered. "The service elevator is directly ahead, about fifty feet. The Bat's room is fifty feet from the service elevator. No sign of them. Let's go."

"Negative, Chuck," BLT said. "You get caught out in that hallway, and you're dead."

"Listen to BLT, Chuck," said Jake, the wind blowing in his face and creating static on the comms. He kept his voice low as he continued. "Two men at your back isn't going to end well for you if those fucks come out of the elevator with assault rifles."

Jake turned his back against the wall and edged sideways to the balcony doors. The curtains were closed, limiting his sight. He pressed his cheek against the wall, and his nose touched the wooden door frame as he observed the inside of the Bat's room through the side gap of the left curtain. His view was restricted, but he saw two men lounging on separate beds, drinking and smoking cigarettes. A third man sat at a desk to the right of the balcony. On the desk was a laptop computer and a Louis Vuitton purse. Jake concluded Jessica was likely in the room because the purse was similar to the one he had bought for her, and a key ring that he recognized as hers was hanging from the purse's handle. The men were speaking Farsi. Jake had learned the language during his time in Iraq. They were complaining about Americans. He held up three fingers to BLT, who responded with his index finger and thumb joined to indicate zero targets were in sight.

"BLT for Chuck." The elevator's thick cables hummed as they carried their load and then fell silent as the doors slid open. "Wait until the men are at the door and then go," BLT said.

Jake and BLT moved into a half-crouch firing stance in front of the balcony doors.

"Go!" Chuck said.

Seconds later, the balcony doors shattered as the door to the suite opened. Chuck fired two shots from his P226 as he approached the two men outside the room at speed. The first bullet entered the ear of the man nearest to him. When the second man turned, the second bullet hit him just above his left eyebrow. The two men, both of Middle Eastern descent, dropped into the room like bags of wet cement.

As the pieces of glass fell from the balcony doors, Jake leaned in and to the right with his pistol at eye level and then ducked back onto the balcony. No sooner had he pulled his head out of the room than a fully automatic machine pistol fired at the balcony. He flattened himself on the floor. He saw the gunmen to the right as they shot at the balcony door. They had been ready to gun down whoever entered the room. Jake felt the pressure of the rounds as they missed his face by inches. He was effectively pinned down. Another burst tore through the balcony door as he pressed his face flat on the cold floor. The rounds cracked into the air like thick winter hail, the tiny projectiles oblivious to their purpose.

A man tucked away in the left corner of the room had fired when the door to the suite opened, and the two men slumped into the suite with gunfire behind them. Dan heard the sound of automatic weapons from the adjoining room. The men in the hotel room reacted surprisingly quickly upon hearing the balcony doors break. The two men on the beds aimed their guns at the drawn curtains and fired. A fourth man at the table in the right corner of the room dove for the floor.

Dan fired at the locked door and pushed it open with his foot. He got a snapshot of the tangos firing at the balcony and held his suppressed Glock 23 at the end of his extended arms at eye level. He fired through the adjoining door, hitting the two terrorists and taking them down with a double tap to the forehead. The men's skulls exploded, and blood drenched the beds as they fell back. Chuck aimed his silenced gun at the man on the floor and fired.

As BLT and Jake advanced into the room, the bathroom door opened. A sixth tango emerged and fired a short, controlled burst from his Heckler & Koch. Jake shot the man in the face and put a second bullet in his throat. The man tumbled back, arterial blood jetting into the air like a sprinkler.

"Get ready to leave," BLT said. Dan entered the suite and headed to the desk. He put the laptop into his pack, along with the Louis Vuitton bag.

"Nice shooting," Jake said as he passed the bodies on the bed. BLT and Chuck patted the dead men down and checked their pockets. The six men had been carrying AK-47s and wore a mix of fatigues and street clothes. All were carrying sidearms in holsters but no radios. Chuck gathered their cell phones, removed the batteries, and tucked the devices in his backpack whilst BLT took mugshots.

BLT's head jerked up when he noticed the leg of one of the men lying in the doorway twitch. He picked up his messenger bag, moved over to the door, and shot the man point-blank in the head to make sure he was dead. "The package isn't here. Let's move out." Jake left the suite and took the stairs down to the lobby.

7

When the shooting started, the hotel guests ran from their rooms. Some screamed, and some were calm, but all hustled down to the lobby and out into the street. Jake stood on the first-floor landing. Below him was the ground-floor lobby, but he remained concealed from the running guests and hotel employees by the reception counter.

He heard the last transmission from BLT above him; they had not found the target. *Where's Jessica?* He checked his cell. She had sent no texts or emails. *Too busy trying on the clothes brought by whoever the fuck she was meeting. Where the fuck is that murdering bitch?*

The next transmission came from Em-Dog. "BLT, you copy?"

"BLT copies."

"I'm bringing the Audi around. Two minutes."

Em-Dog steered out of the rear parking lot and approached the front of the hotel. "Guys, listen up. There are several police cars in front and multiple uniformed cops running through the hotel lobby doors with pistols in hand. You'll have to find another exit."

"Check," BLT said. "I'm with Dan and Chuck. Jake!"

"BLT," Jake said.

"Route up. Now! Em-Dog, we'll come up with something. Be ready to pick us up."

Jake turned around. The stairwell was clear; no more stragglers were heading down past him. He pulled out his P226, shielding it between his right hip and the wall as he backed into the stairwell and ran up the stairs.

Two minutes later, BLT fired bursts from his Heckler & Koch MP7 through the hinges of a locked metal door that led to the hotel roof. The four men stepped out onto the flat roof. All around them, sirens echoed off the buildings. The morning sky, though cloudy, was bright. "Em-Dog, you copy me?"

"Em-Dog copies."

"We're on the roof. Tell me exactly what you're seeing," BLT ordered as he scanned the streets below.

"You need to move away from the hotel entrance."

"We'll cross the apartment buildings to the north," BLT said.

"Copy that. I'll follow on the street."

"Guys, facial-recognition masks," BLT said. "Jake, lead."

Jake led the team onto the roofs of the adjacent buildings four and five floors above the streets of Paris. The glazed-brick roofs were all different heights and gradients. Using fire escapes, drainpipes, and balconies, they moved at speed, climbing up and down and jumping buildings to escape the police.

Jake slowed down and stopped. "We've reached the end of the block," he said turning back to face BLT. They heard shouting on the roof behind them.

"We've been spotted," BLT said, looking behind him.

"This op is going sideways fast," Chuck remarked.

Jake turned to Dan. "Smoke those fucks." Dan removed a smoke grenade from his backpack and pulled the pin. Bright red smoke billowed from one end. Dan placed it next to a ventilator on the roof and ran. The smoke created a cloud between them and the French police.

The roof they were on was under construction—flat with steep slopes on all four sides. Using the ladder on the front slope, they climbed to a set of intersecting iron steps. The fire escape ended adjacent to a three-by-five-foot iron balcony. Jake, BLT, and Chuck squeezed onto it. Dan remained on the ladder. Cracked tiles and broken masonry fell from the roof, narrowly missing Chuck's head. He brushed the cement dust from his latex-rubber mask.

Nearby, police lights flashed. The shouting and commotion on the rooftop behind them were drowned out by the blades of an approaching helicopter. From the ground floor to the fifth floor, windows opened, and faces stared and pointed at the men's masked faces, as if they were animals in a zoo.

"We have to get off this balcony!" Jake said.

"Em-Dog, you copy me?" BLT said.

"Em-Dog copies."

"We've reached an impasse. What are you seeing on the ground?"

"Onlooking civilians, mainly in the buildings. No police presence directly below you on the street. A convoy of emergency vehicles is approaching the area. For now, the back streets are clear. That appears to be your only means of escape."

"It won't take the French police long to spread out at ground level," BLT said. "Once that happens, the street will be locked down."

They heard voices on the roof; the police had made their way through the smoke and were closing fast.

Jake did not hesitate. He forced the window open and rolled into the room, P226 in hand. He hit the hardwood floor and flipped onto his stomach. Ives Saint Laurent fragrance hit his nostrils. He aimed his gun at a movement on the bed. The other men followed in quick succession. A young couple was making love.

"Que diable?" the man yelled.

The woman screamed.

The man had said, "What the hell?"

Jake was also fluent in French. Sensing no threat, he signaled to the other men. They advanced to the living room and through the kitchen to the back of the apartment.

"Activity in the hallway," BLT said.

One scenario was that the building's tenants were trying to view the commotion in the streets. The other scenario was the French police were going from building to building at pace. Either way, opening the door and walking out was not an option.

"Jake, the windows," BLT said.

Jake and Dan pulled the windows up and dropped ropes. They used carabiners to secure them around the windows' central metal frame. Jake gazed at the horizon, momentarily absorbing the nascent rays of the rising sun and the awesome view of the Paris skyline before climbing out the window.

Once outside, he shut out the hubbub. Though the road ahead still had the black look of night, the silence brought a calmness to his mind. There was no path up, and they had no dictated plan to find their way down, but he had always enjoyed this mind-blowing experience. Rappelling was a thrilling blend of adrenaline and achievement. Though he didn't know what he might encounter below, the excitement was no different from rappelling down a natural wonder. He pushed off with his legs and rappelled down. BLT, Dan, and Chuck were seconds behind. Once their feet were on the ground, they ran to the north.

"Em-Dog," BLT said, breathless, "we're on the ground heading north. Pick us up at the next block. ETA one minute."

"Roger that. I'll be there."

BLT, Jake, Dan, and Chuck picked up the pace. When they reached the end of the block, Em-Dog was in situ, the Audi's side door open. The four men climbed inside. The volume of the wailing sirens fell when BLT slammed the door.

Em-Dog turned on his right signal light and, with a deliberate calm, pulled onto Rue du Faubourg Saint-Honoré. They passed the iconic shopping district and cafés, where waiters were setting up tables on the pavement. The sidewalk was crawling with police, and people were standing around pointing at the sirens and police cars. Em-Dog drove at a steady speed and looked in his rearview mirror until the police cars were far behind him and then turned onto the Champs-Élysées. He punched a button on the GPS that would lead them to the airport.

8

Jessica pushed her chair back from the table. The Arab woman placed her small purse on the table and then seated herself opposite Jessica. "Excuse me," Jessica said politely. "I don't know you."

The woman didn't move, just looked Jessica over. "I'm not your enemy," she said. She had a soft British accent, though her tone was forceful. "We want the same thing."

"What are you talking about? You're not … I'm meeting … He … You're not male." *I don't know his name,* Jess said. Jessica heard the voice in her head. *I don't know. Maybe she's a friend of who we're meeting. All I know is that he said he would take care of us. And he did until you fucked things up.* Jessica was not sure where this was going. "Who are you?" she demanded.

"A friend," the woman said, staring intently at Jessica. "I'm a like-minded woman looking for an opportunity."

"In what way are we like-minded?"

"We've both been burnt by Wall Street, and we both feel the way to make Americans listen is to kill."

Jessica did not respond. *Is Jess listening? She needs help.*

"Look, you stand out like a sore thumb," the woman said. "You have eyes on you anywhere you go. We can help you. Of course, there'll be money involved."

Jessica's body relaxed. *Jessica, you're a stupid fuck. All you think about is money. This woman speaks my language. This is about revenge. Step aside. I'll take it from here.*

"Asyd Omar Batdadi asked me to meet you," the woman said.

"It's about damn time," Jess replied. "We've been waiting for days."

"We? You were supposed to come alone."

"Don't fuck with me. I am alone. Do you see anybody else sitting here?"

"Let's talk at the apartment," the woman said. "Asyd Omar Batdadi is waiting. Wait a few minutes and then follow me."

Minutes later, Jess followed the woman, careful to stay several feet behind her. The woman walked at a brisk pace as she navigated through the pedestrians in the immediate vicinity of Place du Marché Saint-Honoré. Jess had a hard time keeping up. When the woman turned a corner onto Rue Saint Roch, she entered a mid-seventeenth-century mansion situated between Place Vendome and Palais Royal. Jess waited a few minutes before following her into the building.

The reception room was like a magazine cover. *Fuck!* Jess thought. *I'm afraid to sit in case I wrinkle the fabric or stain it with something I don't even know is on my pants.* The sofa was cream colored, inlaid with fine green silk leaves that were embroidered so delicately they might have landed there in spring and just sunk in. Jess stared at the couch, knowing it had taken many hours to create the fabric and upholster the sofa. The white curtains were silk *matka*, the kind of white that was untouched by hands and devoid of dust. There was no television, just wall-to-wall bookshelves and chairs arranged around the bespoke fireplace. The black-and-white photographs on the wall didn't appear to be family snaps, but they were arranged to look like such, clearly by a professional. The floor was a highly polished wood, dark and free of dust and clutter. Jess headed for the chair closest to the window.

Asyd Omar Batdadi was six feet three inches tall, a healthy, well-built sixty-year-old. He was known in polite society as An al Alin Hassan. In the past, his face had been round. Plastic surgery had drastically changed his looks, and now beneath his trimmed beard and mustache was an angular face with prominent cheekbones. He was dressed in a Western business suit and regimental tie.

Batdadi's big break had come when a foreign contractor had withdrawn from a deal to build King Abdulaziz International Airport in Saudi Arabia, and Batdadi had taken on the job. By the early 1990s, he was an extraordinarily rich man. He was also a devout man, raised in the strict, conservative Wahhabi strand of Sunni Islam. However, over the years, he had become increasingly drawn to the cool, clear, uncluttered certainties of extremist Islamist ideology.

Batdadi's time fighting the Russians was critical. It was during that period that he'd changed from a contemplative, scholarly man to a respected, battle-hardened leader of men. Though he had yet to fully develop his extremist ideas, the war in Afghanistan had given him crucial confidence and status. He followed extreme ideology in the last days of the year the Soviet tanks rolled into Afghanistan. Batdadi came to the jihad a student and left a man who knew about violence's uses and its effects.

Wealthy benefactors in the Persian Gulf used Batdadi for recruiting, organizing, and orchestrating the operations of the terrorist groups active on Pakistani soil. He served as something of a liaison between ISIS leadership and the criminal and ideological groups who fought against India, the West at large, and Pakistan's secular government.

He was not a member of any of the jihadist organizations with whom he worked. He was a freelancer, a contract employer, the man who translated the general interests and goals of his employers into action on the ground. He worked with different Islamist militant groups, and to do so, he had adopted several different identities.

Batdadi's property was a five-bedroom, split-level penthouse apartment on the top two floors of the mansion. Batdadi was sitting at the desk in his study when his head of security/operations entered the room.

"Good morning, Abdel," Batdadi said. Abdel and Batdadi's other security men were ex-Special Services Group commandos. The Special Service Group was the Pakistani army's primary special operations force, headquartered at Tarbela Cantonment.

"Good morning, sir. The woman named Jessica is waiting in the reception room."

"What is she like?" Batdadi had changed wives like other people change cars. He currently had three Saudi wives—Wahhabis, like their husband—who were more or less permanent. The fourth, however, he changed on a regular basis. The magnate would send his private pilot all over the Middle East to pick up yet another bride. Some were as young as fifteen and covered from head to toe, but they were all exceptionally beautiful.

"Kafir," Abdel said.

"That's not what I am asking. They're all infidels."

"We won't be having sex with her any time soon."

Batdadi laughed. "I will meet with her anyway. It might be fruitful."

"Yes, I understand."

"Six brothers died today at the Ritz hotel for the cause. If she wastes our time … kill her. Is the helicopter ready to leave?"

"Yes, sir."

Jessica was forty-three years old, but Batdadi thought she must have been fifty or more years old as he looked at her blue eyes, in which cataracts were forming, and her wrinkled skin, which had seen too many beaches. Her bio said she lived on New York City's Upper East Side, aspiring to be part of that club. Batdadi presumed she had never really tasted the trappings or basked in the life of billionaires. He also sensed she had never met with a person in power. Yet she intrigued him. Why?

A few of Batdadi's security officers stood around the dining room. Jessica sat by the window staring into the garden, perhaps hoping she would find her answer in a rosebush. She appeared to be underdressed and, more pointedly, lost. Perspiration glistened on her forehead as she glanced intermittently at the armed security men. Her fear was apparent, no doubt an apprehension that, at any moment, the dark-skinned men might take her prisoner and rape her.

Milton Williams, an artist/forger and a friend of Batdadi's and Jessica's, had asked for the meeting a few days earlier, and Batdadi knew why. He had his doubts, but over the years, Milton had helped increase Batdadi's wealth by bringing him forged art he sold to unsuspecting buyers. *Foolish wannabes.* But what Milton had promised him, if played right, was beyond even Batdadi's imagination.

Batdadi had been traveling the world in the past few months, meeting with insurgent groups and international terror outfits in Egypt, Indonesia, Saudi Arabia, Iran, Chechnya, and Yemen, looking for opportunities that would put him in the ranks of Osama bin Laden and Abū Bakr al-Baghdadi. Batdadi was not a member of those terror groups, but terror cells acting under his patronage had executed missions in Jakarta, Mumbai, New

Delhi, Baghdad, Kabul, Tel Aviv, and Islamabad. In August 2010 in Tel Aviv, Batdadi conducted his most notorious operation—an attempted assassination of Israeli Prime Minister Benjamin "Bibi" Netanyahu on behalf of benefactors in the Persian Gulf. The assassin escaped, but not before he triggered a suicide vest on a man in the crowd, which blew up thirty people as they carried away the prime minister.

He walked over to the window, where Jessica was sitting. Simultaneously, the woman from the café entered the room. "You've already met my wife, Natasha. I'm Omar Batdadi."

"Your wife!" Jess said.

Natasha had removed her burka and was now wearing a hijab. She smiled at Batdadi.

He looked directly at Jess. "Do you want something to drink? Eat? How was your journey? I trust the suite at the Ritz was to your liking. How can you be of service?" With the niceties out of the way, he was anxious to know what she could bring to the table. "I am told by our mutual friend in New York that, for a price, you can give me access to Wall Street. To be more precise, HK Bank." Batdadi smiled.

"I'm listening," Jess said.

"You told Milton Williams that, in return for a new identity and safe passage to a country of your choosing, you can get my package into HK Bank."

"Package?" she said. "Don't play games. I know you want to plant a bomb. Let's not mince words. Milton has explained my plan to you in detail. It's amazing, and it can work. We will help you, and you will help us."

Batdadi stepped toward her. "We? Us?"

"Yes." Jess corrected herself. "I mean me. I waited days after a long flight, and I'm exhausted."

Batdadi stepped back and studied her. "You are an intriguing woman. I know we can work together."

She smiled, exposing her stained teeth.

Thirty minutes later, Batdadi, Jessica, and Natasha exited a black Mercedes C63 AMG flanked by two bodyguards. They rushed toward a helipad and climbed into Batdadi's Executive Eurocopter. Its rotors were already turning, and in seconds, it lifted off and headed out over Paris and then banked toward Orly Airport. Jessica sat next to Batdadi in the rear of the helicopter.

"The downfall of Wall Street is closer than you or I could have asked Allah for in our daily prayers." Batdadi could not mask the excitement in his voice.

"What the fuck?" Jess said. When Batdadi looked at her, she raised her cell phone, as if concerned over something she had read.

Batdadi got back to business. "I'm leaving now for New York. Yes! New York."

9

NEW YORK—ONE YEAR EARLIER

Dear Diary,
It's not my fault, so you can't blame me. I didn't want to do it, and I couldn't stop it—at least that's what Jessica told me. Jessica said she could help me make it stop. I went crazy one time because—just for a few seconds—I put a rope around my neck and kicked the stool away. The light bulb fell out, and the rope and I ended up on the floor. I couldn't get off the floor to try again. I didn't want to die, no matter how much I wished I hadn't been born. I even thought of running away. I was scared, but I didn't have any money, family, or friends.

That's what did it—what caused me to do what he asked. It destroyed my relationship with Mom. For years, I endured it, and after a time, it seemed normal and didn't hurt anymore—I mean physically, not mentally. Later, Mom blamed me, said I should've told her I was unhappy. She treated me like I was a stranger—more than that, a means to an end. Mom never hugged me or said she was sorry. I never did convince her that was not what a little boy should do. We argued and argued until I told her that she was ungodly and that she would go to hell. She said I didn't complain when the toys were delivered. That's when it got worse. She died in a car crash, and I had nowhere to live. I knew enough to realize that the only life I had known was now my prison.

Uncle Dicky sent a nice lady to take care of me. Mom and I used to have lunch with Uncle Dicky every week. After lunch we would go to Uncle Dicky's bank. Mom would sit at the desk and work, and Uncle Dicky would take me into another room. He occasionally came to dinner and would bathe me and put me to bed. He liked to get into bed with me. The lady he sent to the house after Mom died made my meals, took me to school, and played with me. I liked her. Sometimes I felt bad because I didn't miss Mom, but I brushed those thoughts away.

When Jessica came to visit in the beginning, she said, "Don't worry, you'll be OK," and that she would help me one day. She said she understood my pain. School friends would invite me to parties and say nice things about me, but I never said yes, and they stopped inviting me. That hurt. I didn't fit in with the Upper East Side crowd or their children. But I got lucky.

I know she wasn't my real grandmother, and if I weren't a sweet little cherub when he came calling, she would not be pleased, but she cuddled me and gave me treats. Uncle Dicky called her Miss Green. She told me to call her Nana Green. It was just us two for a long while.

But what I did with Uncle Dicky, it's not my fault. It's not my fault. It's not my fault. It's not.

I'm scared. Something bad is happening to me. I can't explain it because I don't know if other fourteen-year-old boys feel this way. I don't remember the exact month it started. It intensified after I saw Uncle Dicky late one night. When he saw me looking out the window, he shot me a sorry look before getting in his car and driving away. I wondered for a split second if the moonlight was playing tricks, and any minute I would hear the key turn, the front door click open, and then close. But I didn't hear anything the entire night, nothing at all. What was happening? By morning when I woke up, I was scared. I was scared he was gone and would not come back.

Memory is the worst thing about healing. I was only seven years old, a little blond, blue-eyed boy when it started. Seven years later, I was scared he was gone forever. I opened the window because I woke up hot and wet. I did not wet the bed. My shorts were sticky, and I was trying to remember the dream that excited me yet disgusted me. My dick was still erect when I leaned out the window. The New York air was rancid, and I heard car horns.

Down below to the side of the driveway, I saw Uncle Dicky, one hand on the maple tree. He was leaning over the legs of a boy who was between his thighs. The little boy's hands were gripping the grass. Uncle Dicky's hand was over the boy's mouth. His trousers were down around his ankles. I leaned over the windowsill and stared. Something made Uncle Dicky look up. He zipped his pants while the little boy cried into his hands. I turned to move away from the window, to go and help the boy. I turned back briefly and saw Nana Green come from the house and go to the boy.

I did not see the boy when I went downstairs later that night. I never spoke to Nana Green about what I saw. I understood at that moment that she knew what Uncle Dicky had done because she had let him do it to me.

I did not want that to happen to the little boy. I was scared. I was scared of what was happening to my body and that the pain had been replaced with excitement. Scared because I wanted to do it but even more scared because I didn't want it to stop.

When Jessica took me out for lunch, and I was sure that Nana Green would not hear, I broke down and told Jessica everything I could remember from the age of seven.

Sincerely,

Ambrose

10

Jess pushed her head back into the headrest and closed her eyes. Her thoughts went back to Alice and the moment when she'd plunged the knife into her and twisted. Alice's knees had given way, and she'd gone down, as if her puppet master had dropped her strings. Jessica had politely asked her to leave. She had protected Jessica. Bitch Beth, the so-called therapist, had not helped her. The killings had been easier than she could've imagined. Jess's only regret was that she had not made sure Alice was dead.

She lifted the window shade and was struck by the inky canopy of the night sky's endless abyss. She smiled at the pleasure of the unknown. She was thirsty, and when Fátima, the flight attendant, approached, she ordered a Coke Zero. Jess had acquired a taste for Coke Zero since she had killed Beth's colleague, Steve Lopez Dunhill. Her heart raced. She thought it was strange that, after committing a heinous act, she had developed a liking for something so random. Jess felt it had some psychological significance, but it wasn't exactly something she would go to a shrink about. Jess just resigned himself to a hankering for Coke Zero. She considered it healthier than the red wine that Jessica had poured into her body.

She thought about Batdadi's telephone call. *If I must kill, I will. Jessica's craziness got us here. It's my job to restore order.* Jess thanked Fátima when she returned with her drink. Minutes later, she slid out of her seat and walked toward a section of the aircraft that had been turned into a dressing room for women, including a shower room. She went inside and locked the door.

"Jessica, can you hear me? Fuck! Amazing! This bathroom is amazing. Wake up. We need to talk. Stop the fucking crying. Your constant whining isn't helping. I need to think. Fuck! Stop! I want to know your Wall Street contact. Please don't say it's Jake. I don't want to hear another word about that fucking fake banker! He couldn't take care of you. When you're not emptying your guts, you're crying. I'll be damned before I go back to another shrink. It's not going to happen. Stop wailing. I need to know what you told Jake, and I need to know now."

"Jessica, are you OK? Did you find the clothes I laid out?" Natasha asked through the door.

"I'm not ... I can't spend the rest of my life incarcerated. Fuck you, Jessica. I want a name now!" Jess said under her breath. "I must get a grip. They'll kill me," she quietly admonished herself. She put her head to the door. "Yes, but I can't decide which color to wear."

"The blue will suit your complexion," Natasha replied.

"Thank you."

When she thought Natasha had moved away, Jess walked over to the clothes laid across a chair. She picked up one of the dresses. "What the fuck? What's wrong with you, Jessica? You're making me dizzy." The room felt as if it was spinning. Jess dropped the dress and ran to the toilet.

"Open the door," Natasha said. She did not wait. She used the aircraft key to open the door from the outside and entered. She found Jessica in a sectioned-off room with her head over the toilet, vomiting. "Jessica, are you OK?"

Jess raised her head. "Something has upset my stomach. Nothing for you to worry about." She turned back to the toilet, feeling like she was going to vomit again. "What's wrong? Jessica, fuck! No more pills. They don't help. Can you hear me? I know you're in my head. Stop!"

"What did you say?" Natasha asked. "You don't look good. Are you sure you're, OK? Can I get something for you? Water? Would that help?"

Jess raised her head from the toilet and turned to face Natasha. "Nothing. I was talking to myself. I've felt better, but please don't lose your mind. I'll be OK."

"I can arrange for you to see my personal doctor when we land, but you need to shower and select something to wear. Asyd Batdadi is waiting."

Jess walked over to the clothing Natasha had laid out on the chair. She looked through the dresses and picked up one of many burkas. "What the fuck? You want me to dress like a caged Muslim bitch?"

"Please, Miss Jessica, calm down. We will be landing in a couple of hours in a country where you are now a fugitive. This is the only way we can get you through the security checks without alerting the authorities. Asyd Batdadi—" She stopped and smiled. "Sorry, let me correct myself. Asyd Hassan enjoys diplomatic immunity at the borders and, as such, his wives can go through security without drawing too much attention."

"You're one of many? Aren't you concerned?"

Natasha hung her head. "He's a good man. Sometimes he—"

"Sometimes he's what? What were you going to say?"

"Nothing. It's not important. How are you feeling?"

Jess did not reply, just shed her clothes, and stepped into the shower. When she emerged a few minutes later with towels wrapped around her hair and body, two other women were in the room. Natasha introduced them as Adela and Dalal and said they were personal assistants to her and Asyd Batdadi.

"Please, Miss Jessica, take a seat here," Adela said. She spoke with a thick Arabic accent and had Arabic features—big brown eyes, arched eyebrows, and dense eyelashes. Jess thought Jessica would kill for Adela's small, tight V-shaped jaw, but her long nose was not at all desirable. She looked a lot like Natasha. For a moment, Jess thought they could be sisters. She looked at Dalal, who looked similar. As a matter of fact, she thought they all looked the same. *That's probably why their men don't care if they wear that fucking garb over their faces.* Too tired to argue, she did as was instructed.

"You might be more comfortable wearing this," Adela said, handing her a white terry cloth robe. Adela and Dalal went to work blow-drying and attaching long hair extensions to her short brown hair. Jess studied the results in the mirror and was satisfied. She thought Jessica would like the new look and maybe stop bawling twenty-four seven.

With a full head of hair, Jess's face looked more oval, and it disguised her chubby cheeks. It was a subtle but distinct change. Jess stood and stepped toward the clothes. "Thank you, ladies."

"Miss Jessica, where are you going?" Adela asked. "We're not finished."

Jessica sat back down in the chair. Adela opened a bag on the table next to her. She pulled out several articles and set them neatly on the table, like a surgeon lining up her instruments before commencing an operation. Jess watched her, curious as to what was about to take place.

Adela applied spirit gum to Jessica's nose and tapped it with her finger to make it sticky. Then she added a bit of cotton from a cotton ball to the surface. Dalal used a Popsicle stick to remove a small quantity of putty mixed with Derma Wax from a jar. She rubbed the putty into a ball, warming it with the hair dryer and making it easier to manipulate. Adela applied the putty to sections of Jess's nose. Then she smoothed it out using K-Y Jelly. The smoothing and shaping took a long time, but Jess, not known for her patience, sat still. Adela made her nose long but curled the end inward, like a falcon's beak. Once she was satisfied with the shape, she used a stipple sponge to add texture and then sealed it all. Then she let it dry. Dalal applied dark foundation and makeup over Jess's entire face, highlighting and shadowing and then using transparent powder to finish up.

Jess sat back and looked at herself. The changes were stark. *Fucking amazing.* The overall impact was so significant she looked like an Arab female. Few things on a person's face were more distinctive than the nose. Adela and Dalal had just made her nose unrecognizable. Jess stared at the results in a mirror.

"Madam," Dalal said, the first time she had spoken since entering the room.

Jess had assumed she could not speak English. She turned around and realized that, while she had been staring in the mirror, Adela and Dalal had set up a portable bed.

"Please, can you remove your robe and lie on the bed?" Dalal asked.

Jess resisted the urge to ask if they were lesbians and did as she was instructed. She lay on the bed, naked. The scars from her breast implants had not faded over the years, and the years of not wearing support bras indicated she needed a breast uplift, as well as breast implants more in line with her age and less like a porn star.

Immediately, Dalal began spraying a fine mist onto Jess's body. The mist contained dihydroxyacetone, which would interact with her skin's chemistry to darken it. Its temporary effect would last from three to seven days.

Afterward, Dalal handed Jess her robe and turned to Adela. "Are the contact lenses ready?" Adela stepped closer to the table and inserted dark brown contact lenses into Jess's eyes. She explained that a prescription had been applied to the contacts to skew retinal recognition.

Jess looked at herself, scrutinizing every detail. "Oh my God, are you finished?"

Before Adela and Dalal could answer, there was a knock at the door. They took that as their cue to pack up and leave. Natasha opened the door and waited until Adela and Dalal had walked out before stepping aside to let two men enter.

"What the fuck is Milton doing at this party?" Jess asked. *Jessica, did you know Milton was onboard this flight?*

The men stopped and stared. "Why are you staring at me?" Jess asked, trying to defuse yet another uncontrolled outburst. *Pick up your damn game, Jess!* "Milton," she stepped toward him, "it's been a while. I know we spoke recently, but I haven't seen you … How many years has it been?"

"Jessica." He smiled but did not engage. He turned to Natasha to receive her instructions.

The second man stepped forward. "Miss Jessica, I'm Abd al Hakim. Please, can you sit at the table with your palms turned up?"

She did as he instructed. He took a magnifier from the small bag he was carrying and examined her fingerprints. He removed other items from the bag and, after fingerprinting and cleaning her hand, set to work. He used Sugru, a flexible adhesive repair putty that set strong but turned into a durable silicone rubber, to fill the ridges in her fingerprints. When he was finished, he fingerprinted her again and handed the results to Natasha and Milton and then walked out of the room and closed the door.

Milton had erected a white screen and was removing a camera from its pouch. "Jessica, can you please stand with your back to the screen?" he asked. He took several regulation passport photographs and then walked back to the table and started working on some documents. Minutes later he said, "Jessica, Natasha asked me to introduce you to your new identity, Jamila Hassan." Milton handed her a passport for the Kingdom of Saudi Arabia, a marriage certificate, a birth certificate, and a driver's permit.

Natasha handed her a four-page document. "This document contains details about your background. Make sure you memorize the biographical facts by the time we land."

Jess's eyes widened and gleamed. "Thank you. I did not expect …

Thank you." She took the documents and walked toward the clothing laid out on the chair.

When Jess returned to the main cabin, she was wearing a blue dress and a black burka. The inflight crew was moving around the aircraft, serving drinks and meals.

"I will know by tomorrow. All signs are that we are in position to begin Operation Aleiqi," Batdadi said, continuing his conversation despite Jess's presence. "One of the Khan brothers is with Allah. Alas, Jamal can't attend the burial of his dead brother. The risk is too great, so he can't be with us on the journey."

Jess moved her eyes down to him but realized he was talking on the phone.

"Yes. Get everyone ready to move at a moment's notice. I will brief them in person tomorrow. We can't take any risks." Batdadi lifted his hand and waved to his head of security, Abdel, and then disconnected the call and turned to her. "Ah, Jessica! I hope everything is to your liking."

"Yes." She hesitated as she contemplated the issue of when, how, and where she would be compensated. *Wait, keep a cool head*, she told herself. *Now is not the time.* "Thank you."

"If you uphold your side, my American friend, you will be back on this jet and on your way to a new life of your choice. As you have already seen, we have doctors, identity papers, and more money than you can ever spend," Batdadi said.

Jess! Jess! What did I say? I told you we'd be rich.

Jess ignored Jessica and moved quickly toward the seats at the rear of the cabin. She bent to slide into the window seat but hesitated when she noticed the restrooms. Looking back to see if anybody was observing her, she slipped into a restroom and locked the door.

"Jessica, you bitch! You're going get us killed. Yes, if I die, you die. Did you miss that fucking detail when Batdadi became your new best friend? Fuck you! I don't want to die, and I'm not spending the rest of my life incarcerated because you can't see past your Hamptons lifestyle. I want to know your contact. The fucking money is no good to you if you're dead. We can't talk now, but you will. You'll tell me everything."

Yes, Jess, everything. I'll tell you the entire story.

Jess's heart was hitting her chest hard and fast when she opened the door and slid into her seat and picked up the biographical document Natasha had given her.

11

First Officer Birch stood inside the doorway of the Boeing C-40 Clipper and watched the Audi Q7 pull to a stop on the tarmac. *An extra passenger*, she thought when she saw five men climb out and approach. She scanned the airport grounds, determined there was no threat, and waved, hastening them into the aircraft.

When they were on board, she quickly handed out ice packs and hot towels in preparation for the customs official, who would be on his way to sign off on their departure. The men changed into clean clothes, two smart casual outfits and three suits and ties that had been ready for them in the plane's coat closet. Birch stowed their mission clothing and gear in a concealed compartment below an inspection panel on the floor.

Five minutes later, two customs agents climbed aboard. "Would you mind opening your bags, monsieurs?" one of the agents asked. The other agent stepped forward and looked inside their carry-on luggage. The agent who had spoken turned to Chuck. He had his legs crossed, one arm over his chest, and was stroking his beard, his expression saying, *Why are you wasting our fucking time?*

"Monsieur, please open your suitcase."

When Chuck complied, the agent gently lifted the folded shirts and gym clothes while his colleague checked the passports handed to him by First Officer Birch.

"Merci," he said, handing them back and then moved on to the cockpit to check the paperwork. When he returned to the main cabin, he thanked everyone, and then he and his colleague departed the aircraft.

Fifteen minutes after the door shut behind them, the aircraft was taxiing out of the yellow customs square on the ramp. Fifteen minutes after that, they climbed out of Paris airspace and then flew over the English Channel, leaving French airspace just after ten in the morning.

One full day after the Paris operation, Jake, BLT, Dan, Em-Dog, Chuck, and Alex sat in the conference room on the seventh floor of JSOC headquarters at Fort Bragg. The five men were still sore from the op, but they had each had a chance to go home and sleep for a few hours before heading into the office for the debriefing. Alex silenced the room by rising to his feet, walking over to door, and closing it. Then he returned to his seat. He pulled off his coat and draped it over the back of his chair at the head of the table and then blew out a long sigh. "Gentlemen."

BLT started the debrief, followed by the other operators. For the next three hours, they talked about what they had done, what they'd seen, and what they thought about what they had done and seen. The consensus was that they had all done extremely well to react to the drastic change in the operation, literally at the last minute.

Alex quietly observed the team through most of the discussion. After the five operators had finished, he stood up and raised his hand to silence them. "You've gone over what happened. But now we need to talk about the downside. Although some bad guys were eliminated, it doesn't mean the FBI will let this go if word gets out that we were involved." Alex paused to let his words sink in. "As you might expect, the media have picked up this incident, and they are speculating that two terrorist factions butted heads. The guests at the hotel reported they saw men crashing into rooms and shooting at each other. Our analyst researched what French authorities know, or think they know, about what was going on. The judicial police are investigating this, but DCRI is fudging, not granting interviews of their people on the scene to investigators, so the police aren't getting anywhere. And so far, this is not pointing at us. The video evidence has not identified you guys. So far, no guest has come forward with a cell phone close-up shot of any of you. If and when that happens, we'll cross that bridge. So, that's the good news. Now the bad news—they're going to dig a lot deeper. I'm sure that doesn't surprise you."

Alex put a bottle of water to his lips, quenched his dry throat, and then continued. "OK, let's talk about where we are now and next steps. According to intercepted communications from French security officials, Batdadi was suspicious something was about to go down, and his men were set up to wait and see. They had over three hundred rounds of ammo between them. There were no suppressors on their machine pistols. As you experienced, those fucks were cued up to shoot their way out. Because of your quick actions, the lives of several cops and civilians were saved."

"What about the Bat?" Jake asked.

"He's disappeared. Unfortunately, police on the street prevented any realistic pursuit."

"Batdadi and his men were not there to commit any sort of terrorist act," BLT said. "They were there because of Jessica. What we're missing is the connection. Why is Batdadi interested in a 'head bunny,' a low-level criminal?" He looked at Jake. "Jake, I make no apologies. She is and always has been a fucking crazy bitch."

"Damn!" Jake said, clasping his hands together. "And your point?"

Alex let Jake's comment hang. "It's obvious that Batdadi came to Paris to meet Jessica, though we still don't know why. And for the second time, the target evaded us."

"Hold up," BLT said.

Ignoring him, Alex stood up, leaned forward, and put his palms on the table. "Make no mistake, you guys did your job. And yes, we must get ahead of Batdadi. But we can't let anything like this happen again. A running gun battle in the Ritz and on the streets of Paris? Goddamn it! There were cameras, witnesses, police, and civilians in the way. This isn't what we do. This debacle could compromise the CIA's reputation."

"Alex!" BLT said.

"No!" Alex raised his hand. "No matter the reason, we've seen the outcome. I've made myself clear."

Jake had been on adrenalin for the past thirty-six hours. *It's not like we came home in body bags*, he thought as he listened to Alex. *Things worked out OK, even though the Bat and Jessica got away. I suppose that's the point. We didn't get what we went for. We didn't get him—or her. Alex crash-landed us. We were lucky. This time, we prevailed. Next time, it could turn into a disaster. Since Alice died though, I've lived one day at time.*

The meeting was broken up by a knock at the door. Caterers entered the room and laid out sandwiches, fresh coffee, water, and an assortment of snacks on a side table.

Alex placed a hand on Jake's shoulder when he got up to get some food, along with the other men. Jake thought he was about to be to be dismissed from the team. After all, he had been brought onto the op for a specific purpose, and the mission was fast going south. He'd been expecting it ever since Jessica had evaded them and had not communicated with him in thirty-six hours. But instead of his marching orders, Alex had something else in mind.

"Jake, you outperformed our expectations on the op, given your limited training three days ago and lack of field operations these past years. We've had an uptick in OPTEMPO, and I want you to stay on the team. I see no value in continuing your evaluation." Alex held a handout to stop Jake's response. "We all value your knowledge and input, and I know it helped us enormously in Paris. You demonstrated that you are absolutely one of the team now, and we need you out there with us."

"I appreciate it," Jake said and then got up and walked over to the food table.

The men ate and talked before filing out of the conference room, coffee and water in hand.

Jake caught up to BLT in the hallway. "Hey, BLT, you got a minute?"

"Sure, what's up?" Just then BLT's cell phone vibrated. He picked it up. "Yeah? Sure, OK. Be right there." BLT looked at Jake as he hung up. "Alex needs us at his desk. We can speak later. The guys and I will be at Paddy's Irish Pub in town."

It was just after seven when Jake pulled into the parking lot and parked a black Suburban opposite the pub. The sun had sunk lower in the sky, the light of day giving way to the dark of night. As Jake crossed the parking lot, crickets chirped and mosquitoes buzzed as streetlights clicked on. The tavern was popular with the law enforcement community.

When Jake arrived, the locals were having a party. Thunderous music spilled out when he opened the door, the bass thumping in time with his heartbeat. As he approached the bar, over the roar of the music, he heard distant, hazy chatter. He could not make out any words, but he heard the laughter of BLT, Dan, Em-Dog, and Chuck, who were drinking at the bar and reliving the events of the Paris op.

Shortly after Jake joined the guys, three women turned their attention away from the party and strolled over to Jake and the others, who were riding high.

"You had something on your mind earlier," BLT said, turning away from the other men in their group.

Jake swallowed the beer in his mouth. "Yes." He looked directly at BLT. "Are we good?" He continued before BLT could respond. "I returned, as requested, to the same people. Everything has moved on in my absence. I wasn't foolish enough to imagine anything would remain the same or that my friends would be excited to embrace me and chat, catching up like we never missed a beat." BLT listened attentively as Jake continued. "It's all too obvious that the 'gaping' hole I left on departure has long since healed and scarred over. I'm no longer part of the team's natural flow. Everyone's out of kilter, and there's an awkwardness I never expected. Was it so wrong for me to make an effort to forget? To leave the past behind?"

"I've been around the block a few times," BLT replied. "I'm not—we're not—judging you, but when the bullets are flying, we need to know you can still operate as part of a cohesive unit." He raised his hand to stifle Jake's response. "You're good. You can get the job done and lead the guys. I almost pity the mujahedeen." BLT raised his glass to his mouth and drank and then lowered it onto the bar. "We're done here."

Throughout their conversation, Jake had continually scanned the room and now homed in on two women in the party crowd. The women were pushing away a man's unwanted advances. When they continued to refuse to dance with him, the man put his glass on the table and went to the restroom. Moments later, the two women left the dance area and walked over to the bar.

"Ladies," Chuck said. He turned toward the bartender. "Drinks for the ladies." He placed a hundred-dollar bill on the bar. Chuck was a charismatic Irishman. For reasons Jake could not fathom, the girls loved his short, curly black hair. He had grown up in Wisconsin on a dairy farm. He was the life and soul of the party, a joker with a great sense of humor. He had already drawn five women to join them at the bar.

When the local guy emerged from the restroom and passed the bar, he looked at one of the women who had rejected him and was now talking to Chuck. He stopped and pulled her away. "She's with me," the man said.

"Really? It didn't look that way to me," Chuck replied.

The man released the woman and rammed his body into Dan, knocking his and Chuck's drinks out of their hands. Their glasses shattered, and the beer splashed the women and Chuck.

Quick to anger, Chuck locked eyes with the local. BLT looked at Jake. Chuck was the last of the bare-knuckle fighters. "Poor judgment," BLT said.

Jake nodded. "Truly poor judgment." He turned and looked at the other locals, who were crowded around the bar. "Fuck them all. I'd rather get my ass beat than look like a pussy."

In that frozen second between standoff and fighting, Jake saw the locals' eyes flick from him to BLT, Dan, Em-Dog, and finally Chuck. The faces of Jake and his companions were unreadable—no fear and no invitational smirk. Jake calculated and was banking on the locals making a predicted mistake, and they did.

The locals flew at Chuck, ignoring the other guys. The locals expected it to be thirty to one, over in a bloody flash, and then they would go back to their cave. They did not intend to kill him, just make him yield and then lick their boots and do their bidding. But things didn't go their way at all. In seconds, Jake had taken two, BLT three, and Chuck five. Snow would've been stained darkly with the flow of blood from the locals. No butchery, just expertly immobilized zealots.

Jake looked around. *Impressive.* His training was holding up despite his time in civilian life. There was no pleasure on his face as the fight spilled out of the bar. Jake and his cohorts were a force to be reckoned with, and that night they did the reckoning.

Fifteen minutes later, Jake maneuvered the Suburban, carrying BLT,

Chuck, Dan, and Em-Dog around ghostly sedans. Atop the white bodywork, red-and-blue lights flashed brightly in the gathering gloom, drawing attention to two burning, flipped-over cars and first responders carrying locals into ambulances.

12

Jake walked into the conference room and found BLT, Chuck, and Dan. Em-Dog entered shortly thereafter. "Is this about last night?" Jake asked.

Dan shrugged.

OK, Jake thought. *You have your suspicions, but you don't want to be the first to explore the possibility that Alex is about to walk into this conference room and give us all a roasting.*

When the guys were under the command of the Navy SEALs hierarchy, they would have been summoned to the captain's mast. The captain would listen to what they had done and hand out a nonjudicial punishment, if warranted. The punishment would be prescribed by military law and could be anything from a stern "don't do that again" to a reduction in rank or correctional custody. They weren't under the classic command structure, though, and if Jake's hunch that the meeting was about the previous night was correct, he could only guess their fate.

The door to the conference room flew open. Alex strode in and slammed a file on the table. When he looked up at them, his face was red, and his eyes were narrow, rigid, cold, and hard. His focus was somewhere behind them, as if they had become invisible to him or he could not bear to look at them, like they had crossed some invisible line and deeply offended his sensibilities. The bond between them was not immune. Anger was just the start.

He picked up the file and slammed it onto the table again. "Goddammit! Twelve locals were hospitalized. Y'all caused thousands of dollars of property damage too." He continued for several minutes, telling them how truly fucked up they were. "I'm ashamed of y'all," he said finally, sounding like a parent. "The only reason you're not in jail is several witnesses say you were not the instigators." Alex held still; his eyes locked on Chuck's. "Don't let it happen again. Now get out of here."

Chuck stood and quickstepped to the door. Just then there was a knock, and Chief Analyst Martin "Marty" Burnette entered, almost bashing the door into Chuck's face. "Excuse me," Marty said and then headed to the table, where he set up his Microsoft Surface. "Please gather around, boys. The facial-recognition software came back with a hit on John Doe."

"And?" BLT said.

Marty tapped the keyboard, and one of the pictures taken by BLT's digital camera in the Ritz appeared on half of the twelve-inch screen.

"Who is he?" Jake asked.

Marty worked on the keyboard and brought up a photograph of twin brothers Jamal and Abdul Khan.

"The master bombers!" Jake said. The Khan brothers stood side by side in the photo holding bomb parts. Silence filled the room as dread crept over them like an icy chill.

"Holy shit!" BLT said.

"Facial recognition says there's a 97 percent chance that John Doe is Abdul Khan," Marty said. He moved his index finger on the touchpad and then clicked. A picture of the Khan brothers approaching the Paris Ritz appeared. "This was taken by a security camera twenty-eight hours before the Paris op."

"Both brothers were in Paris, and now one is dead," Jake said.

Marty looked up. "Yeah?"

"The Khan brothers are also connected with the Bat, Jessica, and the meeting in Paris," BLT said. "I hate to state the obvious, but we need to find out what the fuck is going on and why that crazy bitch Jessica is in the middle."

Alex ran his hands over his head. "We need to know more about Jessica and the Khan brothers' activities."

The others nodded in agreement.

"BLT, I'd like you and Jake to speak to Sandy Argo at the National Counterterrorism Center," Alex continued. "She'll have the most up-to-date intel on the Khan brothers." He picked up his file and then hesitated. "Jake, I've received the FBI's update on their investigation. I've emailed you a list of Jessica's contacts in recent years. Something might jump out."

BLT and Jake reached Liberty Crossing, the name given to the campus of the National Counterterrorism Center (NCTC), just before noon. They halted at the front gate and handed their IDs to the security guard, who checked their names against the visitors' list on his monitor. The guard opened the gate, and BLT steered their Suburban into the complex. Numerous agencies worked together at the NCTC, compiling, prioritizing, and analyzing data that came in from intelligence sources across the US intelligence community, as well as from foreign partners.

The soft clicks of Sandy's heels hit the marble floor as she crossed the lobby to meet BLT and Jake. The walls were covered with gray and ivory wallpaper and motivational photography set in silver frames. The NCTC director extended her hand first to BLT and then to Jake. "Hi, and welcome to Liberty Crossing." She was an attractive woman who looked to be nearly forty, with long brown hair and a petite build.

"Sandy," Jake said as he shook her hand, "I'm Jake Logan, and this is Rob Dempsey." She guided them through the visitor sign-in process. Then they took the elevator to one of the meeting rooms. The room was tasteful in a corporate way—nothing interesting enough to cause offence no matter what a person's preferences might be. It was clinical for identically clinical workers in clean-cut suits. They sat at the circular table in the center of the room. "Coffee? Water?" she asked, reaching for the coffee pot on the table.

"No, thank you," Jake said.

BLT put his hand out and took the cup of coffee she had poured. "Thank you," he said. He placed the cup on the table and then reached into his breast pocket and pulled out a photograph.

"The Khan brothers," she said as he slid it across the table. "What else am I looking at here?"

"The guy on the right, Abdul, was confirmed dead forty-eight hours ago," BLT said. "The photo of the brothers was taken outside the Ritz Paris hours before his demise."

Sandy looked up at Jake and BLT with curiosity. "Paris?"

BLT nodded. "That's right."

Her eyes were no longer quizzing; they pierced BLT. "Why don't I know about this sighting of the brothers and the death of one?"

BLT shrugged. Alex had asked them not to mention the Paris operation, so he couldn't tell her he had taken the photo of Abdul Khan minutes after his death and how that image had made the connection to the Khan brothers in the facial-recognition software.

"Belgium's Special Forces Group were following the brothers two weeks back," Sandy said. "It was a 'wait-and-see' op, but they lost them after days of surveillance."

Jake and BLT stared at her in astonishment.

"Yes, they missed an opportunity to take them off the streets," Sandy continued.

"SFG had eyes on the Khan brothers and didn't eliminate the threat?" Jake asked. "How fucked up is that?"

"Intel reported a sighting of Asyd Omar Batdadi in Paris a few days ago, and we believe he was there to meet the Khan brothers," BLT said.

Sandy multitasked, using her electronic tablet while listening. She paused, and her eyebrows rose. "That's not good—"

She was interrupted by a knock at the door. An analyst entered, placed a file on the table, and then turned and walked out, closing the door behind her.

Sandy pulled three photographs from the file and placed them side by side on the table. "The man on the right is Batdadi. This was taken on the day we now know you received your intel on Batdadi, sighting him in Paris." Sandy looked up to gauge their interest. "That's also him on the left. The photo was taken in Pakistan at or about the same time the Paris photo was taken."

BLT looked up at Jake in disbelief. "A double in Paris? Or could the one in Pakistan be the phony?"

"Yes and no," Sandy said. "Look at the center photo taken in Saudi Arabia twenty-four hours before the other two photographs. This strongly resembles Batdadi, notwithstanding plastic surgery. So, Batdadi was in Paris … or was he?"

"Unless we go in and get DNA ourselves, we'll never know if we have the right person," Jake said.

BLT nodded in agreement.

Sandy looked directly at Jake and BLT. "The CIA intel is based on what little is known about the man. Yes, the intelligence can detail the terrorist acts he's behind, but other than the name and the photos, there's literally no bio for the guy. I'm pleased to know you guys have been working on this, albeit without the full picture."

"Hey, we can't often talk about what we are and aren't involved in," BLT said. "Sources and methods, right?" He sipped his coffee. This information was important, another piece of the puzzle. He was energized. He placed his cup on the table. "We need to report to Alex."

"Thank you for your time today," Jake added as they stood up.

Outside the gates of the NCTC grounds, BLT sat in the Suburban and wrote up his report on the afternoon meeting for Alex. "The only reason Sandy agreed to the meeting was because she wanted to learn something from us," BLT said without looking up.

"She takes a read on all the people she meets—or should I say attempts to do so. Goes with the territory," Jake replied as he read the email from Alex containing Jessica's recent contacts. "Hey," he nudged BLT. "This guy, Milton, was in Egypt when Jessica was living there with a CIA dude."

"And?" BLT said.

"He has a shady—correction—a *criminal* background."

13

Waking up was no longer a pleasure. There was a fleeting moment when Jessica was whole again, and then the feeling would evaporate like steam. Her drooping eyelids, leaden with sleep, would snap open violently, as if she'd been woken by sirens wailing. *Don't know how long I've been unconscious or what Jess has done. I remember the arguments and then … and then what?* By the time her eyes were open, her brain was overwhelmed all over again, as if it were all new, fresh, and raw. Jessica closed her eyes and wished she could linger in that blissful ignorance of the first seconds of waking.

She moved her palms over the soft sheets. Her eyes were still shut as she soaked in the warmth of the covers. Slowly and reluctantly, she uncovered her face, blinked, closed her eyes, and blinked again. Streaks of sunlight penetrated the window, blinding her. Jessica basked in her senses and the fragrant, fresh linen. Aside from her breathing, she heard nothing. She sat up, stretched her arms above her head, and yawned.

Jessica looked about in amazement. "Where am I? Jess! Is this my new bedroom?" A smile spread across her face as she continued to take in the room. The king-size bed looked like a snowdrift, white and feathery with four dark oak posts. French windows opened onto a balcony and were draped in white linen. "OMG!" She stared at the beautiful mural on the wall above the fireplace. "Jess, thank you!" She swung her feet off the bed, closed her eyes, and dangled her legs above the deep, luxurious, off-white pile carpet. She put her feet down on the carpet and explored its sumptuousness with every step she took toward the bathroom.

Jessica let out a sudden, sharp cry. She put her hand on the washstand to steady herself, causing an old-fashioned bowl and pitcher to fall and break, the fragments hitting her legs. She stared at her face and neckline in the gilt mirror on the wall. Displaying intense revulsion, she screamed with her entire body. Her eyes were wide with horror, her mouth rigid and open, and her face gaunt and immobile. She clenched her fists and dug her nails into the palms of her hands. "I'm black!"

Brick by brick, Jessica's walls tumbled down. She stepped back, causing the bathroom door to shut. Sobs punched through her, ripping into her muscles, bones, and guts. She pressed her head against the door as her heart was yanked in and out of her chest and her body slipped to the floor. Tears burst forth like water from a ruptured dam, spilling down her face.

"Jess?" She raised her head and looked at the window, hoping the light would soothe her. Jessica grabbed her head. She felt static in her cavities, the side effect of constant fear and stress. She sounded like a distressed child, raw on the inside.

Natasha pushed the bathroom door open and found Jessica curled up like a baby in a crib. "Jessica!"

She did not reply.

Natasha knelt, lifted Jessica's head, and gently placed it in her lap. "What's wrong? Talk to me, please," she said, stroking her hair.

"Jess once told Beth that sanity is just a limited mind, that sanity is a mental operating system accepted by the masses as within normal parameters."

"Jess?" Natasha said.

"I'm not like you."

"This Beth, what else did she tell you?"

"I have something different. I can shift from one operating system to another invisibly. You won't ever know which one I'm using because I don't have to tell you a goddamn thing." *Go, Jessica! Fuck the shrinks and do-gooders. Plans? You're not part of their plans.* The voice in her head was strong.

Jessica looked at her brown hands. Her eyes dripped tears. She stiffened her body. "I can do this. I will get revenge. I will." She lifted her head and looked at Natasha. "If the shrinks can't read my mind, neither can you. We're done. No more cozy chitchats. You want us on your side. You need us on your side."

Jessica pulled away from Natasha and walked back into the bedroom. Natasha followed but headed straight for the door. She held it open, allowing a waiter to wheel a breakfast trolley into the room.

When the door closed and Jessica was alone again, she sat at the table and raised her hands, tears welling in her eyes. *Jessica, stop! Stop now! Do you know what you are? A superficial racist bitch. And stupid! Stating the obvious, you're white! You can't turn black. What difference does the color of your skin make anyway? Scared you won't be accepted at your parties in the Hamptons? The color will fade, but if you don't tell me the name of your contact, I will permanently scar our face.*

"Jess, does the truth imprison us or set us free?"

What the fuck are you talking about?

"One thing we know for sure—the truth can hurt. Ask a drug addict or a sex addict who has faced friends and professionals in an intervention."

Your point?

"The addict arrives home or at work to discover a room full of people well known to him. The addict takes one look around and knows what has happened."

Where's this going? You're hurting my head.

"One person takes the lead, and then it's on—that is, if the addict doesn't get angry and leaves. Even then the addict has a head-on collision with the truth. The truth is the addict is ruining his life and the lives of his friends and family."

Fuck! Jessica, you don't have any family. You're crazy.

"Let me finish, Jess. The addict is faced with a mirror of himself and the love and concern of others. Hopefully, the addict will see the truth in their eyes and words. Some do hear and turn their lives around. Facing the truth about our negative side is difficult though."

Fuck you. I'm not your negative side.

"I'm not saying you're negative or bad. Facing the truth about our negative side is difficult, but we can't improve without knowing the truth, even when it hurts. If we learn the truth, it does really set us free."

What the fuck? I clean up your mess, and you want me to do better. I'd rather you just said, "Thank you."

"We need to face our demons. We need help."

I won't ask again.

Jessica fought against her hand as it reached for the carving knife on the table. She wrapped her fingers around the handle. Struggling with its weight, she tried to resist the force that was directing the blade toward her cheek.

I'll cut you!

She reached up with left hand and grabbed her right wrist. "No, Jess!" She pulled her right arm away from her face. The knife slipped from her hand. "Ambrose," she said. "Ambrose will help us."

14

The lingering light was obliterated by the rapidly falling night. Hues of fiery red and crimson transformed into a vast expanse of blackness that engulfed the town behind Farooq Abboud. His journey had started in Dunmore, Pennsylvania, on Interstate 81. As he raced southeast through the Poconos, he relied on the dark and the fact that section of the freeway was lightly populated to conceal him. He had to be careful not to draw attention.

He passed through densely wooded country, except for the swampy areas in southern Wayne Country. The only development he passed was a commercial strip just south of Matamoras, west of the Delaware River. It was 9:00 p.m., and he'd been driving for two hours, but Farooq was desperate to arrive at his destination as soon as possible. He gripped the steering wheel. The man who had summoned him to the council must have had a good reason. "Yes!" he said. "At last, I get to advance the word of Allah. I will not let this man down or keep him waiting."

A wealthy Arab, Farooq was twenty-nine years old and six foot two. His facial features were typical of his ethnicity—big eyes, arched eyebrows, and dense eyelashes. But he differed in one respect; his jaw was a long, tight V with a five o'clock shadow. He was slim and athletic, and women found him stunning.

The next thirty minutes brought him to the New York border. For the first mile, the road ran along the New Jersey state line. Then it curved to the north. He glanced at the GPS map on the center console to confirm he had not deviated from the preprogrammed route. His orders were that the contact would meet him across the Hudson River at Newburgh.

Farooq was born in Southport, Connecticut. His wealthy parents had moved from Dubai to Washington, DC, two years before his birth. He'd spent his early years in the United Arab Emirates embassy in DC. From a young age, he'd excelled and developed a fascination with missiles, satellites, and aerospace. Upon graduation from high school, he was accepted at Harvard University, where he studied chemistry, physics, and technology. At age twenty-two, he went into the private sector. He was hired as a project manager / engineer by Lockheed Martin in Pennsylvania, an American global aerospace, defense, security, and advanced technologies company. Farooq's work was his life.

Over the past two years, everything had changed for Farooq. At a cocktail party he attended with his parents at the United Arab Emirates embassy, he had been introduced to An al Alin Hassan. Hassan had talked at length about Farooq's work at Lockheed Martin. He had also broached the subject of religion, which had pleased Farooq, as his social circle had incrementally narrowed as he had become increasingly serious about his Islamic faith. That night Farooq had lain in bed and replayed Hassan's observation that Farooq's potential had not been realized. He had thought about his place in this world and what legacy he would take to the afterlife. He desperately wanted a different direction in life. The next day, he took Hassan's business card from his wallet and called him.

He also had renewed confidence. He put aside his fear that, when he died, in time, he would be forgotten, that he would live an unimportant life surrounded by people who would not go down in the history books. *No, he told himself, Allah has given me strength to martyr myself for the cause.*

Farooq turned left onto an unlit side road and then parked his car. He checked his watch. He was on time.

He jerked when the glare of headlights shone into his car, stinging his eyes. Seconds later, the beams dipped but continued to illuminate a path through the clearing. Two shadows appeared in the rearview mirror, their spirit-like forms flickering through the light. The figures approached, one on each side of his car. Farooq rotated his head when he heard a tap on the passenger window. He lowered it.

"Please leave the keys in the ignition, Mr. Abboud."

Before he had released his grip on the steering wheel, the man on his side opened the car door. "The car up front will take you to your destination."

Farooq's heartbeat increased. He had not seen the other car or heard it approach, but he did not question their instructions. He stepped out of his car and moved toward the car in the clearing ahead of where he had parked.

As he neared the vehicle, Farooq noticed the rear door of the Mercedes was open. He bent over and slid into the back seat. To his surprise—he had not sensed anybody following him—the door slammed shut behind him. The car reversed and turned toward New York City. Farooq closed his eyes, assured he would be an asset in the cause of Islam and, God willing, achieve martyrdom.

Farooq arrived at the United Arab Emirates consulate on 5th Avenue in New York just before 1:00 a.m. He went through security and then took the elevator to the thirty-second floor. If he had ever known failure in his life, it didn't show. When he stepped onto the elevator, everything from the way he held himself to the way he spoke to the look of unassailable confidence in his eyes said he could do it. He took in his surroundings. *I would not have been asked to come here, in this way, if it were not important,* he thought.

Hassan was waiting when he was shown into the room. He stepped forward and embraced Farooq. "Allah supports our war against the infidels of this country. The time is at hand, and with your help, Allah will bless our cause," Hassan said. "Please, sit." Both men sat on the sofa. Bottles of water were set out on a side table.

Farooq beamed. "Tell me how I might help the cause."

"I gave careful thought to our recent discussions and—"

"Yes?" Farooq asked.

"The C-4 explosives you have amassed."

"Yes, what do you want me to do? I can bring this weapon to you. Just give the word."

"Wait, not so fast, my brother. I have a specific need—"

"Speak, what do you need?" Farooq said, unable to control his excitement.

"What would be the impact of your weapon—let's say a backpack full—in this very room?"

"The blast would blow out the windows and at least the floors above and below." Farooq smiled; he had pleased Hassan. "We are blessed, Allah willing. This I can do."

"Excellent!" Hassan reached to the side of the sofa and grabbed a four-wheeled Tumi carry-on suitcase and a messenger bag. Farooq watched, curious as to what was coming next. "The C-4, would it be stable if concealed in these receptacles?" Hassan asked.

"C-4 has a texture similar to modeling clay and can be molded into any shape. Yes, it would be stable. An explosion can only be initiated by a shock wave from a detonator."

"Can we detonate it remotely?"

"Yes, using a fail-safe that links the suitcase and the messenger bag to cell phones. If the devices fail to go off at the designated time, a handler can trigger it remotely. Hassan, my brother, tell me when and where."

"We won't speak of the target building tonight. We have much to discuss, but I have other business to which I must attend. Please, rest and eat. We will go over the details later. Allah has been good to us. Let's pray together and give thanks for the bounty of this night."

15

"Dissociative identity disorder is a natural response to being unable to solve problems, Jessica," psychiatrist Amira Bajwa said.

"What the fuck are you talking about? Why are you here? Who told you I have DID?"

"You and your case are internationally renowned, Jessica. You've received a lot of publicity recently."

"So, I'm a celebrity," Jessica said.

"I wouldn't categorize it quite like that, but as I mentioned at the start of this session, I'm a psychiatrist. My life's work is devoted to the treatment of mental disorders. I want to help you."

"I'm not sure about talking to you. Jess—"

It's OK. Talk to Amira.

"In childhood, we are more creative. The part of our brain that dreams at night has more access to our daytime thinking, and we can dream up the most wonderful fantasies, even live them in a way. It's what small children do all the time," Amira said, ignoring Jessica's reference to Jess.

"Go on," Jessica said.

"For the most part, we fail to continue using our imagination—or, rather, it gets 'educated' out of us. The connections between the subconscious and the conscious mind weaken, like anything does when not used. In times of problems and/or stress, the brain panics and tries to reconnect them. The result is 'awake dreaming' or psychosis. And since the person is already in crisis, it's difficult to handle."

"So … Jess is my subconscious, and there's only conscious me? OMG! What are you saying we do?"

You fucking bitch. Stop! Don't get ahead of yourself. Just listen if that's not too complicated for you. If you don't, I'm sure Batdadi will hasten your meeting with Allah. Oh, I forgot. Just because you're black that doesn't make you Muslim. So, I'm thinking hell is a better resting place!

"Oh, sorry, my dear. You misunderstand," Amira said. "We can't make Jess go away. My work is stopping the destruction of the connections, so you can see your path forward."

"But—"

"Let me finish. Above all, you need to be loved and have the freedom to pursue your dreams, your imagination, without fear of judgment. We can cure everything with whole and connected minds—everything."

"You mean Jess and I can be friends?"

"Yes, something like that."

"Beth did say we could coexist."

"Bethany Jones, your previous psychiatrist?"

"Yes. Jess called her 'Bitch Beth.'"

"Our approach to curing mental illness has been wrong for so long, speaking to the conscious mind when it was the one underneath that needed to talk."

"You mean Jess?"

"Yes, Jess has a voice, and you ignore her at your peril."

Way to go, Amira! I told you you need me more than I need you.

"We have to talk to the subconscious, soothing the entire mind."

"Selling and creating art was my livelihood. I had plans to open an art gallery." Jessica thought about how she used to sit in a room full of art all day long. "Being surrounded by original art enhances my creative expression. I've even produced a few pieces of my own."

"You can still make your dreams come true."

"I lived vicariously through my Upper East Side and Hampton friends. I had the designer outfits and the most perfect shoes ever made. It was as easy as A, B, C finding men on the internet, but …" Tears swelled in her eyes. "They didn't stay, and I had to freeze my eggs."

"Jessica"—Amira put her hand on Jessica's knee—"my dear, we know about the egg freezing and acquired your eggs—they're safe. Help Jess help us, and we'll give you the life and the family of your dreams." She smiled at Jessica.

Fuck you, Jessica. Take her offer. Yes, life was good at first, and then you spent more time on the internet, drank red wine, and swallowed pills. Your midriff became softer and fatter, and the depression began. I told you to go back to work. You had status then. You were someone. Now who the fuck, are you? Some over-the-hill woman desperately buying bleaching solutions for your hair and expensive wrinkle-reduction creams. You think you had the best of everything, but your "friends" scattered when the depression deepened. It was mental illness, after all. They didn't go all at once, but their calls became less frequent, until they stopped altogether. Revenge I will get, and it starts with that fucking banker, Jake. So, you will accept the offer.

"Anyway, Dr. Amira—"

"Just Amira, please."

"Mental illness, being crazy, loopy, insane, it sounds amusing from the outside but not so much from the inside. Imagine the worst nightmare you ever had. Take a moment to recall it. Then imagine you're unable to wake from it because you're already awake."

Stop the bullshit, Jessica! Accept the fucking offer!

"Jess, let me finish. All those bizarre ideas that make so much sense when you're asleep start to make sense with your eyes wide open. I'm not going to tell you too much more right now. Please don't be offended, but I don't know you very well yet. Later on, sure. But Jess wants to work with you, and I want to be her friend, so I'll talk to Ambrose."

Jessica, I'll take it from here. You'll be OK. We'll be OK.

When Jessica heard Jess in her head, she was tired and gave way.

"Maybe there's some aspect of this that worries you?" Jess asked Amira. "You look almost sickly. Oh, I get it. You think I might drive you crazy, that Jessica and I switching was not part of the plan. Plans! No plan means you'll go crazy. Hmm … well, I won't lie to you. That's what it means for some people, but only if they aren't with me. I can work without a plan. Anyway, once you have some kind of nervous breakdown, your brain is weakened. And you don't want that; trust me. Plus, you could go off on almost any tangent. It can ruin your life for years, and sometimes you don't really recover. I don't recommend it, not for anyone, least of all you. You're so nice! I think you're adorable! But we need some ground rules. You need your 'plans.' Asyd Batdadi has 'plans,' but don't fuck with me."

"Jess, I didn't mean to … The agreed course was I talk to Jessica, get her onboard, and move forward. If I—"

"You think I'm angry with you? Oh no, not at all. I forget these things faster than the Flash can run, ha ha. No, seriously, I'm not the kind to hold a grudge. Glad to see you're looking composed again. I didn't like that rapid changing thing with Jessica at first, not cool. You want to know more about my mental illness, but you're scared to ask, right? How did I know that? It's obvious. People find it as fascinating as those cop shows with dead bodies draped all over the place. I'm not saying you're morbid, though, not at all. I like you! I used to watch those cop shows myself, until I figured out their role in keeping me 'asleep.' All that fear seems exciting at the time, but it isn't good for anyone. It just makes us feel good about ourselves for not being barbaric monsters instead of actually getting off our backsides and doing something positive. That's partly what I mean by 'sleeping.' I prefer being fully awake. Everyone's much safer that way. Trust me."

Amira reached out to shake Jess's hand but then pulled back. "Jess, if you or Jessica need to talk, I'm on call." She stood up and walked out of the room.

Natasha was waiting outside her office.

"Jessica is onboard," Amira said. "The other personality, Jess, believes she can control her. It's risky, but I believe the rewards outweigh the pitfalls."

16

One day after BLT and Jake returned from the NCTC, Alex entered the conference room, ten minutes late for their scheduled meeting. Jake and the other Paris operatives were already there, as was Marty from the analyst team. All the men were sipping coffee and chatting when Alex arrived.

"There's an interesting new development from Jake's identification of Milton Williams as a person of interest," Alex said as he walked across the room and placed his file on the table. "Jake, bring the room up to speed on Williams."

"Milton Williams, art forger and former colleague of Jessica Brooks, aka Jess. For over ten years, Williams, through intermediaries, duped several museums into accepting fakes into their collections. The forgeries made headlines around the world. The FBI investigated known art thieves and suspects connected to organized crime. Agents followed leads across the United States, Europe, and Asia. Williams's name came up as a suspect, but then he disappeared without a trace."

"Did you have any contact with Williams?" Chuck asked. "Friendly or otherwise?"

"In a crowded room, Williams is conspicuous. It's as if he parachuted in from Milan, Paris, or some other fashionable place that none of the rest of us has ever visited. In whatever conversation he's in, the other person is enthralled, yet afterward they don't recall anything important about what he said. He can converse without leaving any verbal 'fingerprint.' Make no mistake, morals are a weakness, and no one has ever accused him of having them."

Alex closed his file and looked up at Jake. "Thank you. Jake highlighted one other recent contact of Jessica's, Tom Pérez."

"Who?" Em-Dog asked.

"A CIA operative in Egypt," Marty said. "He started his career as an intelligence reports officer in the Office of Near Eastern and South Asian Analysis, focused on providing support to countries in the Middle East and North Africa. Five years later, he moved over to field operations as an Egypt specialist."

"Tom dated Jessica," Jake added. "She lived with him in Egypt for just over a year."

"And you know this how?" Dan asked.

"She emailed me bragging about her new boyfriend when they were in Cairo."

"Williams has been living in Cairo since he evaded law enforcement," Alex said. "I guess it's his forgery heaven, a city filled with rich, unsuspecting Arabs. Intelligence from the CIA and other agencies says he's living among terrorist groups and has added money laundering to his résumé. I'm splitting hairs here. Until recently, he showed no interest in supporting terror against the West." He removed a photograph from his file and laid it on the table. "Pérez took this image of Williams and two men in an open-air café. Do you recognize the man in the shade under the umbrella?"

The men at the table looked at each other.

"Batdadi or his twin," Chuck said.

"Fuck!" Dan exclaimed.

Em-Dog looked at Alex. "When do we go?"

"No team. Chuck, you take this," Alex said.

"Sounds good to me. And Pérez?"

"Jesus Christ, he lived with a woman diagnosed with two distinct personalities for over a year. Jess exhibits all the traits of a psychopath, and Jessica is at best a narcissist. She walked out, so maybe there's nothing there, and he was just thinking with his balls," Alex said.

Chuck looked at Jake.

"Contact was made with Pérez three days ago. Shortly thereafter, he submitted this image, among others." Alex pointed at the photograph on the table. "We reached out with follow-up questions, but he's gone silent."

"He must be pretty fucked up, or he knows something we don't," Jake said. "He was tracking Williams. Jessica's electronic communications indicate she reached out to Williams while she was living in Cairo. We know Williams, Pérez, and Jessica arranged to meet for dinner. We can't confirm they broke bread together. That being said, Pérez knew Jessica and Williams were friends. Jessica is on the most-wanted list. Do you see where I'm going?"

"The more we can learn about Batdadi, the better, but in this business, we don't trust anyone," BLT said.

"At this stage, I make no accusations," Alex replied. "We need what Pérez knows and a sense of how long he's known it. I agree with BLT that our priority is Batdadi. Trust but verify. Pérez must come in."

"Check," Chuck said. He quickly gathered his belongings and exited the room to go down to the support desk to draw documents, cards, and cash.

The remaining men looked at Alex to ascertain his plans for them. "The C-40 is fueled up at Pope Airfield," he said. "I'd like you to go to Cannes tomorrow to set up covert surveillance on a safe house we believe is owned and used by Batdadi."

The meeting broke up soon after to allow the men to prepare for the upcoming operation.

17

Private jets generally landed at Cannes Airport, but the C-40, a larger aircraft, landed at nearby Nice Airport, cleared customs, and then parked. The four operators loaded their gear into a Bell OH-58 Kiowa, a single-rotor military helicopter that was waiting to ferry them to their destination. Thirty minutes after disembarking from the C-40, Jake, BLT, Dan, and Em-Dog were back in the air, watching the cool of the evening wash over fresh ocean waves as they kissed the sun-warmed sand. Jake savored the moment together.

Initially, the helicopter flew low along the Mediterranean coastline of France's southeast corner. Soon, they headed out over the sea in full view of a major yachting and cruising area with several marinas along the Cote d'Azur. The chopper touched down on a helipad in Cannes Bay that pointed out toward the sea at the height of the old port.

A Mark V Special Operations Craft pulled alongside the helipad. For the second time that day, the four operators unloaded their gear. Captain Gary Mitchells of the Special Warfare Combatant-Craft Crewmen welcomed Jake, BLT, Dan, and Em-Dog onboard. The sea was perfectly calm, like a peaceful lake, and its soft murmurs were scarcely audible. The waves seemed to be asleep. A darker blue line marked the curve of the horizon.

The craft set course for Batdadi's safe house. The flat sea stretched in all directions. Seagulls wheeled overhead, carried by the cool ocean breeze. His villa was in the Californie neighborhood of Cannes. It was set on three acres of beautifully manicured ground and offered total privacy and tranquility in addition to breathtaking views of the city, the mountains, and the Mediterranean. The Mark V was to be used as a reconnaissance platform for the operators to observe the safe house and approach from the sea. The plan was to get a closer look when night fell.

BLT touched Jake's shoulder. "Em-Dog and I will keep watch. You and Dan set up the gear."

"Fuck, you look like tonight will be your last on earth," Jake said.

For the last thirty minutes Jake and Dan had been below deck laying out and checking the equipment the team had brought onboard.

"Maybe I have good reason to think so," Dan replied.

"Is this something we should discuss with BLT?"

"Fuck you! A lot happened when you were filling your coffers on Wall Street."

"Sorry! I didn't mean anything by it. You looked—"

Dan raised his hand, indicating no harm had been done. He leaned back placing his elbow on the table "We were on an op, set to advance onto land. You know the mission 'get from here to there.' Surveyance before a troop landing. They appeared in my line of sight—a pair of eyes sticking out of the mud. My reaction was instinctive. Line up the target right between the eyes with a MK 3 and throw. It hit the man hard and square."

Jake nodded. "Go on."

"Suddenly, I was thrown forward and dragged down deeper into the Furat Canal."

"Iraq?"

"Yes. I'm not sure how deep it was—I wasn't interested in looking at my depth gauge—but I knew I was heading for hell. That entire area was booby-trapped. If one of theirs went down, they would take one of us—fucking human shields. The man, plus a heavy weight, was attached to a rope, and I was trying to remove it."

"What the fuck?"

"I was able to separate from the rope at about ninety feet," Dan continued. "The man vanished into the deep water, along with the weight."

"And your psychological evaluation said what?"

"Fuck you. What did yours say, Mr. Wall Street? I didn't run."

Just then the door to the cabin opened. "Boys," BLT said.

Jake and Dan continued to check the gear as if words had not been spoken. Eventually, Jake moved away from table, still irritated. He stared at Dan. *Fuck you! I was out of the loop, but I can still kick your fucking ass.* True, Jake had taken time out and pursued a career on Wall Street, but his days had started at 4:00 a.m. with Michael Murphy physical training—pushups, chin-ups, triceps dips, stomach crunches, and flutter kicks, along with daily runs. The only weight he used was his own body. He was confident about that night's dive. All his land-based physical training would translate well into the water: The flutter kicks had maintained his strengt' to push the fins. The runs had built up endurance for long surface swin and any underwater attacks using scuba.

The silence broke when Em-Dog clicked the cabin door open.

"We have a problem," he said as he threw his Steiner binoculars on chair. "Batdadi's property has a CONTROP scanning and observ; system. It provides a virtual fence over the water. It may detect us b we reach the boundary."

"CONTROP detects swimmers and small boats, but that's n(we'll approach," Jake said.

"When directed, we'll launch west of the virtual fence," BLT said. "We'll have a two-mile swim to reach the beach. Our presence will not be detected if we use rebreathers." Using rebreathers meant their exhaled breath would be recycled through chemical scrubbers, eliminating bubbles. "Once we hit the beach, our route is through the mountain passes. Questions?" The room remained silent. "Good. Be ready to go in fifteen."

The odds were even that one of the four operatives would inadvertently cross the virtual fence. The margin of error was small. No one made this a concern, though. As the Mark V approached the dive location, Captain Mitchells was on deck with BLT and his team, ready to signal the [...]

One by one, BLT, Em-Dog, and Dan jumped into the waters of the [Medit]erranean. Captain Mitchells lowered weighted, watertight boxes [from th]e side to Dan and BLT. The ocean was no longer calm; huge currents [roll]ed across the surface, the wind tearing white, moonlit spray from [the wave]s.

[Em-Dog ju]mped but broke the surface awkwardly and went under before [he could] collect his box. At a depth of ten feet, he did not have the [moon or s]tars to provide navigational guidance. He checked his dive [watch to f]ound the direction to the target. He lined his body up with [the bearing on] his compass and followed the other divers.

[His strokes] were compact, seemingly effortless, and soon became [routine. Every]thing was the same, silent other than a barely audible [hiss that] emanated from his rebreather. He focused on what [he was doing, resisting t]he momentary urges when his mind wandered. The [swim was ex]hausting. *My mission is to get to the shore equipped and in sufficient physical condition to fight on arrival.* He swam on, pushing his fins, his heart pounding, his timing as good as it would get.

One hour in, Jake felt sand beneath his fins. He was the first to arrive on shore. His muscles were tight, and he was dehydrated. He turned back and watched the other divers come on shore. The wind speed had increased and whipped the sea into tempestuous waves. Its powers unleashed a tumult of breakers that roared and smashed into the beach with unchecked fury.

BLT used a faint red flashlight to find an old, overturned, scuttled boat. Earlier that day, Captain Mitchells had concealed four backpacks under the boat, which rested against the rocks. The operatives shed their diving equipment, bundled it together, and placed it under the boat. They placed several rocks around the boat and on top to make it appear as if it had been abandoned. The operatives, who carried the watertight boxes in their backpacks, had a two-mile hike to the Bat's villa. Jake and the other men stood and looked on as the mountains loomed before them, their cold gray crevices holding the unknown.

18

The mountain path was wide where the sandy soil was soft and then narrowed into the rocky passes, where it wound up and around the mountain. Steep as it was narrow and rocky in a chaotic way, each footfall required enough strength to prevent Jake from falling into a steady rhythm. Sometimes the path was barely visible, no more than a mild disturbance in the dirt, but it led up to the peak, the only destination Jake, clad in night-vision goggles, had in mind.

As Jake came around the mountain, the path ahead was covered in loose rocks, each one washed smooth by the stream that had once run freely over them. Jake braced his feet, attempting to guard against the inevitable rolling in random directions, but his ankles tumbled left and right regardless. Thick, dark green boughs arched over the path from each side. During the day, their dappled shade provided relief from the harshness of the midday sun. At night, they did little to make the steep incline any easier. Jack lifted his eyes to the path ahead. After rising sharply, it turned out of view, likely carrying on in the same way.

In silence, Jake and the other operatives made their way past moss- and lichen-covered boulders sprawled in Mother Nature's rockery. At that hour, there was no trace of civilization in the wilderness, apart from the well-worn path. Jake's spirits were high. He cared little about the mud that stuck to his boots or the backpack that dug into his shoulders. His lungs bursting with fresh air, he tilted his head up and observed the stars in the black sky. There were no clouds and no horizon to delineate the sea behind them. The path faded into a void of mist and bare twigs.

Suddenly, the path rose steeply before disappearing at a rocky outcrop ahead. BLT looked at his compass, moving it to the left or the right. He slipped and then righted himself before gravity took him down onto the sunbaked rocks.

For the past hour, they had climbed across the top of a col, the path winding back and forth until they found themselves on the other side, where long mountains stretched on. The path went along the summit of the col and then dropped down. They followed the path until it came out of the mountains at the edge of a forest. The forest adjoined a field, where horses were grazing. Directly in front of the field was Batdadi's compound.

Around 1:30 a.m., BLT took up a vantage point that gave him a frontal view of the villa, using the forest for cover. Dan headed to the rear of the compound. Forty-five minutes passed before Dan's voice came through their earpieces. "Go, Dan," BLT said.

"Guard on patrol in the grounds behind the villa."

"Three in front, one in the guardhouse, one outside the villa, and one on patrol," BLT replied. "The front perimeter and grounds. The house appears to be uninhabited. Cameras operational. Given the CONTROP scanning and observation on the beach, the level of security might run to motion- and acoustic-monitoring equipment."

"Will remain in situ," Dan said.

"Copy that," BLT replied.

Jake and Em-Dog had removed the contents from the watertight boxes simultaneously with BLT and Dan's communications. Jake handed

Em-Dog a pair of video glasses and a remote control. Em-Dog put the glasses on and sat with his back against a tree.

"I've placed the helicopter on the landing pad," Jake said.

Em-Dog signaled his appreciation with a thumbs-up. Using a remote control, Em-Dog made contact with the infrared camera on the toylike, radio-controlled helicopter. It lifted into the sky, the payload attached to its belly. Once over the property, it would be invisible. Though quiet, it still posed a degree of risk.

Em-Dog moved his fingers over the toggle pad on the remote control until he had a view of BLT crouched in the forest below. BLT and Dan were his eyes on the ground. Jake sat next to Em-Dog with his laptop, waiting for Em-Dog's signal.

"Go," Em-Dog said.

Jake viewed transmissions from the helo's camera and then created an endpoint in its memory, a home to which it would return at the end of its mission. "Set," Jake said.

BLT's voice came through their earpieces.

"Go, BLT," Em-Dog replied.

"In position." BLT was now kneeling beside a tree ninety feet to the right of Jake and Em-Dog. He scanned the grounds around the guards using his M4's infrared scope. "Dan," BLT said.

"In position." Dan was to the side of the pool house using the night-vision scope on his submachine gun to scan the grounds behind the compound.

"All clear." Jake gave the green light to start the helo's approach.

Em-Dog flew the helo over the property. From an elevation of over a hundred feet, he could see the heat signature of Batdadi's security guards on patrol below, just out of earshot of the device. The helo's destination was the air-conditioning vent on the villa's roof. Em-Dog scanned the roof and then carefully landed the aircraft and shut down its engine. Jake reached into one of the airtight boxes, retrieved a second remote control, and handed it to Em-Dog. He turned on the remote, which connected to his video glasses, projecting an image from a second camera on a microrobot attached to the helo's underside. He entered several commands on the controller to detach the microrobot from the helo and power it up.

The robot moved like a six-legged insect. It was four inches long, two inches wide, and one inch tall. He tested the robot by turning its video camera in all directions and then commanding it to move forward, backward, and to the right and left. He raised his thumb to signal to Jake that the bug bot was operational and then put down the remote and moved his hand in the grass until he touched the helo controller. He picked it up and instructed the helo to return to the helipad.

Over the next fifty minutes, Em-Dog flew three more bug bots to the air vent on the roof. When the helicopter touched down on the helipad, he removed his googles. "Four bug bots in place."

"Roger that," BLT said.

Back across the water in the team's safe house he would oversee the operation of the robots in the air vents.

Jake and Em-Dog sat in the back of an Audi Q7. BLT was at the wheel with Dan at his side. The vehicle turned right into the grounds of a rented nineteenth-century French villa at 4:00 a.m. that morning. For the moment, exhaustion was a luxury the team could not afford. BLT and Jake still had to set up the remote equipment for the bug bots. They drove through the gates into the garden and parked in front of the house. At JSOC's request and because the team was always armed, the perimeter of the grounds was not patrolled, but the property was wired with cameras, security lighting, and motion sensors.

In different times, Jake would have liked to spend a summer at the estate. Behind the villa was a swimming pool with outdoor seating. The iron gates on the perimeter of the walled property led to a private beach. The villa was set away from the crowds of Cannes, just to the south tip of the bay. The surroundings were tranquil, hills behind the property and water in front. *Paradise*, he thought. But relaxing and enjoying cocktails in the sun was not why they were there.

It was just after 5:00 a.m. when BLT and Jake started setting up the remote equipment for the bug bots. Exhausted, Em-Dog and Dan had crashed in one of the bedrooms. BLT had studied the architectural plans from the developers of Batdadi's safe house to determine the best entry points for their bug bots. Provided no wire mesh was in their way, the attic vents were the best route.

The lifelike bug bots could move up and down the ductwork in the air-conditioning system. BLT tested the bots on his control pads, guiding them into the roof vent and to their target location. The laptop's video quality was patchy, but it would suffice. As the bots moved into position, the audio picked up clicking when the AC units kicked on or off, confirming the microphones were working. The sound quality was good, as evidenced by the soothing sound the AC units made. After two hours, the bots were positioned in the kitchen, dining/living room, office, and master bedroom AC units, as planned.

"Are we done?" Jake asked.

"Fifteen minutes," BLT replied. "I need to adjust the tilt of the cameras for optimum view."

Jake closed his eyes and dozed for just over ten minutes. When he forced his eyelids open, BLT was still working the control pad. "Problem?" Jake asked.

"The camera only gives a narrow view of the floor cabinets in the kitchen and a partial view of the entry hall."

"Microphone?"

"Good."

"We'll have to rely on the audio recording then."

"Right. I was powering down the cameras and microphones when you decided to rejoin the party."

Jake raised his middle finger in jest. Before BLT could respond, Dan and Em-Dog entered the kitchen. Jake hit the fridge while BLT set up a conference call with Alex in North Carolina.

When BLT ended his call, he joined the other men in kitchen. "Dan the chef has made omelets," Jake said.

BLT's eyes moved to the table, where Jake and Em-Dog were eating huge omelets and French bread, washing it down with beer.

After breakfast, Jake and BLT crashed on the sofa, both worn out. Em-Dog and Dan returned to the surveillance equipment.

19

Abdullah Omar had made his mark on the first day of the job. Now, the landscaping company viewed him as an asset. He often did the work of a team, increasing the company's bottom line.

Two days earlier, after leaving his family home in the North Bronx with only his bike, he had ridden to Hunts Point, a neighborhood located on a peninsula in New York City's South Bronx. He located the building and the room that had been rented for him. It was twelve-by-nine, smaller than his room with an en suite bathroom at his parents' house. The room was stocked with food, a bag, and clothing.

Hunts Point was the sort of neighborhood where everyone either drove decades-old cars with bald tires and smoking engines, rode bikes, or took the subway to get where they needed to go. At night, it was not safe to go out unless one had the protection of one of the gangs that controlled the area. It was where most of the men and women who cut the lawns, cleaned the pools, washed the clothes, and cleaned the houses for the wealthier folks in Bronxville lived. Abdullah had ventured out that night to seek a job with the Green Landscape Company. Employment secured and feeling pleased with himself, he approached the entrance of his building. Two men obstructed his path to the stairwell.

"Need a fix, bro," said a man who towered over Abdullah at six foot five. The man gazed down at him. His foot was on the steps that led to the front door. He had the physique of a basketball player. A jersey hung off his chest and stopped short of his pants, which rested several inches below his waist. The other man was stocky. He leaned on the rail, his feet extended across the step. "Help a bro," the tall man said.

Abdullah did not engage either man. His first instinct was to glance over his shoulder, confirming nobody was behind him. Turning his head, he scanned the gun bulges in their pants. *I can take them. They will fail, armed or not. If they attack, can I let them live? Killing them will complicate the reason I'm here though.* He moved forward.

The stocky man pulled in his foot, allowing him through. Abdullah advanced three steps up.

"Need a fix, bro," the tall man said again.

Abdullah moved to his right and made eye contact with the man, who spoke with an Ebonics dialect, the English creole spoken by African Americans. He guessed they were natives of the coastal area of South Carolina or Georgia. He shook his head and replied in broken Arabic that he didn't understand what the man was saying, though he did. He did it to throw them off, to make it harder for them to communicate with him. He calculated that frustration messed with the mind. Then he spoke in his native tongue, which seemed to catch them off guard.

"Where's you from?" the tall man asked. He pointed to the sky and opened his arms like a bird, imitating an aircraft.

The stocky man broke into laughter. Then he stopped suddenly and lunged forward, moving with a speed that was surprising for a person who bordered on obesity.

Abdullah grabbed the man and lifted him off the steps with one arm as if he were a small dog. He placed a blade against his throat, drawing a trickle of blood from the man's carotid artery. Then, with a sudden movement, he propelled the man into the street. The tall man stepped back, turned, and ran, leaving the injured man crawling on the street.

Later that night, Abdullah sat on his bed. The air-conditioning in the room did not work, and sweat dripped off his face. He sipped water from the bottle on his nightstand. From the bag left for him, he had retrieved three cell phones. He swiped the screens on the phones. One had a message that said, "Memorize and carefully dispose of this phone. Cell phone two is to make an emergency call. Destroy the phone after use. The remaining phone is to receive further instructions."

He paused and memorized the message.

After a blisteringly hot day, the sun had finally set. The window was open, and the relief it offered from the humidity was palpable, the cooling breeze creeping into the close confines of his room. Nighttime had always been when the demons residing within him came out to play, bringing out the worst in him. *Things are different now*, he thought. *Allah has decided to shield me from darkness and pain*. His heart was throbbing, his soul a bird in the sky. With every moment came peace, and with every breath he took, exuberance. *I will not let him down*.

Abdullah took a long breath and lay down. The frail bed frame squeaked and groaned, trying to support his weight. His door was locked, a thin panel of glass in front of it. If someone came for him in the night, he would not be surprised. He slept clutching a Tokarev pistol. If someone came for him, he would kill. It was his life now, as he planned it to be.

Two days later, Abdullah started work with the Green Landscape Company and labored for fourteen hours, for which he received the minimum wage of fifteen dollars per hour, paid in cash at the end of the day. He took the money, signaling his gratitude, but the money was not why he was there.

He did not eat the first day and only accepted a bottle of water. On the second day, he brought his own food and several bottles of water. Each day, he cycled half a mile to the location where a truck would meet him and the other men and then ferry them to their destination for the day. He worked even when the other workers sought relief from the humidity and the sun beating down on their backs.

The ten-acre home was in Bronxville, Westchester County, New York. He pushed lawnmowers, hefted bags of yard debris, and loaded them onto trucks parked in the service area behind the mansion. He observed that the landscape trucks, unlike the other service vans, were not allowed to come through the front entrance. On his first day, he had kneeled at the edge of the Olympic-sized pool at the rear of the property. The water was warm, and for a split second, he imagined himself swimming laps in it.

On the other side of the pool was a guesthouse. Although it was a distraction, he could not stop himself from watching the attractive, slim, but curvy maid who was tasked with cleaning the guesthouse daily. Her beauty was stunning, and but for her Hispanic features, she would not have appeared out of place. He forced his mind back to the matter at hand. Sweat ran down his back and into his eyes. As he surveyed the mansion and grounds out to the perimeter, the other workers stopped for water or shade breaks, a luxury he could not afford. In his mind, he placed all the buildings onto a map, but uppermost was the professional security team, which included three armed and alert men. If an incident occurred, they would respond immediately. Though he searched, he could not see any obvious weaknesses.

He finished weeding the flower beds in front of the house, applied mulch, and moved to the trees adjacent to the main gate. He leaned a ladder against one of the trees and pruned the overhanging branches. He was close enough to the main gate to see who was coming in and the alarm pad and surveillance camera mounted there. The sliding wrought iron gate adjoined the seven-foot walls that surrounded the estate. Atop the walls was barbed wire.

He had also noticed that security guards attending the gates in the rear and front entered a security code to allow guests, the landscaping company, and service vehicles to access and exit the estate. He'd reached out to prune a branch tangled in barbed wire when a laundry van pulled up to the gate. He carefully observed the six-digit security code when the guard punched it into the alarm pad.

As the gate was closing, a black Porsche Panamera driven by a chauffeur approached. The chauffeur used a remote control to open the gate and then slowly drove up to the house's front entrance.

"CEO of HK Bank, Baron Prescott," Abdullah whispered. He climbed two steps up the ladder to get a full visual of the car.

A man in his in his late fifties emerged from the car. Abdullah thought the man was somewhat tall for his build. If he were a few inches shorter, he would be more handsome for it. It was as if he had stopped growing, only to be stretched six more inches on a medieval rack. His face was mostly obscured by the stack of documents he was carrying.

Stop staring, Abdullah admonished himself, turning back to pruning the tree branches. He climbed down the ladder and moved it, enabling him to see the surveillance camera. His eyes moved down the metal pole to which the camera was attached. He was not sure whether it was a wireless security camera that transmitted a video and audio signal to a wireless receiver. Unless they were battery-powered, many wireless security cameras required at least one cable for power. *You're overthinking it*, he admonished himself again. *Yes, it's true, Prescott would have the best money could buy, but if there have been no incidents, an update could still be on his to-do list.*

Moving close to check it out, he saw that the power line disappeared into the ground, and he figured the cables ran beneath the ground but adjacent to the wall, either inside or outside the compound. He moved closer to the wall and weeded the dirt around the pole. It did not take long to find the trench that housed the power cable and ran under the gate to the wall's outer boundary. He assumed the power line would be encased in hardened pipe.

He moved closer to the pool, put his bag of lawn debris in one of the trucks, and paused to drink from a cup of water he filled from one of the large orange water coolers. He glanced at the Panamera. Prescott emerged from the house to retrieve a briefcase from the back seat. Using his right hand to hoist his lithe body, he placed the bag on the Panamera's roof.

Prescott had the look of someone who Abdullah didn't even want to lock eyes with, let alone cross. His facial features were devoid of warmth, like they had been stolen at birth, and his blond hair was so closely cropped that, from a distance, Abdullah had thought he was bald. Prescott's eyes met his not with humility but with a blunt refusal to avert his gaze first. Abdullah's musings stopped when he realized he'd made a mistake. He had watched Prescott for a few seconds too long. With Prescott's trajectory set for him, he decided to busy himself tidying his tools. But as he went to take them back to the truck, he heard footsteps behind him and felt a hand squeeze his arm.

"You're done here. Finish gathering your tools and get your ass back to the truck." He rotated to see one of the security men and a second one approaching. His eyes moved down to the gun under the guard's jacket. "I won't ask again," the guard said.

Fuck! I've screwed up the job, my reason for being here. Abdullah fell to his knees and hurriedly gathered his tools. He moved away without engaging the security guard. After he had put some distance between himself and the guard, he looked back. The guard had walked off toward his employer. How long had security been watching him? He could not be sure. "My cover is blown," he whispered as he hauled his tools onto the truck. He closed his eyes and prayed.

Thirty minutes later, the truck stopped abruptly. He opened his eyes, realizing he had fallen asleep. Despite his worst fears, his boss man had not pulled him off the job or reprimanded him. Another ninety-degree day had left his coworkers drenched in sweat and heading to air-conditioned bars. He did not join them. He still had his job and would return to his room to give praise to Allah.

That night, Abdullah cycled to the parking lot at MNR Fleetwood Station and used the keys he had retrieved from the bag he found in his room the night he arrived in Hunts Point to open a black MINI Cooper parked at the lot.

The estate was isolated and, apart from the security guards, deserted. He parked away from it. Then he stood behind an elm tree and observed the estate with a pair of night-vision optics that had also been in the bag. He paused for a moment and observed the starlight and the silvery moon. The trees' shadows danced upon the estate's walls, their leaves flickering like candlelight, creating a new picture from moment to moment. Amid the perfume of the summer blooms, he felt the cool of the evening wash over him as fresh ocean waves kissed the sun-warmed sand. He savored the moment.

He snapped back and turned his attention to the estate as he climbed the elm tree. He was on a dry run to learn valuable intelligence. Soon, he would translate that intelligence into action. He was ready and wished it could happen that night instead.

One hour later, he climbed down the tree, walked back to the MINI Cooper, and drove back to the parking lot.

20

New York—present day

Dear Diary,

I was surprised when she called. At first, I thought she forgot me. Then I remembered she had her own problems. Jessica's face had been on the TV for days, but that had gone quiet. We talked and laughed. She said she didn't murder those people, but she had to go away until she could clear her name.

Jessica said she would like me to visit her. She asked if I was still staying at Uncle Dicky's house and if I still spent time with him. I answered yes to both questions. She asked if I was happy. I hesitated. What did she mean? Am I happy? No, but how many people are? If she was referring to spending time with Uncle Dicky ... no ... yes ... it's complicated. Jessica didn't push for an answer, and I felt more confused.

She said I should come and visit her and that she would call tomorrow. I didn't think she would call—her being on the run and all—but she did. She also sent a car for me.
Sincerely
Ambrose

21

"Jessica, the doorbell. Ambrose is here." Jess looked over at the clock. It was almost 9:00 p.m. and dark outside. She raced to the window, curious as to why he was pressing the bell repeatedly, like it was an emergency. Jess cracked the shutter just enough to see a black limousine drive away. She crossed the room, opened the bedroom door, and went out to see what the commotion was about. Standing in the lobby was Ambrose, in tears.

Jessica? What's your problem? Our—your—future is at stake. Find out why that little fuck is babbling. Now!

"Ambrose? Sweetie, what's wrong? What happened? Are you OK?" Jessica rushed forward and put her arms around him.

"Jessica, I can't live at Uncle Dicky's house anymore. I've done and seen things I can't live with. I can't comprehend the purpose of my life and …" Ambrose let out a deep sob. "He's cheating on me. I need to get as far away from him as possible. I want to die."

Not a problem. We can help. I'll tell Batdadi we're good to go.

Ambrose collapsed in Jessica's arms. She hugged him. "Who's cheating on you?" she asked. "It's going to be OK. I'll help you." She was not sure whether her words comforted him or if she had just been played, but

Ambrose broke free from her hug and turned and opened the front door, revealing two giant suitcases.

What the fuck? You suggested dinner. Fuck, Jessica, did you say he could move in? Not part of the proposal. Still, we can make it work. Get your head out of your ass and get the bags. Fuck! I need a plan for Batdadi and the shrink.

Jessica stared at the suitcases. "He means it," she whispered. "Ambrose is intent on getting free of Clint."

"Thanks," Ambrose said and then ran out to the suitcases and pulled them inside. He paused, wiping beads of sweat from his brow.

"Ambrose, when we spoke yesterday, why didn't you give me a heads-up that things weren't good with Clint—Uncle Dicky?"

"I was scared you would try to talk me out of it. You always said you'd help. I just need to figure some stuff out."

Jessica looked over her shoulder at Batdadi's man, who was standing in the kitchen doorway. He nodded toward Ambrose's suitcases. Jessica smiled. "Thank you."

On second thoughts, Jessica, he can stay one night, and then he must go home. He's useless to us without Clint. One night, do you understand?

"Yes."

"Sorry, did you say something?" Ambrose asked.

"No. Are you hungry?" Jessica walked over to the stairwell and sat down, looking at him as she awaited his answer.

"Let's hit the kitchen" Ambrose said. He did not wait for her. He disappeared into the kitchen and emerged a minute later with some roast chicken and a bottle of Coke to wash it down. "Jessica, would you mind if I went to bed? I'm burnt out. We can talk tomorrow." He walked over and hugged her. "Thank you," he whispered into her ear.

The next morning, Jessica awoke to someone tapping on her bedroom door.

"Yes?"

"It's me, Ambrose."

"Come in."

Ambrose walked in wearing swim shorts and looking disconcerted. "Good morning, Jess—"

"Don't call me Jess," she snapped.

"Sorry, I didn't … Your hair and skin color. Sorry, I was tired and upset last night. What happened to you?"

"Last night when you were begging to stay, my appearance didn't bother you?"

"I didn't mean … It's just—"

"I'm black. Get over it. It's no more shocking than you coming over late for dinner and then announcing your plan to move in. And I apologize if my looks don't please you. You're not the only one with a problem."

"Sorry, Jessica, my bad."

"I can help you, but you must go home. Maintain contact with Clint—Uncle Dicky—for just a while longer. You must do something for me. If you do it, you'll never have to see him again. We'll both be OK."

"Do what? Are you serious? You're kicking me to the curb?"

"No! You can leave you luggage here and come back when you've completed your task."

"You haven't told me what you want me to do."

"We'll talk about that later."

Amazing! Jess said. *You handled that like a pro. You can achieve so much when you get your head out of your ass.*

Jessica walked into the dining room, sat down at the table, and poured herself some coffee. She missed the cup momentarily when she saw Ambrose doing laps in the pool. He glided through the water like an Olympic swimmer. She grabbed her napkin and mopped up the spilled coffee without taking her eyes off him. She regretted reaching out to him, but Jess had threatened to have Dr. Bajwa destroy her frozen eggs.

When he climbed the ladder and got out of the pool, she was struck by his lean body. His abs were perfectly ripped, and her eyes moved down to the erection bulging in his dripping-wet shorts. "Will you fertilize my eggs?" she whispered. "Give me babies?"

Stop! Jessica, he's a minor. A child molester, that's what you are. I want no part; do you hear me?

"Jess, I didn't mean ..." Tears welled up in her eyes.

She turned away when Ambrose walked through the patio door with a beach towel wrapped around his waist.

"Hey, Jessica." He bent over and kissed her left cheek. "The pool is fantastic."

"Yes," she muttered.

He walked to the other side of the table and sat down. "Who owns this house?"

"A friend. He needs our help," Jessica blurted out as Ambrose poured coffee while biting into a piece of toast. She paused and took a deep breath. "Do you think Clint would take you to the New York Stock Exchange?"

"Hmm ... yes. Uncle Dicky always promised that was one of the places he would show me when I was older. Why?"

"Stop asking questions. Jess hates questions."

"I thought you didn't like being called Jess. Anyways, Uncle Dicky said he would show me the New York Stock Exchange. In fact, after I saw him with the little boy in the garden, he was nice to me the next time he came to visit. He mentioned there was a social event coming up at the New York Stock Exchange and asked if I wanted to go."

I'll take it from here, Jess said.

"Special event? When?" Jess asked.

"I don't know for sure, but it was sometime this month."

"Good. When you go home, call Uncle Dicky, and tell him you would love to go and that you'll meet him at his office for a bit of fun."

Jess, Clint does things that Ambrose doesn't like. You called me a child molester, and now you're proposing—

"Jessica, this is too deep for me. I don't want to do that anymore," said Ambrose.

She moved closer to Ambrose. He had crossed his arms and his hands rested on his shoulders. She turned the chair to face him and looked into his eyes. He appeared confused, and she detected disappointment in response to what she had asked of him. "You're confused about your sexuality. I hear you, and I understand. This will be the last time. Do this, and you can swim in beautiful pools for the rest of your life."

22

Jessica kissed Ambrose goodbye later that morning. "Love you," Jessica said. "I want both our lives to change for the better, just do this little ask for me—you won't have any regrets, I promise." After the car drove away, she walked back into the lobby and headed to her room just as the housekeeper called to her.

"Miss Jessica, we're serving lunch in the dining room."

"Thank you," she replied as she turned and briskly walked into the dining room. She abruptly halted when she saw a man, who stood approximately six foot two, there, his back to her. Before she gained her composure, he had turned and was staring at her. Jessica was stunned. He was the most beautiful man she had ever seen. His wavy black hair fell above his ears and framed the perfect features of his face. He appeared neither Middle Eastern nor Western but a mix of the two. Instantaneously, Jessica was drawn to his eyes, an emerald green. *Who is this man?*

In a British accent, he said, "I'm Khalil Hassan and you're … Jessica. Please sit."

Still mesmerized by him, Jessica took her seat at the table.

"An al Alin Hassan's son."

Jessica expression was one of confusion.

"Oh," he said, "you know my father as Asyd Omar Batdadi." In his forties, Khalil Hassan had been privately educated at boarding schools in the West. After, he had been admitted to Oxford University. He had learned the ways of the West and preferred them. He was seated at the end of the table. "The room is quite lovely isn't it?" he asked. "This room was once graced by members of the British royal family."

The phrase *OMG!* almost slipped from her mouth. She smiled politely. "Will your father be joining us?"

"Alas, he has business to attend to and can't join us. Would you like something to eat?" Khalil rang a small silver bell, and a servant appeared. He instructed her to serve the hot plates. "Jessica, may I pour you some wine. It's a pinot noir. Or would you prefer white?"

"Red, thank you," she replied. "I thought alcohol was forbidden by the Muslim faith. Does your father know you drink?"

"It is forbidden, but why do you think I follow the Muslim faith?"

"I … I just thought."

"I'm of Muslim descent. You just thought—"

"I'm sorry." said Jessica. "My bad." She smiled.

"I don't wish to talk about my father. I've him to thank for all this," said Khalil as he swept his arm and took in the room. "But I would much rather talk about us."

"Please, Khalil. Don't play games with me."

"No games. If I didn't want to know you better, I would not be here, believe me." Khalil's eyes moved to the doors to the dining area. They were closed. He glanced over his shoulder—his father's security men in the pool area were talking among themselves. He said, "You are an intriguing and attractive woman, Jessica."

Jessica blushed. She put her fork on the plate. After she had chewed and swallowed the food in her mouth, she said, "Do you know why I'm here?"

"No … Yes. I don't care. I just know what I'm feeling here and now." He took a sip of wine.

"Maybe …" Jessica searched for words. She had not lost sight of the fact that she was here by Asyd Omar Batdadi grace. "I've made a commitment to your father—I must see it through."

Thereafter, they ate lunch and made small talk. When the servant arrived to clear the table, Khalil left the dining room but not before he bent and whispered into Jessica ear, "Give us a chance."

She felt his breath warm her ear and her heart beating against her ribs. She let go of the breath she didn't realize she'd been holding. Jessica's hand fell to her side and gripped his.

Khalil father's home was one of the largest on the Atlantic coast, ten acres on prime waterfront. He had been summoned there to talk about him playing his role in the family business. He was eager to please his father but was happy in his medical career.

In the rear grounds, by the pool, he had seen Jessica lounging. She was Caucasian, notwithstanding her tanned skin, and her body was slim but curvy. To Khalil, her face was extremely attractive. On that day her hair was dark, luxurious-looking, and done up in a ponytail. She had slipped off her dress, which sat next to her as she lay back on the chaise. He thought her to be a sensual woman, and in that moment, he married her with his eyes and soul.

Until now, he had not engaged with Caucasian women romantically. He found himself mesmerized by this woman, but he was expected to marry a woman of his ethnicity and faith. Theirs would be a forbidden love. But nonetheless, he lunched with her, and later that night he went to her bedroom and lay on her bed watching her as she slept.

She was serene, and with every breath she took, in his heart, he realized she was the woman he wanted to explore life with. Suddenly, she moved. He thought, *Does she sense my presence?*

Her eyes opened and when she did not scream, he lifted the sheets while shedding his clothes and slipped into the bed.

Khalil engaged in intimacy with Jessica in secrecy at his father's home. She lay in his arms, and he kissed and caressed her until she fell asleep. Resentment toward his father emerged. His feelings for the woman were intense and rapidly growing. He was determined to develop the relationship. In the early hours of the morning, he kissed her until she opened her eyes. "I'm leaving for London tomorrow. I will wait for you there—until you've concluded your business with my father."

23

Abdel informed Batdadi that the package hadn't arrived yet. Farooq, the delivery boy, had been professional, but he had detected something in his voice when they'd last spoken. "I can't let this fall apart. Operation Aleiqi will not fail. This is my destiny. The world will speak my name alongside those of Osama bin Laden and Abū Bakr al-Baghdadi." He turned away from the window and peered at Abdel. "Get the package." He turned back to face the window and observed Ambrose climbing out of the pool.

Abdel walked out of the room and took the stairs down to a basement room. Two of Batdadi's men were seated at a large desk playing Tables. The board on the desk was elaborately painted, but otherwise it was similar to a backgammon board. The man in possession of the dice released them and then placed his hand over them to stop the dice from rolling and focused on Abdel as he entered the room.

Abdel pointed to the man with his hand atop the dice. "You, go to Farooq's home in Pennsylvania and wait there. If he doesn't show up in New York today, find and kill him." He pointed to the other man. "You, come with me."

The men hastily got up and followed Abdel through a door that led to the garage.

Ahmed, who stood five foot eight, opened the door of one of the four vehicles parked in the garage. Once inside, he was about to close the door when Abdel handed him several throwaway cell phones. Abdel walked across the garage to another car, where Ibrahim, also of Arabic descent, was fastening his seatbelt. When the garage door opened, the cars drove through the outer gate and headed in different directions.

Abdel drove through New York, waiting for word from Farooq that he was en route to the rendezvous with the package. He made several calls to Farooq with the throwaway cell phones over the next two hours. He had just turned onto 42nd Street when he finally heard Farooq's voice.

"A man threw himself in front of an oncoming train."

"What? What about the package?" Abdel asked.

"I have the package. The trains are delayed."

"Batdadi will not tolerate any more delays. You can't afford any more failures."

Farooq was silent on the other end.

"Call me at the rendezvous. Goodbye." Abdel disconnected the call.

A slow, misty rain accumulated on the windshield. He shifted gears and drove toward the meeting place. An unusually high number of uniformed police officers were on the street.

"What do you see?" he yelled at Ibrahim.

Ibrahim stared out the window.

"Allaena!" Abdel swore.

"Look," Ibrahim said. "The police are showing photos to people passing by."

"Who are they looking for?"

"Allaena, do I look like Sherlock Holmes?" The second the words fell from his mouth, a frightened look appeared on his face. Abdel's wrath would be forthcoming. Abdel did not reply though. He hit redial on his phone instead. Farooq answered on the third ring.

"The package has arrived," Farooq said confidently. "Where are you?"

"Approaching." Hanging up, Abdel continued toward the shopping mall. He stopped one block before their destination and got out. Ibrahim slipped into the driver's seat. He watched as Abdel picked up speed and turned into the shopping mall. When Abdel was out of sight, he turned on the signal light and drove off.

Forgoing the elevator, Abdel took the stairs to the residential apartments. No one used them, and he didn't want to be forced into awkward conversations with shoppers or neighbors. Batdadi owned many such residences through shell companies around the world.

He reached Farooq's floor and made sure no one was in sight. He swiped his card to enter the floor and then the apartment.

Farooq was standing to the left side of the door. A smile beamed from his face, and he gave Abdel a bear hug. Abdel pushed him aside and closed the door. Farooq walked over to a large suitcase that was sitting next to the counter in the kitchen.

"Is that it?" Abdel asked.

"Yes. Inside is a carry-on case, a messenger bag, and a vest," Farooq replied.

"Excellent work."

"Sorry about the delay."

"It wasn't your fault, and you're here now. I would like a glass of water."

"Yes." Farooq made haste to the refrigerator. Abdel swiftly pulled out a 9mm Glock, silencer attached, and put a bullet in the back of Farooq's head. His knees bent, and he slumped to the floor. Abdel detached the silencer from his gun and tucked them both into his jacket. He moved to the package, extended the handle, and pulled the case toward the door. When he opened the door, he heard the movement of people coming down the hall toward the elevator. He paused until he was sure the people had boarded the elevator and then pulled the package into the hallway.

Abdel entered the stairwell and carried the package down to the wet streets below. Outside the building, he turned and walked up a block, putting distance between him and the mall. The street was less busy, and Ibrahim was waiting on the opposite side from where Abdel had left him.

A sense of relief hit when he opened the car door and loaded the package. Farooq's end could have been his but for the package in the back seat. He believed Allah was guiding him. Allah was on his side, as he'd always been.

Ibrahim swerved through the traffic, cutting off a honking cab. The wet streets softened the sounds of the tires as the car stopped at traffic lights. Abdel turned and looked at the package.

"An accident," Ibrahim said. "We must work around it."

"No rush. The priority is to get the package to Asyd Batdadi." Abdel leaned back, sitting sideways, and staring at the package. The lights changed, and Ibrahim punched the gas, zooming off into the traffic ahead.

24

"All the cams and mikes are operational," Em-Dog said. "We're in, dude. We'll get the goods! Trust me."

Not taking any chances, Jake pulled a low-tech monitoring device from his duffel bag. He had set up a Steiner spotting scope on a tripod. The loft space looked out over a stretch of saltwater separated from the sea by a low coral reef, where Batdadi's safe house was located. The distance between the villa and the surveillance target was just under a mile but not too far for Jake to observe comings and goings from the sea. The Steiner scope was in front of the window. Comfortably positioned on his stomach, he could see the back of Batdadi's compound. Jake released his grip, pushed himself to a standing position, and walked over to Em-Dog, slapping him on the back. "Let's join the others."

When Jake and Em-Dog entered the room, BLT had his phone on loudspeaker. "Your transmissions are live," Alex said. He was now able to listen in on his end. Anticipating that Batdadi would speak in his native tongue, he had an Arabic-speaking analyst ready to go.

BLT put the phone on mute and directed his gaze toward Em-Dog and Jake. "Head out to the airport and pick up the gear on the C-40." BLT put his head back down and continued his call with Alex. "Any news on Chuck?"

"No. He hasn't checked in, but we have no reason to think anything is amiss. Y'all are in France to monitor Batdadi, and I want to focus on that mission. Is the team up and running?"

BLT looked up when the door to the house clicked shut. "Have faith. When he comes to France, we'll be on him."

"Our intelligence is that he arrived in France this morning," Alex said.

BLT put the receiver down and turned to Dan, who was just settling his head onto the sofa.

"What?" Dan said, raising his head.

"He's here."

Dan jumped to his feet and immediately activated their surveillance equipment. All the cameras came to life. There was some activity in the house, though none of their cameras revealed the Bat. They waited and watched the video feeds. Their patience was rewarded thirty minutes later when they heard men speaking Arabic.

"We're going to get him," BLT said confidently.

Dan nodded, not taking eyes off the feed.

They had been monitoring for thirty minutes when a flurry of excitement took over the general chatter in the house. Men tightened their ties and took up positions in the corners of the room. More men appeared through the front door carrying bags. Finally, a tall, well-dressed man entered the room. He greeted the other men with a kiss on the cheek and a handshake, and then he and another man moved to another room, where they engaged in deep conversation.

"That's him," Dan said. "The tall man is the Bat."

"Are you sure?" BLT asked.

Dan signaled with his middle figure. BLT ignored the rude gesture.

"I'll call Alex and let him know you've confirmed the Bat."

"Fuck Alex. The Steiner is set up. Grace screwed up. We should've shot that fuck back then." Dan pulled out his earpiece and ran to the loft.

He peered through the spotting scope at Batdadi's safe house. The room had thinned out—he zoomed in on the three men who had headed out. "Muscle," said Dan. He moved the scope and focused on the Bat. BLT was at the surveillance equipment watching Batdadi take off his suit coat while engaged in conversation with the man who was beginning to look like his second-in-command. In the background, he observed three men pass on the outside of the doorway. He switched to the feed in the hallway, but other than men standing in doorways, it was empty.

Thirty-five minutes after Em-Dog and Jake left, there was a knock at the door. Dan was in the loft, so BLT went to answer it. By then, Em-Dog and Jake should've been inbound and had probably ordered food, so he displayed no concern about his security. As he looked through the peephole, he saw a bike on its side on the pathway and a man with a large food bag on his right side.

"May I help you?"

The man's accent was thick but not so bad that BLT did not recognize that he said he had a pizza delivery for Monsieur Dan. BLT smiled and opened the door. At that moment, he saw another man to his right. He went to slam the door shut. Too late. The delivery man flung the bag aside, leveled a Beretta at BLT's head, and pulled the trigger.

From around the side of the doorway, two men burst into the house, handguns held high. The man holding the Beretta stepped over BLT and then paused and looked back at the dark blood and brain matter oozing from the gaping hole in BLT's head. "I hope you enjoyed your stay on the Riviera."

Dan's hands were tied behind his back, and his ankles were tied to the legs of the chair in which he was sitting when the Bat appeared. "Welcome to the beautiful Riviera." He had ordered his men to seat Dan with his back to the front entrance in the hallway. BLT's body lay immediately behind him. The Bat seated himself in front of Dan, his legs crossed and his arms behind his head. He was in his comfort zone. Dan was helpless and at his mercy. The other three men stood behind him, carrying pistols in their shoulder holsters. Batdadi smiled at Dan as he looked up.

"The others are onto you," Dan said. "They will come behind me, and they will stop you."

Batdadi laughed. "If Allah wills. I investigated your background. May I call you Dan? Ex-Navy SEAL, rogue CIA operative. I met with a friend of yours, Tom. He did not have much to say. I ordered him tortured for information about your plans. Alas, I gave the order to eliminate him because your future plans are not so important to me now that we're having this meeting. You see, you're one of the few who know my identity. A problem that's easy to solve."

"Fuck you!" Though Dan's hands and feet were bound, he tried to lunge at the Bat.

Batdadi quickly stood up and stepped out of the way.

The guards behind Batdadi moved in and pulled Dan upright and then looked to Batdadi for instructions.

"You and the other infidels of the west have plagued our lands for too long. Now the caliphate has returned." Batdadi nodded at his men. They drew their pistols and fired repeatedly at Dan. Then they stopped suddenly and looked at the off-white walls, which were covered with a crimson spatter of blood.

25

Em-Dog had just loaded the last bag in the Audi. He and Jake were in the process of fastening their seatbelts when the sat phone in the SUV rang.

Jake answered it. "Yeah?"

"Jake," Alex said. "We have a problem."

"What's up?"

"We've just translated the conversation from Batdadi's safe house."

"And?"

No answer. The phone went dead.

Assuming it was a hotspot or some other interference, Jake decided to wait for Alex to call back.

Minutes later, Em-Dog exited the airport and turned into traffic, where they suddenly found themselves caught behind an accident up ahead. Sitting in the Audi, they were grateful for the relief the air conditioner gave them from the brutal heat. It was clear they were not going anywhere soon. In front of them for several miles was the Cote d'Azur.

Finally, the sat phone rang again.

"Alex," Jake said, anticipating it was him calling back.

"Batdadi knows about the safe house, and his men are headed there," Alex said, his voice urgent.

Jake pounded the dashboard. "Fuck!"

"I called BLT several times but got no answer. Tried Dan too, but nobody picked up."

"Fuck! Fuck! We're in gridlock. Christ! It can't go on for much longer, but even then, we're ten minutes out. Fuck!"

Em-Dog slammed his hands into the steering wheel. "Fuck! Fuck!"

The fear that something was wrong traveled in Jake's veins but never made it to his facial muscles or his skin. Em-Dog had pulled onto the shoulder to let a police car pass, its blue lights flashing. Jake studied the sea, lost in the rhythmic percussion of the waves against the sand.

As Em-Dog pulled back onto the road, Jake's eyes were fixed on the horizon, his face aglow with the last orange rays before twilight beckoned the stars. They continued for half a mile before turning right onto the winding road that led to the rear of their safe house. Em-Dog parked the car out of sight. They crossed the grounds, Jake leading and Em-Dog keeping a safe distance between them.

"Batdadi?" Jake whispered, surveying the silent house. He looked back and signaled Em-Dog to move forward and then mounted the three steps to the door.

Batdadi?

It was warm in the dining room. His single thought fell into silence like a stone landing in a deep crevice.

"Batdadi?" he whispered.

Nothing. Even the air conditioning was silent. That afternoon, no one had been there to turn it on. He looked down at dirt tracks on the floor. Followed by Em-Dog, Jake went into the kitchen. He smelled cigarettes, stale and long since burned out. They saw BLT's coat on the chair by the window. The chair was pushed askew, as if he had gotten up suddenly.

Jake glanced at the equipment they had set up to monitor Batdadi. The footprints approached the table and then made for the hallway. Heart thudding, Jake followed them. He pushed the door open and saw his fellow operatives' bodies. Dan was tied to a chair, which had fallen back on top of BLT. They lay in a pool of dark, congealing blood. The putrid smell initiated a gag reflex in Jake. He raised his arm to his forehead as if to block his vision, but there was no way to undo what he saw—BLT's sunken eyes. Jake's hands wanted to tremble, but he would not allow them to do so. He tightened his grip on his P226 and stepped back into the kitchen.

Em-Dog held his head over the kitchen sink and tried to compose himself. Jake sat with his head between his legs, still clutching his gun. In their line of work, they had seen death over and over. A corpse was a corpse, unless that corpse was someone they cared about. That was when their emotions emerged and when they experienced trauma.

Jake raised his head. "We have to find a way to do our job." He pulled out the sat phone and called Alex. "Our operation here is compromised." That was an understatement. After he explained what they had found at the villa, he called First Officer Birch and informed her they would need thirty minutes to remove any traces of their activities from the safe house and that she should have the C-40 ready to go.

By the time Jake finished the calls, Em-Dog had broken down the surveillance equipment and retrieved a large duffel bag from the kitchen closet. It contained everything they needed in the field—light-blue latex gloves, flashlights, paper bags, body bags and tags, an instant camera, green biohazard suits complete with hood and air-filtering gear, plastic sheeting, shoe covers, and several other items.

Wearing shoe covers and latex gloves and carrying paper bags, sheeting, and body bags, Jake and Em-Dog walked into the hallway. They cut the restraints off Dan and wrapped him and BLT in the sheeting and placed their bodies in the body bags. After shedding the shoe covers and latex gloves in the paper bags, they carried the body bags outside.

"I'll meet you out front," Em-Dog said.

When Em-Dog went to collect the Audi, Jake closed the door behind him and started a final sweep of the villa. Sadness drained through him, traveling to every cell in his body. As he made his way back to the dining room, fatigue was engraved on his face. His sorrow grew more profound with every loss he encountered.

He stopped and glanced in the mirror, lost in his reflection. No longer could he see the inquisitiveness, the desire, the fire that used to illuminate his eyes. All that remained was the deceiving, hollow soul that was reflected through his tears, the emotional scars leaving no room for his true self. He was a shell of a man.

"This ends. Either I'm going to die or Batdadi is, but I will end this," he said to his reflection.

Jake walked to the back entrance and closed the door, keeping in his soul what was pure about his friends and locking the dirt behind him.

Em-Dog parked the Audi close to where BLT and Dan's bodies were lying. Time slowed once more, as if Jake needed a "photograph," a keepsake to give him strength in rough times to come. The silence of the night made his blood cold as the night air crept through an open window. His head snapped in an instant from gazing with unfocused eyes at the body bags in the back of the SUV.

Though it was useless, Jake tensed against the shaking of his limbs. He did it instinctively, trying to suppress for a few moments what he could not. He drank in the silence to counteract the rage that threatened to engulf him. On an op of this kind, thick silence would normally focus him, especially on an inky night devoid of moonlight or stars. But that night it worked like a salve. He felt the rage. The more absolute the silence, the stronger its medicinal effect. *They must be eliminated. Batdadi must be eliminated.*

Once Jake and Em-Dog arrived at the airport, they boarded the plane with their fallen heroes, and then Captain Green called the tower to let them know they were ready to execute their flight plan. First Officer Birch had taken care of customs details, with the help of twenty thousand euros.

26

Ambrose climbed out of a taxi on the Upper East Side, between Central Park, 5th Avenue, 59th Street, the East River, and 96th Street. Once known as the Silk-Stocking District, it was one of the most affluent neighborhoods in New York City. He admired the park and the beautiful apartment buildings, surprised Jessica had not lied about changing his life.

He found the apartment building and, fondling the keys in his pocket, took the elevator to the apartment on the sixteenth floor. He opened the door and confirmed that the studio, though small, was as Jessica described. "I love it," he said, smiling. "I could never afford this without help." *Help, she promised to help.* He looked out at Central Park. *And she did.* "It's all I need."

Ambrose put his hand over his mouth when he noticed the hundred-dollar bills stacked in the corner of the room. *Is that what I think it is?* He laughed but then stopped when his phone rang. He grabbed his messenger bag and headed for the door. *Abdel, I've had my grand tour. I can see the bathroom and the kitchen later.* He locked the door and headed down to the lobby and out into the cool afternoon.

Central Park was in front of him, the sidewalks filled with people walking to and from the park. He opened the door and stepped into the black Mercedes parked on a side street one block from his apartment.

"Is the apartment to your liking?" Abdel asked as Ambrose settled into the back seat.

"I love it," Ambrose said, his smile widening.

They continued their short journey to the United Arab Emirates consulate on 5th Avenue in silence. Upon arrival, Ambrose passed through security, escorted by Abdel. They took the elevator to the thirty-second floor.

Although Ambrose was tall, he found Abdel's six feet and body weight of two hundred pounds intimidating. He also found him wanting in the social skills department. *If I help, if I do … if I do what? These are serious people.* He glanced at Abdel and then looked away quickly. Adrenaline flooded his body. His heart pumped like it was trying to escape his chest. He thought his heart would explode, and his eyes widened with fear. His body urged him to run fast to anywhere but there. He leaned into the corner of the elevator and inhaled deeply. *Let's face it, there's nothing I can do. It's too late to change my mind.*

Ambrose followed Abdel into an office. A man was leaning against the front edge of a large desk, his arms folded. Like a laser, his eyes locked on Ambrose, who immediately recognized him as Asyd Batdadi. Ambrose had seen him staring at him through the windows at the house where Jessica was living. It was his first time in a room with him. *His eyes!* They were black, like a crow's. He wore an expensive suit. His cufflinks matched the gold of his watch. His dark eyes never left Ambrose.

"Let's get started," Batdadi said. "Do you have everything?"

"Yes," Abdel replied.

A third man entered the room. He was in his thirties, thin, with dark skin. His eyes were black, and his nose resembled a beak. He was wheeling a large black suitcase. The man jerked his head toward Ambrose. "Your phone."

Ambrose felt his heart pounding again, fear and insecurity seeping into his system. *I wish Jessica was here. Oh God, I wish she was here. Calm. I can do this. I must do this if my life is to change.*

"Come, come," Batdadi said, waving Ambrose forward. "Tell me about your relationship with the president of HK Bank, Mr. Clint Morris."

Ambrose looked at him, "Excuse me?" *Jessica! You told him.*

"Do you know him well? Is he a good friend?"

"Uncle Dicky? No! I hate him. It's not my fault," he blurted. "Mom and I used to have lunch with Uncle Dicky every week. After lunch, we would go to Uncle Dicky's bank. Mom would sit at the desk and work, and Uncle Dicky would take me into another room. I didn't want to do that." Ambrose did not stop for breath. "When I lived at Uncle Dicky's house, I saw him one night." Tears formed in his eyes. "He, Uncle Dicky, had one hand on the maple tree. He was leaning over, the legs of a little boy between his thighs. The boy's hands were griping the grass. Uncle Dicky's hand was over the boy's mouth. His trousers were down around his ankles. Afterward, the little boy cried into his hands …"

Ambrose lowered his head, unwilling to share more. He did not look up when the door opened. The footsteps behind him approached and stopped ahead of Ambrose. He saw the body of a man waist down. The man's hand reached out and handed a cell phone to Batdadi. He did not look up when Batdadi approached and pushed the phone into Ambrose's hands. Tears fell from his eyes as Batdadi put his hand on his shoulder. "My child, you've endured much, but your pain will be your strength."

Later that evening, Ambrose wheeled the large black suitcase into his Upper East Side apartment. He kicked off his shoes, flopped down on the sofa, and called Jessica.

"Ambrose, are you OK?"

"Yes, I'm so happy. Thank you for asking." He waited for her to reply as if her words were golden, perhaps some elixir he's been waiting all his days to hear.

"What the fuck are you talking about? Where are you?"

"On the Upper East Side, in my new apartment. I love it."

"Oh, I'm pleased you like it. So, I'm guessing you spoke to Asyd Batdadi."

"Yes. At first, I was petrified. He appeared to be thinking so deeply, already with a strategy that's several moves ahead of what I'm capable of."

"And? Did he tell you what he wants you to do?"

"Yes. In his words were kindness, a concern that what was done to me was wrong and should be made right."

"So, you'll help him—and me of course."

"Yes, yes. Let's have lunch next week. I'll show you the apartment."

"Thank you. Love you. Bye."

27

Cairo, Egypt, nine days earlier

In the searing heat of the midday Egyptian sun, the Cairo market overflowed with lunchtime diners and shoppers. The aroma of grilled meat wafted through the air, mixed with smells from the coffeehouses that inhabited the streets and alleys that wrapped around the mosques and ancient buildings.

Men entered a boisterous neighborhood coffeehouse, the chairs spilling out into the center of the alley. They played backgammon and chess and smoked hookahs and cigarettes while drinking coffee.

Milton Williams, a silver-haired, thirty-eight-old American, sat at a table under the shade of an umbrella between two Middle Eastern men. They did not stand out among the crowds of black, white, Arab, Western, and Asian people moving through the alleys. Occasionally, Williams glanced at a Westerner sitting alone and sipping Turkish coffee. He studied his face and mannerisms. Something about the man gave him pause. Williams had not survived these last years by being oblivious to men following him. The two men on either side of Williams were his protectors. Their eyes shifted right and left more than those of the other patrons.

Williams watched as the man pulled his sunglasses case from his shorts and placed it on the table.

"Milton."

Williams turned to Batdadi, the Middle Eastern man to his right. Batdadi had already pushed his chair away and was standing in preparation to leave. The three men strolled off into the marketplace, leisurely and relaxed.

"Abdel," Batdadi said.

Abdel needed no further instruction. He broke away from the two men and doubled back to the coffeehouse.

"I believe the sunglasses case on the Westerner's table is a camera," Batdadi said. "He placed it there for one purpose only—to film us. When the man you were watching picked up his cell phone, I understood this to be his play."

"Shit," Williams said.

"The cell phone transmits a Bluetooth signal to the camera in the sunglasses case. What I don't know is if he caught our image."

"The man is CIA," Williams said.

"How can you know this?"

"Because he's a past acquaintance of Jessica's."

"You know this how?"

"Facebook. She posted her life on Facebook. She emailed me and told me she was living in Cairo with Tom Pérez, who worked for the CIA. The photos coincide with the email. We must get out of Egypt. Let's not push our luck."

"Abdel will take care of this."

Abdel followed Tom through the winding passageways of Cairo's Old Town, careful to keep his distance. His target entered an apartment across from a walled residence in an upscale neighborhood. Standing there, Abdel surveilled the building and the intermittent sightings of his target in the window of an apartment on the sixth floor.

The light ebbed, and so did the heat of day. A swirl of pink and lavender transfigured the sky as the perishing ball of light sank below the horizon, leaving behind a dark silver-orange color. The remaining phosphorescence from the gradually draining sky danced along the apartment building's glass windows.

When a light came on and the target closed the blinds, Abdel darted across the street. He waited until a young couple entered the building. Distracted by their affection for each other, they did not notice Abdel move forward and wedge his hand between the door and its frame to stop it from closing.

He waited until their footsteps faded and then stepped inside. Abdel was halfway up the staircase with his 9mm Glock in hand by the time the door clicked shut behind him. His hand slipped into his pocket, and he attached a silencer.

Rock music blared from the target apartment. *Infidels. Obnoxious and inconsiderate.* The vocals surged through Abdel, heightening his hatred for Westerners. He focused on the door. It had six-inch-wide planks of wood around the frame, down the center, and across the middle, creating quadrants. Flimsy plywood filled the four sections. The door's chipped brown finish was scratched and dented. It had a brass-colored lock and doorknob that were dulled with age and greasy fingermarks. Abdel concluded that the door's function was privacy rather than to keep intruders out. He crouched and began to pick the lock.

A plasma screen was in the corner of the room, from which the loud music emanated. Tom sat on a sofa surrounded by a mess. His foot tapped rhythmically. He picked up the remote and then dropped it when Abdel entered. "What the fuck?"

"Unless you can move faster than a bullet, shut up." Abdel stepped forward, his weapon pointed at Tom. "Are you alone?" Abdel searched the studio apartment with his eyes without waiting for an answer, keeping the Glock pointed at Tom's chest and then brought his eyes back to Tom. "Oh, Mr. Pérez, the tourist, you've been productive. I would like to know with whom you shared those photos." Abdel reached for the notepad on the table. His eyes did not move as he looked at the shock register on Tom's face.

"What the fuck? I have no idea what you're talking about."

"You're a liar, and that's the problem. Your mouth is foul, like that woman, Jessica." Abdel kept his gun aimed at Tom's chest. "Tell me what you told the CIA. Everything."

Tom did not speak, just looked at the MacBook next to him on the sofa.

Abdel sighed, as if disappointed with Tom's lack of cooperation. "Password." He pointed to the computer.

When Tom shook his head, Abel lowered his weapon and shot him in the thigh. Tom's face closed in a grimace. He groaned as his skin turned pale. Blood oozed down his leg, forming a pool around the sofa.

"I won't ask again."

Tom wiped his hands on his shirt and reached for the MacBook. "You already know. I uploaded your ugly mugshot to US Intelligence. Kill me if you must, but I won't give you the password." He pushed the computer onto the hardwood floor.

"So be it." Abdel fired twice in rapid succession. There was an explosion of pink as Tom took both rounds in the head and slumped over.

28

Chuck dropped his bag on the bed and gazed out the balcony window. He was impressed by the view of the Nile and downtown Cairo. *Later.* He did not have time to step onto the balcony. He grabbed his key card and headed down to the lobby of the Four Seasons Hotel.

He had arranged to meet Tom in Khan el-Khalili, a major souk in Cairo's historic center. The marketplace was originally the site of a mausoleum, but now ancient and modern mixed together. Time was not on Chuck's side as he wound through narrow, winding alleyways, arriving at the restaurant five minutes late.

He entered the restaurant, and the maître d' welcomed him. "Tom, a reservation for two," Chuck said, slightly out of breath.

The maître d' held out his hand. "This way, sir."

Chuck walked closely behind, taking care not to disturb the other diners. He surveyed the packed room. An old couple eating side by side, one glass of wine each, studiously bent over their meals. A group of young women in their twenties collapsing with helpless giggles as a stern woman dining alone nearby looked on and frowned. Businessmen in gray suits, ties pulled loose, lighting cigars.

When the maître d' halted, Chuck spotted the note on his table. On the note were doodles, his name underlined, the address of the restaurant, and the time he'd agreed to meet Tom. Chuck grabbed the note, turned, and bumped into the backs of several patrons as he hurried out of the restaurant.

Years of training and experience in the field had sharpened Chuck's instincts. At the restaurant's entrance, he had seen a lone, muscular Middle Eastern man leaning on the building across the street. He did a sweep of the marketplace. At 9:20 p.m., the crowds had thinned out, and the people shifting through the alleys moved leisurely. They did not stand out, but to the trained eye, the single man at twelve o'clock periodically checking the entrance to the restaurant did.

When the man broke away from the wall, Chuck pushed past two men entering the restaurant and moved toward the alley. As he turned into the alley, he saw the man following. *He's onto me.* Chuck increased his pace. He could lose the man in the darkness and the foot traffic of the Khan el-Khalili. He turned into alleys and narrow covered passageways that twisted through the market, heading north for the bank of the Nile.

As the shops and tents fell away, he glanced periodically over his shoulder. He had not seen the man on the last three occasions. Out of sight was not out of mind though; Chuck had to consider that the man might be ahead of him.

He slowed and walked along the bank of the Nile. Hotels towered above, and restaurant tables spilled away from the buildings toward the river's edge. Diners laughed and admired the view from under canopies. He wondered what had happened to Tom and why the man was tailing him.

He turned right onto a quiet cobblestone street. The sound of a kicked stone caused him to look back. He saw his tail thirty yards back. He turned left and made his way back north. He navigated through a market, staying parallel to the Nile to avoid losing his bearings.

Chuck paused in the entrance of a mosque to consider his options. He thought about turning and confronting the man, but he was concerned about the proximity of civilians. He had to act quickly because the man was closing in, and Chuck was unaware of his intentions. He moved into the open and turned down to the next alley, away from the crowds. Once in the dark, he picked up his pace.

Chuck glanced back, brought his head forward, and abruptly came to a halt. In front of him, no more than twenty feet, was the man, a pistol in his right hand. *I can take him. Yes, take him now without any commotion. No! Then I won't find out why he's pursuing me and why Tom was a no-show.*

Chuck dropped to the cobblestone pavement and rolled into a sprinter's stance. The force of his right leg propelled him, and he ran across the street and down the adjacent alley. He ran into an apartment building and up the stairs in the entryway, taking three steps at a time. He paused on the second floor to take a gulp of air.

The building was six stories tall. He heard footsteps behind him and continued running. His only escape was to access the roof to the connected buildings.

On the fifth floor, he slowed down, no longer hearing footsteps behind him. He feared another ambush if he continued climbing. Out of breath and trying to outwit his pursuer, Chuck opened the window to the fire escape and made his way out onto the iron ladder. *Fuck!* He heard the man and then saw him coming up. Chuck grabbed the rung above him and began to climb, his pursuer right behind him.

As the man closed in, Chuck kicked his leg. The man slipped but continued to climb. Seconds later, Chuck thrust himself onto the flat roof, the man hot on his heels. Their eyes engaged. When Chuck reached for his gun, the man launched himself forward. Chuck continued to raise his arm, but the man knocked the gun away just as Chuck fired. He punched Chuck in the jaw. Chuck fell backward, his feet flying into the air has he fell. The man lunged forward to attack before Chuck could regain his bearings.

The force caused Chuck to fall back. His perception of time distorted. Everything slowed down until there was nothing but him and the rooftop above. Time seemed suspended and then speeded to impact. His head hit the cobblestone, and his bones shattered. Darkness followed, swallowing him whole.

29

Shaking his watch from under his sleeve, Ambrose checked the time. It was almost noon. He closed his eyes. The sun was already overhead. He felt the warmth on his face and heard the chatter and laughter of people going about their busy day. A breeze stirred and brought with it the scent of hot dogs from a street vendor. He tried not to think about Uncle Dicky, but as soon as the moment began, it ended. After his meeting with Asyd Batdadi, he lived for revenge.

Sexual abuse, yes. It was wrong, I didn't want to do it, but I did it anyway, only to be rejected. "That boy … that poor boy." Ambrose closed his eyes against the horror of it. *Jessica said there were only so many dark corners in a person's mind to hide such experiences. She doesn't know that, from time to time, I did coke. Now, I choose revenge. I love my new apartment. Revenge is the reason I got out of bed this morning. I don't think it's the healthiest way to deal with my issues, but unfortunately, the human mind—my mind—doesn't have a delete button. If only for a little while, I need to forget. I want to be free of Uncle Dicky and maybe …*

Ambrose hurried down Wall Street and went through the revolving door into the lobby of HK Bank. At the reception desk, he asked that his arrival be announced to Clint Morris.

He seated himself on a leather sofa and waited for Uncle Dicky to escort him up to his office. The lobby had the air of a morgue, an interior designed to give the bank a sense of grandeur. The scant smiles and sparse use of flowers served only to increase the hostility of the environment. Ambrose closed his eyes. *This place, the bank, defines Uncle Dicky.*

"Ambrose," Clint called.

Ambrose snapped back from his thoughts. A beaming smile on his face, Uncle Dicky waved him over to the security gate. He had arranged for Ambrose's security pass. A guard opened the barrier, and Ambrose walked through, pulling a carry-on suitcase behind him.

"Taking a vacation?"

Ambrose looked down at his bag. "Yes. A friend invited me to the Hamptons for the weekend." It was a lie, but he did not want to hesitate before he replied. The truth was, he had always wanted to visit the Hamptons. Jessica mentioned the town in every conversation. He followed Uncle Dicky off the elevator and into his office.

Ambrose should have been repulsed by him. In his midsixties, Uncle Dicky was five foot six with dark, wavy hair and a muscular physique. His most distinctive feature was his neatly trimmed beard. Like his hair, it showed no sign of gray. Ambrose suspected he had a personal stylist from a high-end salon on call to maintain its dark color.

He did not resist when Uncle Dicky turned around and put his lips against his. *Look at me, know me, love me. I keep praying, hoping it shows in my eyes and that you'll be able to decipher my feelings.* A few seconds passed before Uncle Dicky pulled his lips away, unzipped Ambrose's pants, and bent him over his desk.

"Are you looking forward to the reception at the stock exchange?" Uncle Dicky asked a few minutes later once he had zipped up his pants and straightened his tie. "Many prominent heads of banks are attending, including my friend, James Mackinnon. Did I mention he's chairman of the Federal Reserve?"

"Yes." Ambrose forced a smile. Then he sank into a dark place. *Your lack of eye contact should've warned me. It's not natural to avert your gaze from the one you love. It gave you distance from my heart and soul, enough to allow you to abuse me. It's the depravity you crave. You make me feel dehumanized, just another part of your life to be in control of, to perform a vice with. I'm done!*

He picked up his messenger bag and moved behind Uncle Dicky toward the door. He stopped briefly, turned, and glanced at the suitcase filled with C-4, standing in front of the sofa.

Ambrose sauntered with Uncle Dicky to the stock exchange. As they approached, James Mackinnon joined them. Along with other dignitaries, they meandered toward the security barrier.

30

Acquiring a membership at the Equinox fitness club was expensive but not onerous. The luxurious club was inspired by the adrenalin of the nearby trading floors. The converted Art Deco bank featured a plush, elegant interior designed by David Rockwell, and it welcomed the affluent.

The club's most desirable feature was its view of the New York Stock Exchange building across the street. Jamal Khan could have watched the events unfold from the safe house, but he preferred to be there. He wanted to trigger the detonator himself. *These infidels killed my blood brother.* This would be the closest he had been to any of his bombings. *For and in the name of Abdul Khan I do this. Yes, Allah willed Asyd Batdadi to risk all to bring me here. I, Jamal Khan, will not fail. Allahu Akbar!*

In the past weeks, he had undergone plastic surgery and had drastically changed his looks. For the past two days, he had frequented the studio, cycling. Today, he cycled on one of the stationary bikes placed strategically throughout the gym for lone cyclists. The display pad on the bike registered the miles, and though he pedaled, it felt automatic. His legs remained in motion, but his thoughts stayed in the moment, rehearsing the events about to unfold. Farooq's work was excellent. He had examined every detail. Alas, Farooq's delay had caused Asyd Batdadi to doubt his loyalty to the cause.

Farooq had packed Ambrose's suitcase with C-4. The boy had confirmed that the bank did not inspect bags, and there was no security screening.

At 12:45 p.m., Jamal received the first text message from Ambrose. "Your gift was delivered."

A minute later, he spotted Ambrose wearing, as instructed, dark-blue pants, a white shirt, and a quilted vest with a messenger bag over his shoulder. Clint Morris strolled in front of him. In addition, Farooq had molded the C-4 into the lining of the boy's vest and the lining of the messenger bag. Jamal had anticipated that, when the boy went through the first security checkpoint, a cursory inspection of the messenger bag would take place. The boy had been instructed not to add anything to the bag other than the iPad, which had been placed inside in advance. Jamal focused on James Mackinnon as he joined Clint and the boy. A smile illuminated his face. Ambrose and the other two men walked to the security gate and joined other guests in line.

The crowd of people faded out of sight as Ambrose entered the security barrier. Jamal predicted the boy's messenger bag could not pass through the secondary security screening in the foyer. There, Ambrose would be screened by metal detectors and/or millimeter wave scanners. There would also be explosive-detection machines, but inside the foyer was sufficient.

He dismounted the bicycle, put on a sweatshirt, and set off toward the steps of Federal Hall. Two minutes later, he looked out at the large bronze statue of George Washington made by John Quincy Adams Ward. He thought it ironic that the infidels of this Congress had forgotten that their forefathers had, on this site, claimed entitlement to the same rights as the people of Britain. "America failed miserably to confer the same rights to their Muslim citizens and residents of the United States of America," he whispered.

Jamal was prepared to martyr himself. He had spent his last day ritually cleansing himself and preparing to enter Paradise. He'd read from the Koran and had found the courage to do Allah's will.

At 12:55 p.m., he received a second text message from Ambrose. "Red roses."

On the day he had met the boy at the United Arab Emirates consulate, he had instructed him, among other matters, to wait to send his text reply until after he, Jamal, had sent the second text. The text would be the boy's cue to discreetly place the bag and leave. The plan had been good to the point when Ambrose entered the stock exchange. *The boy exceeded all expectations. It's a shame he must die, but I can't take the chance that they'll find the bag. He will die for the greater good.*

Jamal swiped the screen on his phone, tapped three numbers, and sent encrypted radio signals to the detonators in the suitcase, the messenger bag, and Ambrose's vest.

Jamal closed his eyes and took a deep breath. He felt adrenaline pump through his veins. Exhaling, he stood up. "For Abdul, Allahu Akbar! Allahu Akbar!" His hand emerged from the pocket of his jogging pants, revealing a dead man's switch. He pressed the button and armed the device strapped around his waist.

Three seconds later, the steps of Federal Hall shook as an explosion rocked the building, sending shards of glass; chunks of stone; and pieces of bone, blood, and human flesh in every direction.

A second explosion erupted inside the foyer of the New York Stock Exchange, followed by a third at HK Bank, where an orange fireball punched through the building on the forty-sixth floor. The deafening shrill of alarms erupted. The blast took out the side of the building and the roof. Windows shattered, and a deadly rainfall showered down thousands of pieces of glass, steel, and stone.

31

Bronxville, New York, five hours later

The temperature was expected to reach one hundred degrees. The sweat rolled off Abdullah's brow. He wiped his forehead with the back of his hand. His clothes were drenched, even though he had worked for only half an hour. He kept his head down and put his back into digging holes for the trees that would arrive later that morning. He was not as far as he would have liked to be. He had lost time when his employer had confronted him about the previous day's incident with security. The landscaping company extracted from him the work of four men, and that was the sole reason he still had a job. *I am one man, paid a wage that can barely keep me alive, one reprimand away from losing this job.* He focused on the success of the previous night's reconnaissance, the bigger plan.

Looking at the workers next to him, he felt sorry for them. People with power, infidels, would always take advantage of those without means. Money meant nothing to him. He was there to serve the will of Allah. He would surrender his life to Allah. Sweat trickled down his neck. The tree holes complete, he moved over to a hedge and clipped with an enthusiasm that signaled his thanks for the opportunity to work.

He ran his eyes along the top of the edge, zooming in on the Porsche Panamera parked in front of the house. He had learned from his chats with the maid that Prescott had a chef and two maids who worked for minimum wage and lived in the servants' quarters. No family lived there. Prescott was divorced, and his daughter and son had not returned home after college.

The rear door to the house opened, and Prescott emerged. He looked more tanned than the day before, and his muscular calves bulged below his shorts. His shirt was untucked, no doubt his way of showing he was a casual, run-of-the-mill man. Prescott crossed the grounds and worked his way toward the guesthouse. *Those flower beds and bushes need trimming*, Abdullah thought. He clipped but made no noise. He had worked his way to the window when he heard moans and groans.

He paused and looked around for security guards. His path appeared clear. He raised himself onto his toes and looked in the window. The blind was partially up. Prescott was naked. The woman was wearing only her bra, her panties around her ankles. She clenched a chair, her body bent forward. Prescott was standing behind her. He pushed into her violently and then slumped onto her back. Seconds later, he hastily freed himself from her and pulled on his shorts. She gathered her clothes and walked toward the bathroom. Prescott put on his shirt and slipped out the door.

Abdullah continued observing. The maid he had watched on his first day emerged from the bathroom fully dressed, catching the tears that fell from her eyes with a tissue.

Minutes later, she came out of the guesthouse. He bent down and started to weed. As she passed, she hung her head. Then she stopped and turned. He nodded at her, his gaze partially down but his eyes on her. She smiled radiantly, though her cheeks were red from crying. They both turned to see a security guard. When Abdullah realized it was the same guard as the day before, he stood and hurried away from her. The guard turned and headed in the opposite direction. Abdullah glanced back and watched as she walked away. She did not look back. "I'm Abdullah," he whispered, "Abdullah Omar. And you are?"

That night, the humidity was as bad as ever. Opening the window offered no relief, and the tenseness in Abdullah's muscles made him feel more like a mannequin on his mattress than a man of flesh and bone. He wanted so much to melt into the maid's soft form, wrapped in eiderdown, and drift off to sleep. *PFC Omar could date her. I could rescue her, take her home, but ...* His thoughts wandered to different a time.

That night, he went into the target building under cover of darkness with an escort. Orders! So-called orders. He hated the sand and just wanted to go home to his work shed with the radio blaring and solder a new gadget. Insurgents were getting blasted with missiles from the flyboys, but this one had to look like the insurgents themselves had done it. The bomb he carried was comparatively crude to what he normally produced, and the materials were inferior, but it would take down the house and the multicar garage and leave the swimming pool a cracked wreck.

He followed his orders and nestled it into a key pillar and then stopped at the sound of a child's laughter. It came from an upstairs room. The laughter was pure, unrestrained joy, Allah's child. As he was about to arm it, his hands trembled. He would be murdering one of Allah's children. He stopped himself from laughing uncontrollably. He froze. When he recovered, he walked out past the jarhead team with the device under his arm, not even trying to slink into the shadows. Somebody pointed an

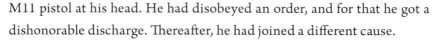

M11 pistol at his head. He had disobeyed an order, and for that he got a dishonorable discharge. Thereafter, he had joined a different cause.

Stop!

He jolted out of bed and headed for the door.

Abdullah looked up at the six-foot walls that surrounded the estate. The barbed wire atop them twinkled in the darkness. In the moonlight, it looked more like a prison than a billionaire's compound. The night sky wasn't an issue; he had mapped every inch of the estate, right down to the flower beds. Abdullah closed his eyes. *Allah, let your will be done.*

He approached the service gate, slithering along the wall. It did not have electronic monitors or surveillance cameras. There were two security guards, one in front of the main gate and the other patrolling the front and rear of the property. The rear guard passed the service gate at twelve-minute intervals, intelligence he had gleaned the night he'd surveilled the estate. A cursory glance confirmed that the surveillance camera remained directed at the gate. He planned to go over the wall using a parkour technique. Abdullah waited for the guard to approach the gate and then move away.

He stepped back across a stretch of grass and faced the wall. "Three, two, one," he whispered and then sprinted toward the wall. The momentum was crucial. As he reached the wall, he pushed off the ground with his leg and then hit the wall with his other leg and pushed. He planted his foot on the wall, engaging it to change his horizontal motion to vertical movement, and pushed up the wall. Abdullah took a deep breath. *You can do this.* With his other leg, he ran another step up the wall and grabbed the top with both hands. He took another deep breath and pulled and then pushed as if he were climbing out of a pool. He put his foot on top of the wall and brought the other leg up into a squatting position. Moments later, he had regained enough energy to hold down the barbed wire, careful not to grab a barb. Twisting his feet around, he vaulted over and dropped silently onto the other side.

He looked around; the coast was clear. The guard would be somewhere past the front of the property and would be approaching the service entrance soon. He zigzagged across the lawn and waited by a clump of bushes until the guard came back around. When the guard passed him, he struck. The guard slumped to the ground, blood running from his head. The wound was fatal. Abdullah wasted no time taking the man's handgun and his MP5 submachine gun. As he looked at the guard, he did not feel anything. *I kill you as you killed innocent children. Sleep. I send you back to your maker, with Allah's blessing.*

Abdullah advanced toward the residence. He stopped when a noise emanated from the guesthouse. *Don't let it distract you—it's not your business.* A light went on in the guesthouse. The guard patrolling the front gate turned and looked toward it. Abdullah ducked behind a shrub. When the guard pivoted back, Abdullah crept up to the front door of the residence. The sounds coming from the bedroom window inside the house were the same as the ones that had come from the guesthouse.

He opened the door and slipped inside. The house was dark, but he could see his way to the staircase. He made his way up the stairs. The bedroom was immediately on his left, and the door was open. He crept closer to the doorframe and peeked in. A table lamp illuminated the room. The maid was bent over the bed. Abdullah recognized her auburn hair falling around her naked body, highlighted by the moonlight. Her face was buried in the bed. Prescott's hands gripped her shoulders as he thrust violently against her flawless, petite frame.

Restraining his instinct to attack Prescott, he turned away and went back downstairs into the living room. He quickly surveyed the room and then set to work with calculated precision, connecting the right wires to the right place in a color coding that only he understood, using a trigger he had designed. Then Abdullah walked out of the room and out the front door. He had done what he had come to do.

He stood behind a bush and looked at the Porsche Panamera. He had one more task before he headed out. He bent down and placed a package behind the wheel.

As he entered the security code into the keypad at the gate, he counted the seconds in his head. Ninety seconds later, his MINI Cooper in sight, he turned back to see a rising ball of orange-red flame baking the startled air. The blast lit up the night over Bronxville. Abdullah didn't stay to watch it as he started the car.

He smiled. *Goodnight, Baron Prescott, CEO of HK Bank. Farewell, sweet maid. It was my sincere pleasure to set you free.*

32

The Wall Street bombing was all over the news. From where Jessica sat on the terrace, she could see the television screen inside. According to witnesses, there had been three explosions. Cell phone cameras had captured the aftermath. Office workers and tourists were covered in blood. Some wandered around in a state of shock. Others lay in agony on the ground. Some people had lost limbs, and some had died.

"Jess, have you seen the carnage? I didn't agree with this. Where's Ambrose? He hasn't reached out since yesterday," Jessica said.

Shut up! They'll hear you. What exactly did you think would happen? You set a chain of events in motion that neither you nor I can stop now.

"No! I promised him. What about his Upper East Side apartment and … the money?" she whispered.

Oh, let me see, Ambrose is gone. So, you think you can walk down to the local police precinct and tell tales? Think again. Here's what you're going to do—button your lip. Understand? You're walking a fine line. Ambrose's fate can and will become yours.

Jessica's face was solemn. Everything had gone wrong. There was no way back. The air became soupy, hard to breathe. A glossy sheen coated her eyes, and her thoughts scattered like an electrical storm in her head—too many short circuits to make any sense.

She rolled off the lounger and crossed the estate's extensive grounds. She felt the need to move. If her limbs were moving, the anxiety would dissipate, or at least she could ignore it for a while. She slowed to the end of the estate's main dock, where one hundred feet out to sea in deep water, Batdadi's yacht was moored. With the mansion behind her and the sea ahead, she buried her consciousness in the rhythmic rising and falling of the ocean.

Inside these walls, Jess existed, coursing through her veins, uncontrollable and destructive. Jessica appeared calm, but her eyes cried out for help.

Give up. It's over.

"Help me," she uttered. Jessica shook her head violently. *This is unproductive.* She had to cogitate, find a path out of her plight. *If I flee, I'll be caught by the FBI.* She tried to recall Jess's precise words. "Shut up. They'll hear you." *Who? Asyd Batdadi and Abdel aren't home. Is Jess spooked? Frightened that Amira will sedate us? She could do that with the aid of the security guards.* Jessica had no doubt that Amira was in communication with Asyd Batdadi. *So, if I stay, I'm as good as dead. I have only two options—back or down.*

Her feet ceased traveling forward and rested on the edge of the dock. Jessica glanced behind her in despair. Her end was at hand. The colors on the horizon swirled and blended as her head tilted toward the sea. "Jump! End it now," she whispered.

Stop! You're fucking crazy. Crazy!

Jessica put her hands over her ears. "Roses are red, violets are blue, I'll sink to the bottom, and so will you. Call me crazy if you will, but I know who I hear, and he's my eternal friend."

No!

Jessica's lips curled into a smile as she realized she had finally escaped. With a single movement, she pushed forward and jumped. She only cared about bringing an end to what was behind her. The setting sun clouded her vision, and then the world tilted. The crimson rushed into burnt orange, and the wind hammered her face. Her eyes were sucked into the backs of their sockets with the sudden acceleration. She looked down and saw a deep, dark abyss. The sea reached out to her with extended arms, beckoning her to drop. She closed her eyes, certain of her fate.

Wall Street was the location of the first terrorist strike. The second was five hours later in Bronxville. An unmitigated success, there were no consequences because of the bloody body count, such as large-scale indiscriminate arrests. Wall Street was a bonus, and everything had proceeded according to plan. Now it was time to begin Operation Aleiqi.

Batdadi and Abdel had met with Malik several weeks before the carnage in New York. A heavyset man in his midthirties, Malik, Batdadi thought, had become more affable, and he feared he had lost his killer instinct. However, still loyal, and hardworking, he had not succumbed to the ways of the infidels and prayed to Mecca five times a day.

Batdadi had sent Malik to the United States three years earlier. Six months after entering the Unites States, Malik had married a Caucasian American and found a job as a heating, ventilation, and air-conditioning engineer in Washington, DC. His parents were Saudi by birth. He had been born in the United States and raised in the UAE, where he had become renowned in the fields of biochemistry and molecular biology— that is, until anger fed by Bin Laden had radicalized him and set him on another path. Years of training in a terrorist camp had made him a trusted sleeper agent. In the last eight months, Batdadi had activated him.

Batdadi's informants in the Emirates' institutions had been fruitful, and if he sought information about anyone or anything in the UAE, it was his for the asking, which was how he'd learned the schedules of several international journalists.

At great risk, he had traveled to and from the UAE under the name An al Alin Hassan. The project managers of the assault on New York were Batdadi; Jessica; and his top man, Abdel. He and Abdel had worked out of what had become his safe houses—the UAE embassy in Washington, DC, located in the North Cleveland Park neighborhood, and the UAE consulate in New York.

Other sleeper agents, unbeknownst to their counterparts and working in the docks throughout the United States, had successfully evaded authorities and imported sarin, considered a weapon of mass destruction. Though production and stockpiling of sarin had been outlawed in April 1997 by the Chemical Weapons Convention, the reports of its total destruction were exaggerated. Batdadi laughed. *Thanks to my faithful partner, the Russians, although it's a rumor that they have aerosolized sarin.* He could not have been more pleased with how events unfolded because now Operation Aleiqi could be completed.

Malik had taken him through the technology, which was simple yet deadly. He examined the humidifier, an electrical appliance designed to increase humidity in a single room or an entire building. He played with a prototype, the same as the one Malik had installed and connected to an HVAC (heating, ventilation, and air conditioning) system.

Batdadi opened his laptop. "I'll push the initial launch button myself."

"It's your right," Abdel said. "You are an esteemed leader. You will, as you have always done, lead by example."

Batdadi did not look up from his laptop. "Very good," he said.

33

The sun shone incandescently, and the virescent color of the summer day under its glare was offensively bright, cheerful, a conspiracy to show him the world would go on without them. In his grief, Jake thought it should not. Everything should be as gray and as foggy as his emotions, cold and damp with silent air. But the birds still chirped, and flowers still bloomed.

He walked through Arlington National Cemetery like a silhouette of himself, wishing he really was as insubstantial as the shadows, so his insides might not feel so mangled. A tear flowed from his eye. He was not ashamed. BLT, Dan, and Chuck had been his family. They were gone now, their lights extinguished forever in his heart. For three days, he had stood in silent grief and awaited the start of the funeral services.

Words from a military chaplain, tributes to their lives, and their loved ones had brought a fresh onslaught of sadness. Their caskets were draped in the United States flag. The casket team served as honor guards in a ceremonial role over the remains and as pallbearers.

Three men, among some of the most lethal servicemen Jake had known, were buried amid the graves of heroes, soldiers. After their burial service came the tradition of Navy SEALs "pinning" the casket with Trident pins.

Later, Jake closed the door to his apartment and dropped his bag on the floor. In the kitchen, he cracked open a bottle of beer. He opened his mouth to gulp it down and then paused and placed it in the sink. A few minutes later, the air was thick with the scent of freshly brewed coffee. He poured himself a large mug and sank into the sofa, bathing in the caffeine kick. *Take one minute at a time, grab a quick shower, change your clothes, and then check in with Alex.*

Stripping down, he dropped his clothes in the laundry basket and ran a bath instead of a shower. Steam filled the bathroom, warming the chilled ceramic floor. As he waited for the tub to fill, he observed his scarred body in the mirror—the bruising had by and large faded. He turned away quickly, lacking the time and the mental energy to acknowledge his body was broken. He took an Epsom salt soak from the medicine cabinet to detoxify his skin and ease his aches and pains. He stepped into the tub and allowed the water to massage his muscles, which were long past cramped.

The water soaked into his skin, and for the first time in a long while, he closed his eyes. He pushed everything out of his mind and drifted into sleep, awakening abruptly when he slipped under the water.

Moments later, he stepped out of the bath, toweled off, and swallowed a couple of Advil from the medicine cabinet. He walked into the bedroom, the towel still wrapped around his waist, and slumped into bed.

Jess awoke from a blackout, feeling like she was hooked up to a power cable. No languor or slow warm-up. The transient dulling was not a dream; it had obliterated the fall. Deep in the water, her senses were altered, the sound lazy and the sea too dark to see much at all.

The brine flowed past her limbs. She kicked against the pressure of the water. That deep in the sea, the water brought a chill to her skin. *It's even colder than I could've imagined.* With the increased pressure, the water felt like mud.

As Jess glanced toward the surface, her heart rate increased. She had never been that deep before. *I've seen darkness before. This isn't like that. This is the darkness that robs you of your best senses and replaces them with paralyzing fear.*

Seconds felt like minutes. Jess's legs were tired, and she struggled to reach the surface. Pain migrated around her body, burning and throbbing. Panic sent her heart hammering against her ribs. Her head pounded, and her cells screamed for oxygen. She fought and forced herself up. *I must take a breath. I will see tomorrow.* With a final burst of exertion, she broke the surface and gulped air.

For the next few minutes, she struggled to orientate herself to her surroundings. Silhouettes of birds flew across the magenta sky. The sun was half into the water, but its reflection in the sea made it appear whole, and the mauve of the dusky sky intensified. The powerful currents flowed away from the shore and pulled her out into the ocean. She looked back toward the dock and recognized she was caught in a rip current and the danger it posed. She did not fight it though. Instead, she swam parallel to the shore toward Batdadi's yacht.

Slowing to consider whether she had made the right decision, she treaded water for a bit and then turned onto her back and floated. Darkness was when the finned predators came out. She had to make a decision—continue forward or bypass the yacht and swim back to the dock. Night was the best time to sneak aboard. Daylight would leave her exposed to Batdadi's security. *I've survived too much to die now.* She was confident it was enough. To date, her life had been marked more by tragedy and insanity than anything approaching normalcy. As she swam toward the yacht, her strokes were compact, seemingly effortless.

Jess lifted her head out of the water and then turned onto her back and used small strokes to move closer to the yacht. No security guards were visible on the main deck. She drew close enough to touch the yacht's hull. Still in the water, she moved down to the starboard side and stopped at a porthole. She pulled herself partially out of the water and peeked inside.

A dark-skinned man in his early sixties sat at a table, eating. He had dark, wavy hair, which was rapidly going gray, and a thick mustache. He ate slowly, chewing his food methodically while reading a book. Next to his plate was a cap bearing an Arabic merchant's insignia on the brim. *The captain*, she thought. *One man. Kill him.* Jess sank back into the water. She imagined plunging the fork into his chest.

Jess dog-paddled toward the yacht's stern. Gripping a ridge, she pulled herself up, the water falling beneath her feet. Head positioned up, adrenaline coursed unchecked, urging her to raise her leg adjacent to her hand. She pushed until her core was resting on the rail.

She swung her legs over the rail and landed on the deck. Jess rolled and then crouched on the port side. She quickly detached a gaff from its long rope and crept toward the stairs leading down to the captain's cabin.

She turned the doorknob; it was unlocked. She kicked it open. Her eyes homed in on her target as she threw the gaff. Stunned by the opening door, the captain attempted to jump to his feet, but it was too late. The gaff knocked him back. Jess advanced, grabbed a knife from the table, and plunged it into his throat, severing his jugular vein.

34

Insomnia haunted Jake's nights. The activities in which he engaged brought extreme stress, as did the losses he had recently experienced—Alice, ten months earlier at Jess's hand, and now BLT, Dan, and Chuck in the last couple of weeks.

He sat down on the floor with a file spread in front of him and studied the most recent intelligence reports from the NCTC dealing with the recent attack on Wall Street. At 2:20 a.m., his phone rang, breaking his concentration.

"Yeah?" he said in an annoyed tone.

"Jake, it's Alex. I have good news."

"I'm listening." Jake dropped the report he was reading.

"I just learned that Jessica and at least three others are in the Hamptons. This is a moving target. Batdadi's yacht is moored off the coast with at least two people onboard. Intel is patchy—it's not clear whether we are dealing with six people or four because two boarded the yacht. Our people are working on it."

"And … what are we going to do about it?"

"I've planned a mission. The authorization to go came from the commander in chief no less. The loop is tight. We don't want information to leak out to them. Expect the kill or capture to take place within the next twenty-four hours."

"How did you find them?"

"The FBI retrieved a cell phone from the Wall Street crime scene with an interesting digital footprint. The phone was found on one of the victims, identified as Ambrose Wilson. He was captured on CCTV entering and leaving HK Bank. Records confirmed he was there to meet Clint Morris, the bank's president of corporate finance. As you are aware, Morris had a relationship with Jessica through his wife."

A phone holds a thousand memories, Jake thought. *Not just in the voice calls but in the pictures, music, and text messages.*

"Jake?" Alex raised his voice, several seconds having passed.

Jake took a deep breath. It was the monumental news he had been waiting for. If everything worked according to plan, this was the beginning of the end of Jessica's reign of terror. He spent most of the night talking to Alex. In addition to everything they discussed, Alex put Jake on notice and ended the call when he said, "Don't stray too far."

After the call with Alex ended, Jake walked into his bedroom to change into some workout clothes. He had not done laundry recently and was down to his last pair of socks. He found his Nikes in the closet and clipped his pager to his waist and headed for the door. He locked the door behind him and made his way to the building's gym. Workouts helped Jake to relax and clear his mind. As he pulled up and down on a bar, he pushed the events of the last days from his psyche. Fifty minutes later, Jake had built up a sweat from a combination of push-ups, dips, pull-ups, dead lifts, and crutches. In fact, he was in better shape than he had been when he was in the SEALs.

After stretching out his legs, he hit the road for a ten-mile jog. The final leg of his workout ended with a ten-mile swim at the recreational center, where he kept a fully equipped locker. After his swim, he showered. He was beyond fatigued. He stood under spray and let the hot water bounce off his body. His mind was numb and his legs weak. He leaned against the wall and allowed his body to sink down. For several minutes, he sat trying to blank out the deaths that had plagued his life.

Jake snapped back when he heard voices in the bathroom. Standing, he turned the faucet all the way to cold. Blood raced through arteries and shocked his body back to life.

Jake toweled off and dressed in shorts and a T-shirt. In the snack bar, he downed a bottle of water followed by a bottle of G FUEL. He checked his pager and headed back to his apartment where he checked his phone for calls from Alex.

Waiting was an aspect of the job he did not like. *The call will come. Until then, I need to sleep—no ifs and buts. There's nothing I can do for now.*

Jake lay on his bed; he thought about Jessica. What role did she play in all of this? Would he kill her if it came to that? He was tired—he drifted off to sleep.

35

As the setting sun slipped below the horizon, two army CH-47D helicopters hovered over a special operations craft, a riverine. The craft was rigged to the underbelly of the helicopter with a sling and would be used by the Special Warfare Combatant-Craft Crewmen. Jake was seasoned in the use of the MEATS (Maritime External Air Transportation System) insertion and extraction delivery system. Alex had briefed him in advance that the clandestine mission would be at night without air support. He was amped up and excited to see some action.

It was a perfect night for a drop. The ocean was cold but calm. The Combatant-Craft Crewman lowered the boat and then dropped a ladder down from the helicopter into it. Jake, Em-Dog, and the SEALs, all with flippers strapped to their thighs, and their boat team lined up. The second the riverine was launched, they descended the ladder into the boat. Once everyone was in place, the crew fired up the powerful diesel engines and headed for Batdadi's yacht, moored one hundred feet out from his residence.

In the dark of the night, the high-speed assault craft arrived off the coast. Four of the six SEALs, Jake, and Em-Dog swam to Batdadi's yacht. The SEALs made an assessment and then communicated their plan. Minutes later, they boarded the yacht. With the SEALs in place as a backup, Jake advanced stealthily and positioned himself outside the captain's cabin, his P226 pistol in hand.

Jess swung her head toward the door when she heard it click closed.

"Put your hands on the table," Jake said.

The yacht was designed with a contemporary and sophisticated feel. Its floor-to-ceiling windows and skylights offered a seamless sense of openness to the outside world.

As Jess slowly raised her hands, she tilted her head up slightly and caught sight of Em-Dog. She eyed his weapon, a .40-caliber semiautomatic Glock pistol. It was pointed at her head. His bleak gray eyes were framed in the passionless face of an executioner.

With her hands on the table, she turned back toward Jake. "Jessica?" she murmured, "Jake is here." Her voice was kind and soft. "I saw the anger and heard the intensity in his tone. There's a great deal of emotion behind his words. I'm not taking the fall for this. Say you're sorry and that you'll be a better person if he'll forgive you." Jess retreated.

The chatter was barely audible. Jake had no way to decipher which alter ego was present.

Jess, its time, the time I knew would come sooner or later and dreaded. I have to say goodbye to the only person who looked beyond my flaws and, for a time, bankrolled me. I want my frozen eggs. How am I supposed to make him love me now? If I find the courage to ... If Jess ... if everything you said is right, there's no going back. I can't right this wrong with sorry. Dr. Bajwa said, Khalil said ... I know you can hear me. I'll try to reason with him. But, Jess ... Alice, Ambrose, all those dead people.

Jessica looked into Jake's eyes. "When the world was falling apart around me, you made me feel as if it wasn't so bad. When I thought nothing could make me feel better, you managed to put even the slightest simper on my face. I wish ... I could go back to when we first met, so I could do it all over again—differently. I pray for babies. I can't help that because I have this place in my chest that feels empty, like a black hole, pitch-black and barren. I'm lost, and it's the only way for me to be found again."

What? There's a gun pointing at your head. Babies? Fuck! I'm going back to shore. Jess yelled in her head.

Jessica's elbow dropped to her side. Under the napkin on her lap was a 9mm Glock. Jess had removed the pistol from the captain's person before she had thrown him overboard. She'd thought it would be perfect for dispatching anybody who boarded the vessel. At first, the metal had felt cold in her hand, even icy, but after minutes of cradling it, the gun felt more like a part of her than a tool of death. Where the weapon was now positioned, it was a discreet deadly force.

In that frozen second between Jessica's words and her elbow dropping, Jake's eyes flicked to the bulge under the napkin. Her face was unreadable—no fear, no invitational smirk. He pulled the trigger on his P226.

The entry wound was small, but the bullet exited and splintered the surface of the portrait behind her. "Target engaged," Jake said.

At first, Jessica didn't realize she had been shot. The bullet had gone right through and struck the portrait behind her. Her collarbone was shattered, her rotor cuff destroyed. She was bleeding, but the bullet had struck her with such force that her wound was mostly cauterized, and the blood loss was minimal.

Jake figured she was nauseous from the shock. She struggled to her feet, holding her useless arm, and then stumbled and fell to the floor, screaming in pain.

Jake bent down and grabbed her gun. She stared at the pistol, which was pointed at her. "I've been shot!"

"I know." He did not hide the joy in his tone.

"You bastard!"

He ignored her as he spoke into his headset. "Send a stretcher."

"I'll kill you. I swear to God!" She spat and tried to kick him and then fell back, moaning and clutching her arm.

The SEAL team members, Jake, and Em-Dog slipped over the side of the yacht and swam to shore. A fifth SEAL from the assault craft was on the beach waiting for them. When they emerged from the water, he passed out water bags. As they loaded up their gear, he outlined the strategy for their mission and what they could expect until they entered the mansion, where intelligence reports and infrared sensors indicated three hostiles. "Apart from initial floor plans, we have no intel on what the inside looks like," he said.

Just after midnight, the SEAL team, Jake, and Em-Dog crossed the grounds behind Batdadi's mansion.

"Em-Dog, I want you on my back the entire time we're inside the residence," Jake said into his headset. "We move as a unit."

One of the SEALs kicked open the door that led to the deck behind the house. Another tossed a stun grenade into the room just right of the kitchen.

Boom!

Jake, Em-Dog, and a third SEAL rushed in. Jake and Em-Dog went to the right, and the SEAL shifted to the left alongside the wall. They used flashlights mounted on their weapons to illuminate the dark room. Jake stepped back when he saw movement through a doorway on the left. Em-Dog shifted his light beam. It flashed off the metal of a rifle. He fired two three-round bursts from his M4 into the doorway.

A dark-skinned Pakistani fell into the doorway, his Kalashnikov rifle lodged under his thorax. Jake and the team stepped over the man and moved in a tactical formation down the hallway, clearing the rooms on the left and right. They made a turn and advanced up the staircase on the right.

They were halfway up the stairs when a rifle on the balcony fired rapidly. Jake ducked, and the gunman continued firing. When Em-Dog scooted to the left of the stairs, the SEAL behind him leapt up and fired ten rounds at the target. Jake had never seen a SEAL move so fast. Through the ringing in his ears and the sparks around them as brass bullet casings struck the floor and bounced, he heard a thud when the gunman slumped over the balcony and fell to the lobby floor.

They continued up the stairs and cleared the upper rooms. At the far end of the landing, inside a bedroom, a woman was bound to a chair. Em-Dog found the overhead light and flipped it on.

The woman had a hood over her head. Jake picked up her cell phone from the nightstand, pulled a chair from near the dresser, and sat directly in front of her. Em-Dog stood behind her. Jake signaled Em-Dog to remove the hood, revealing Dr. Amira Bajwa. She blinked as her eyes adjusted to the light.

Em-Dog attached his laptop to the sat phone. A SEAL handed him the SIM cards they had removed from the locked cell phones found on the bodies of the dead men. He uploaded their information to the CIA and waited for the response. The lock on Amira's phone was controlled via fingerprint. Jake placed her finger on the sensor and learned her name from accessing her phone.

"Look at me!" Jake shouted.

Amira made eye contact. He turned his laptop screen with the photos of Batdadi and Jamal toward her. "How come you know these jihadist folks? Where's Asyd Batdadi?"

"I don't know," Amira said.

Jake grabbed Amira's jaw and twisted her face toward him. "Where's Batdadi? This can be easy, or it can be very painful. Where can we find Batdadi?"

"I don't—" Before she could finish, Em-Dog yanked her chair back, causing her head to hit the hardwood floor. Jake nodded, and Em-Dog lifted the chair back in place.

Jake grabbed the back of her head and forced her to look at him. "Who is Abdel?" he asked, holding up Amira's cell phone so she could see the text messages. He swiped up. On the screen was a picture of her with two young children, a boy and a girl. "That's your son and daughter, isn't it? Your blood?"

Amira looked away but not before her face registered recognition, followed by fear, which confirmed Jake's suspicion. He stood up and scrolled through the call log. "Amira, can I call you by that name? Let me explain something. If you don't tell me where I can find Asyd Batdadi, I'm going after your children. People I love are dead, and I'm going to kill your son and daughter."

Amira pushed against her restraints. She spat at him and then learned forward. "You are law enforcement. I don't believe you."

Jake looked at Em-Dog. He put the hood back over Amira's head. Then they left the room.

"Ya Ibn el Sharmouta!" Amira shouted. She repeated the words in English. "Son of a bitch! I will demand the death penalty for you if you harm my children!"

One hour had passed when Jake returned to the room carrying his laptop and a satellite phone. Em-Dog moved behind Amira and pulled the hood off her head. Jake positioned himself on a chair in front of Amira once again and powered up the devices. Seconds later, he had a signal and clear pictures. He held out the laptop, allowing her to see the screen.

"Open your eyes," Jake said.

Slowly, Amira moved her head and stared at the screen. The CIA had used her cell phone and Facebook to identify her children and family.

"Begin Operation Indispensable," Jake said into his headset. A drone had been launched from a US military base just across from the Turkish border.

Amira realized instantly that she was looking at the drone's flight path. Its speed shocked her, and the fact she could identify landmarks terrified her. The realization that her children were near to death hit her. As the drone reached the edge of Istanbul, Amira's resistance changed visibly. The drone was slowed in a residential area.

"Zoom in," Jake said.

The images captured by the drone were detailed. The backyard area was much like those found across the United States. Two little children played by a pool. The clarity of the Spider-Man image on the boy's swim shorts and the girl's Wonder Woman doll lying on the recliner was incredible.

Amira stared at Jake. "You ... you can't."

He opened her cell phone and scrolled through the call log. "Aleiqi has called you several times. How is this name related to the strike on Wall Street?" He rested the phone on his lap. "Let's see what your children are doing. You care about them, don't you?" When Amira did not reply to Jake, he spoke into his headset. "Arm the missiles and eliminate the target." The camera lens zoomed out.

Amira's eyes were moist. She spoke softly as tears fell from her eyes. Jake could not hear her, so he bent forward, putting his hand behind his ear.

"The United Arab Emirates," she said. "Don't hurt my children."

"Where? What about the UAE?"

"Asyd Batdadi is connected to Islamists from the dark age. His benefactors are powerful people with international connections."

"Yes," Jake said, nodding for her to continue.

"Asyd Batdadi and Jess's plans to take revenge aligned. If she delivered Wall Street—and she must have because you're here—he promised to reciprocate and give her revenge on the journalist world. She believed the turning point in her life was the reviews she was given by establishment journalists. I heard something about killing two birds with one stone."

"I need details."

"When Jessica wandered off and did not return to the mansion, Batdadi's security men sought someone to blame, and they bound me to the chair in this room. You arrived and interrupted their interrogation. That's all I know."

Jake looked at Em-Dog and winked, "Abort," he said into his headset.

Another day, Amira would learn of Jake and Em-Dog's cunning ploy.

36

In the aftermath of the Wall Street bombings, the might of the United States was in play, a country was in mourning, and the world was in shock. In his address to the nation, President Dayle Wesley stated that the country would not rest until the perpetrators of the heinous acts were brought to justice. "There's no place on this planet that the arm of the United States can't reach," he said.

His words echoed over and over again on TV monitors playing live feeds from the White House, Wall Street, and Bronxville. It was a day the country thought it would not see again after the 9/11 attacks. The nation was at war against what appeared to be a far-reaching network of violence and hatred that had, once again, sought revenge on American soil.

When Jake walked into the conference room, a group was seated along both sides of the long conference table. He took a seat to the right of Alex.

"We have a team in New York," Alex said.

As Jake listened, he opened his laptop to check on recent updates.

"We're going to need all the help we can get," Alex continued. He turned to his chief analyst, Martin Burnette. "Marty, bring Jake and the others up to speed."

The other participants at the table looked at Alex, confused. He held out his hand, indicating Marty.

"We got the first video from Egyptian intelligence, and the second was shot outside Federal Hall in front of the George Washington statue minutes before the suicide bomb on the steps," Marty said.

"Do we have a time stamp for the Egyptian footage?" Jake asked.

"Yes, February to June, the months leading up to the bombing. There were several sightings at the coffeehouse from which Tom uploaded the images of Batdadi, Milton, and Batdadi's head of security, Abdel. Milton is now in custody, but he's not talking. Taking a step back, Batdadi and Abdel were moving between Syria and Egypt. The last frame shows Batdadi and Milton. Chuck was found dead several hours later and Tom a day later." There was a silent pause before Marty continued. "We identified the suicide bomber on the steps of Federal Hall as Jamal Khan, one of Batdadi's master bombers. His brother, Abdul, was recently killed in Paris."

Jake's eyes remained on his laptop. He did not need intel on Abdul's demise.

Alex touched the keyboard on his laptop, and an image appeared on the wall-mounted TV screen. "Her name is Amira Bajwa," he said, taking over the briefing. "She's a psychiatrist and a resident of Turkey. Over the past few weeks, the NCTC has been picking up chatter of an impending attack somewhere in the United States. Jake had an encounter with Bajwa recently, and she's also in custody." Alex directed his attention to Jake. "Any clue as to what that very big something is?" Alex's facial expression demonstrated he was acutely aware Jake did not know the answer and that his question was more for effect.

"She was brought onboard to evaluate and succor Jessica to accomplish what we now know as Operation Aleiqi," Jake said. "Jessica, also in custody, was instrumental in the Wall Street attack. In return, millions were transferred to offshore accounts. Her condition is reported as stable, but she's been unresponsive during interrogations. As for the 'something very big,' it involves an attack on our First Amendment rights, in particular, journalists. Jessica believed journalists—their critiques—destroyed her career in the art world."

Breakaway groups formed in the corners of the conference room. Jake moved to the other end of the table and sat with Em-Dog and Sandy, reading through reports generated by her organization. Sandy's analysis focused on the recent attacks in New York and speculated that all the disparate cells involved had been run not by Batdadi but, rather, by his operation commander and head of security, Abdel. Sandy handed Jake a report from the Center for the Study of Weapons of Mass Destruction.

"Assad!" Jake's eyes homed in on the paragraph highlighting Syrian dictator Bashar al-Assad.

"Yes, he lies, cheats, and hides," Sandy said.

"It was reported we destroyed his WMDs. What did we miss?" Jake asked. "How much does he have in reserve? And how does he factor in to Batdadi's operations?"

"At some point, Assad's name was in the mix. There was chatter about some of his chemical cache, sarin being weaponized. We thought they were simply rumors." Jake's brow creased with concern as Sandy continued. "The Kurds found and communicated the target site to us. When the inspector went to the site, the canisters were gone. We tracked them to an underground bunker but only retrieved five of the six canisters reported."

"But why take only one canister?" Em-Dog asked.

"Maybe they hoped we wouldn't be able to track it," Sandy said. "We started to connect the dots to Batdadi after his travels to Egypt and Syria, and we believe he acquired the canister for his own purposes."

Sandy opened her laptop and uploaded the Egypt images she had received from Tom. "There's more. The passport Jessica used to reenter the United States was recovered from a Hamptons resident, thanks to your field operations. As you might expect, it's a forged document bearing the name Jamila Hassan. We matched the surname Hassan with ten other Hassans who entered the country on the same day as Jessica. Three Hassans traveled together via private jet—An al Alin Hassan, Jamila Hassan, and Natasha Hassan. Amira Bajwa was also on that flight. We cross-matched data from US Immigrations and Customs with our digital ID library. We are 99 percent certain the passport photograph of An al Alin Hassan is the same as Tom's digital image of Batdadi taken in Egypt."

"Sorry, Sandy," Jake said, looking up. "I'm listening. You said a single canister?"

"Yes."

"The damage WMDs can do doesn't compare with suicide bombers. I'm not making light of the recent attacks, but Jessica's relationship with Batdadi was coincidental. An opportunity emerged. He used Jessica and hit the jackpot, if you will. Nuclear attacks require infrastructure, which is almost impossible on American soil, but bioterrorism requires—"

"Fuck," Em-Dog said.

"Air, water, or food chains."

When the others had left and the door closed, Alex slumped in his chair and closed his laptop, his eyes on Jake, still unable to believe what he had just heard. Minutes earlier, Jake had pulled him aside and said he believed Batdadi had weaponized sarin. Alex had immediately cleared the room, apart from Jake, Em-Dog, and Sandy.

"Aerosolized, meaning it can be distributed through the air?" Alex asked when the door clicked shut.

"Yes," Sandy replied. She quickly summarized the NCC's analysis.

"Analysis appreciated," Alex said, "but it omits the where and the when. We'll have a major problem if Batdadi deploys sarin. How many casualties are we looking at with one canister?"

"As you know, sarin has been used as a chemical weapon due to its extreme potency as a nerve agent," Sandy said. "Exposure is lethal even at very low concentrations. Death can occur within one to ten minutes after direct inhalation of a lethal dose due to suffocation from lung muscle paralysis. We have no doubt Batdadi is going to use a single canister, which suggests he is not interested in mass casualties. He is targeting one or more individuals."

Alex rotated the stylus in his hand. "If we're going to take this to the president of the United States, I want evidence that there's an imminent attack on this country."

Sandy glanced at Jake. "When I approached just before you cleared the room, I had been informed that the folks at Wall Street had discovered traces of sarin among the remains of the suicide bomber, Jamal. The explosion and ensuing fire incinerated the sarin." She looked directly at Alex. "That's not all. Fragments of a reinforced aerosol container similar to a deodorant container were also recovered from the scene."

"How the fuck did we fail to detect importation of a deadly substance?" Alex asked.

"Sarin weaponized as an aerosol in a container akin to a consumer product would have to be transported to a highly secure facility equipped to deal with bioterrorism elements. Our people are in pursuit. A limited number of facilities could undertake such a project or would be willing to assist Batdadi."

"Russians?" Em-Dog asked.

Alex looked at him. "You think that's where the help came from?"

"Maybe the Russians are sowing discord in the world right now," Jake suggested.

"Speculation—we pay analysis to do that bullshit. A target—give me a target!" Alex said.

Jake put his head in his hand as he rested it on the table and closed his eyes. *I pray to God I'm wrong.* He opened his eyes as he lifted his head and said, "If, as I suspect, I have identified the target, the attack will be catastrophic."

"The target?" Alex shouted. He slammed his hand on the desk. "Why are we continually one step behind Batdadi?"

"The president of the United States, at the White House Correspondents' Association Dinner. POTUS usually attends the event," Jake replied.

"POTUS is Batdadi's target, and any and all journalists are Jessica's target," Jake reiterated. He and Alex were alone in Alex's office fifty minutes later. "I don't believe it was her plan when she set out, but Jessica hated the media—her agenda coincided with Batdadi's agenda. Wall Street was the bonus and revenge on me."

"We know what's out there and the target location," Alex replied. "I've brought the White House up to speed. President Wesley will not attend the correspondents' dinner. His people don't want to go public for fear of panic."

Alex's eyes were wide open with a vacant expression. He quickly refocused. "Many HVAC systems have air monitors, which detect numerous airborne pathogens. If a deviation is detected, the air system immediately shuts down."

"That's good to know," Jake said, "but people can still be infected by the time the system shuts down. They should postpone the dinner."

"My thoughts exactly. A C-40 is fueling up at Pope Field. Em-Dog will meet you onboard. I want you to lock this shit down."

37

Jake and Em-Dog arrived at the Ritz-Carlton in Washington, DC, at around 8:00 p.m. that night. The hotel manager met them in the lobby. Men dressed in biohazard suits were already on site. Alex had convinced the relevant people to order an evacuation of the hotel, and the people responsible for the White House Correspondents' Association Dinner had agreed to postpone the event until everybody's safety could be guaranteed.

It's only a matter of time before the news breaks and the media moves in, Jake thought. He was comfortable with that. They might need the public's help to end the situation and neutralize the remaining culprits.

"Weaponized sarin," David Brown, the head of the hotel's security system, said, trying to look confident. "We were informed they might attempt to introduce it through the HVAC system."

Jake nodded. "Yes."

Brown was in his fifties and had a receding hairline. He had worked in security at the hotel for the last thirty years, rising to the head of the department six months earlier. "We have air monitors all over this place. The system can detect deviations and foreign particulates, including sarin," he said. "Where the hell do you think it is?"

Jake and Em-Dog remained silent.

"We have eleven floors, excluding the floor below ground," Brown continued, it was clear he wasn't going to get an answer. "Three hundred rooms, including two hundred and sixty-seven deluxe rooms and thirty-two suites. We have evacuated the hotel, but as you can imagine, the shareholders aren't happy."

"No," Em-Dog whispered.

"Excuse me?" Brown said.

"No, I can't imagine they are," Em-Dog replied.

An HVAC engineer joined them and explained that the hotel had undergone a $12 million renovation, which had been completed earlier that year. "Pete," he said, holding his hand out to Jake. "The engineer who installed the HVAC system is no longer with the company." He handed Jake the engineering plans for the hotel and explained that the central air conditioners circulated cool air through a system of supply and return ducts.

Jake turned to the men in biohazard suits. "Start with the ducts leading to the dining and conference rooms." He pointed at Brown. "You go with them."

Jake moved to a corner, took out his phone, and called Sandy to give her a rundown regarding what he had learned about Malik, the former engineer. After he hung up, he opened the door to the staircase leading to the below-ground floor and ran down the stairs, Em-Dog close behind him.

The below-ground floor was all concrete and had no personality. Near the ceiling were long, low windows, no wider than the arrow slits in a castle turret but lying on their sides.

"Where are you going? Are you looking for something specific?" Em-Dog asked.

"The main supply duct."

"Over there," Em-Dog said, pointing.

Caged off in a concrete room toward the back of the hotel was a heat pump. The air conditioner's main duct was connected to it. Jake examined it.

"What are we looking for?" Em-Dog asked.

"A protrusion on the heating system, maybe the size of an iPod, colored to blend in with the casing."

"You think they can activate it remotely, via a computer or phone?"

"Yes. If, as we suspect, Malik updated the HVAC system, he had access to the air-conditioning room and could do everything that needed to be done." As Jake peered at the components of the air-conditioning system, his gaze focused on a small device attached to the heat pump, the same silver gray as the HVAC system.

"There!" he said to the biohazard men and HVAC engineers, who had joined them in the room. He pointed at a device in a dark corner of the duct about ten feet from the connection to the heat pump.

"They took a risk bringing this shit to the United States," Em-Dog said.

"Terrorism is the only endeavor where a man can succeed once and then declare himself as standing above others in rank, importance, and achievement, not to mention a martyr to the cause," Jake said. "Yes, hitting one place, and with POTUS in attendance, was all Batdadi needed to dine out to the end of his days and memorialize his murderous soul."

As the biohazard team moved in, Jake took a deep breath and then exhaled, though not because his mission had been accomplished. It was far from finished if Batdadi walked the earth. His exhale was about finally reaching the beginning of the end.

They walked out into the courtyard of the Ritz. Members of the public had gathered and were staring at them. The men in biohazard suits had drawn attention, creating a cell phone moment.

"People are starting to get excited," Em-Dog said. "Twitter will be on steroids tomorrow."

38

Jake sat in Alex's office doodling on the notepad on the desk. He had brought Alex up to speed on what had happened at the Ritz-Carlton. Em-Dog sat to his right. Outside the window, the sun was going down.

Although it had been part of his report, Jake repeated it verbally. "The biohazard teams managed to detach the canisters from the air ducts in the dining and conference rooms and the main air duct." He did not look up as he spoke.

"Too close for comfort," Em-Dog said. "The fucking device was dormant, waiting for Batdadi to trigger it. They're cleaning everything up, checking it all out."

Jake stabbed his pen into the notepad. "The threat has been neutralized, but the problem isn't solved and will not be until I cage the Bat."

"We're looking for him," Alex said. "It's only a matter of time."

"Are you sure about that?" Jake shot back.

Alex frowned at Jake's outburst. "That is not constructive. Any ideas where he might be?"

"I can tell you this. He won't walk away from the fight. Not now. We just fucked up his plan."

Em-Dog stood up and headed for the door. Halfway out, he turned back. "We're going to get him, Jake. We have the best people hunting Batdadi. Every possible route in and out of this country is covered. He won't get away."

The evening after the debriefing in Alex's office, Jake flew to Florida. He had no operational reason to go to Naples, but he needed to clear his head after recent events. Florida was not just a state way from North Carolina. It was also a much-needed pit stop. He was seated in a booth at Jack's Bait Shack, his right hand resting against the bulge of his P226 pistol in his pants pocket. On the table was an updated dossier on Batdadi from Sandy. In the last twenty-four hours, they had turned up nothing.

He read the pages in relation to Batdadi's entry to the United States of America. United States Customs and Border Protection recorded that An al Alin Hassan and his wives, Natasha and Jamila Hassan, had traveled to the United States. The documents stated that the United Arab Emirates consulate in New York was their residence for a short vacation. An al Alin and Natasha Hassan exited the United States several days later. He turned the page. At a later date, An al Alin Hassan returned to United States, giving his destination and place of residence as the United Arab Emirates embassy in Washington, DC.

Several pages in, Jake turned three pages back and studied the image on the page. A UAE immigrant working at a hot dog stand outside the embassy had taken photographs with his phone. He had caught a glimpse of the ambassador and a man he believed to be a member of the UAE royal family. *I know Jamila Hassan, aka Jessica, is in Womack Army Medical Center, and the man next to the ambassador is not royalty. He's An al Alin Hassan, aka. Batdadi. He was—and still is—in the UAE embassy.*

Murphy nodded at Jake, signaling he wanted to know if Jake wanted more of the same. Jake did not respond; he had just finished his second Bud Heavy. Murphy would not read his pause as he would with many other patrons as indication he was contemplating whether to have a Bud Light. Jake had told him that light beers gave him gas. He had never considered that doubling his intake of light beer was what gave him gas. Murphy's facial expression did not change when Jake placed a fifty-dollar bill on the table and headed out.

Jake abandoned his Ford F-150 in the Fort Myers airport parking lot and, thirty minutes later, boarded a flight to New York. After leaving the airport, he did not go to a hotel but, rather, to a nightclub. He made himself comfortable at the bar and watched the lights flash as people bounced up and down on the dance floor to the drums and bass.

He saw the watcher just after 3:00 a.m. Jake had just finished his second Bud. A second glance several seconds later confirmed it. The man was sitting in a group with a woman who appeared to be his girlfriend. She was blond, beautiful, and looked like she was twenty years old. Her long legs gracefully crossed, she and the other people in the group were passing hand-rolled cigarettes around the table, inhaling plumes of smoke into their lungs. He continued to observe discreetly until the man went to the restroom.

Jake entered the restroom as the man was zipping his pants. He turned around to find himself facing the barrel of Jake's handgun.

"What?"

"I'm not your type, so why were you gaping at me?" Jake asked sarcastically.

The man stared in silence, his lips trembling.

"I asked you a question."

"The gun," the man said, his voice quaking.

Jake raised his gun level with the man's forehead. "I'm interested in your attraction to me."

"You stick out in a place like this. My friends, we're—"

"Hackers, I know. Where can I find the Wizard?"

"If I tell you, he'll kill me."

"If you don't tell me, I'll kill you." Jake took a step back as urine soaked the man's leg.

"I don't know where he is. He finds you. But I do know that, if you shoot me, you'll never find him."

Jake lowered his gun, turned, and walked out of the restroom.

Frustrated at not finding the Wizard, Jake caught a cab back to his hotel in the Meat Packing District; by then, it was after 4:00 a.m. He opened the door to the balcony. The cacophony from the street pierced the silence of his suite. Sirens squealed, and horns blared above the blast of music from passing cars. The view across New York was priceless. From where he stood, he could see the entire Manhattan skyline. The city that never slept was in full swing.

He showered and shaved. Though he had not eaten in the past twenty-four hours, he did not order room service or go to a restaurant. He wanted to take in the early morning, to breathe and contemplate his next steps.

The route he walked tracked through the Meatpacking District from West 14th Street south to Hudson River Park. He had just taken a seat on a park bench facing the river and was reading his email when the Wizard approached.

For several minutes, they sat side by side. The Wizard's face was stern, even a little melancholy, in repose. His features transfigured when—if—he smiled. Daniel Walker, aka the Wizard, had grown his beard as soon as he could, his way of telling himself and the world that boyhood was gone, and he had arrived in his days of manhood. He kept it neat, as neat as the rest of his hair and his work.

Finally, Jake broke the silence. "I want you to trigger the fire alarm, followed by the air monitors in the UAE embassy in DC."

"There's no way JSOC will allow what you're asking for. Absolutely not," the Wizard said.

An atypical government contractor, the Wizard's interaction with JSOC had come after he had used his computer skills to gain unauthorized access to government data. Law enforcement had described him as a hacker. He had extensive knowledge in that area of technology, especially devices, programs, and computer networks. However, he had not hacked the government computer system nefariously; he had used his mastery to detect other hackers. Thereafter, JSOC had used his skills to take advantage of vulnerabilities in software systems. The Wizard could manipulate a computer system or electronic devices to remotely control them or access the data stored in them.

"Yes, hack the UAE embassy's computer system."

"Let's be clear. You don't have Alex's authorization." The Wizard had avoided a criminal record when he'd agreed to an under-the-radar role with Alex's team.

"I know, and I understand that," Jake said.

"I don't think you do." The Wizard paused. "You're planning retaliation by launching an international incident, unleashing cyber warfare! This isn't a hack, and all is forgotten. Who's writing the checks?"

Jake's patience was exhausted. "Did you get your chai tea latte this morning? Did you bother to look at your phone—the news headlines?"

"Hackers know that your government steals from the poor, but that's to be expected, and we don't say anything. What I will not put up with is when you have a crisis—and I assume it's a big one because you came to me—but you won't give me all the info. So, when you're ready to be transparent about the current predicament, feel free to reach out. Until then I suggest you go fuck yourself."

The Wizard stood up and turned to leave and then glanced over his shoulder. "Here are the facts. State actors have their own in-house hacking teams. They have also been known to hire criminal hackers and offer a lot of money. How about you extend me the same courtesy?"

Jake put his hand on the Wizard's arm. "Just trigger the fire alarm and the air monitors."

"So, you can do what, play judge, jury, and executioner? I shouldn't even be discussing this with you."

"If there was another way to do this, I wouldn't need to ask. Believe me, for the last twenty-four hours, I've been trying to come up with one."

"I can tell you right now that Alex is never going to authorize this."

"The Bronxville and Wall Street bombings. All I need is your help getting Batdadi outside the embassy."

"And … other requirements?" the Wizard asked, turning to face him.

Jake smiled. "If anyone can make it happen, it's you."

The Wizard didn't smile back. "How much time do we have to put this together?"

"I need to go in tonight."

39

Four hours later, Jake used a phony ID to rent a studio apartment in a building situated to the rear of the UEA embassy in Washington. He leaned against the kitchen door and stared at Em-Dog. Jake had filled him in on what had happened in New York.

"I take it you haven't liaised with Alex."

Jake shook his head. "No! He can't be involved. If this goes south …"

Em-Dog looked at him in disbelief.

Jake eyeballed a response. "Batdadi has secured the protection of the UAE. By the time Alex works this through the channels, Batdadi will have done another Houdini."

"You don't even have confirmation he's in the embassy."

"True, and if I'm wrong, the fire alarm will be billed as a false alert, and then you can go on down to the steak house."

"Fuck you," Em-Dog said.

Jake waved him off. "I see only one way to end this, but there are no guarantees. I've put things in motion."

Em-Dog set up a variable-power Zeiss Victory FL scope on its tripod, dragged a vanity table to the window, and placed the tripod on top of it. The scope was mounted on a 300 Win Mag, creating a sniper's nest. He powered up the scope and sighted through it. From his position, he had visuals on the rear grounds of the UAE embassy and into several second-floor windows to the right and left.

He performed a sweep with his gun and then swung back, focusing on the embassy's rear exit. He was satisfied he could take the shot if the target stepped out, but he harbored reservations about terminating Batdadi on embassy soil without explicit authorization. He exhaled a long breath. "Implied authorization—Batdadi murdered innocent Americans." Em-Dog settled into his perch and awaited Jake's signal.

The fire alarm went off, an ear-splitting wail. It rose to a peak and then ebbed and rose to a peak again, undulating like a wave.

"Two minutes before security confirms no fire and deactivates the alarm," the Wizard said. He was in a van parked two blocks from the embassy.

"Copy that," Jake said into his headset. "Activate the air monitors alarm."

"Air monitors activated. Embassy falser code deactivated," the Wizard replied, receiving and delaying the dispatch to the emergency communication facility.

Em-Dog listened to the transmission between the Wizard and Jake as he scanned the embassy's exits and waited patiently to see if anyone would come running out of the building.

Sitting on a park bench, Jake watched the embassy through the lightly falling rain. The tiny earpiece in his right ear was linked to an encrypted voice-activated mobile phone in his right pocket. By touching the screen, he could speak just to Em-Dog or broadcast on all channels. He held his P226 in his right hand, resting on his thigh. He kept the weapon low in the shadows but ready for quick use.

"Are you getting this?" Em-Dog asked a moment later, a hint of excitement in his tone. "The ambassador, Batdadi, and Abdel are on the move."

"Copy that. I'm three o'clock to the guardhouse." Jake had changed location and positioned himself on the avenue at the rear of the building, assuming protocol would dictate an evacuation to the rear of the embassy.

"CCTV cameras disabled," the Wizard said.

"Roger that," Jake replied.

He crossed the avenue to the building that accommodated the guard who controlled the entrance to the grounds behind the building. He pulled his mobile phone from his jacket pocket and changed the channel, so his words went only to Em-Dog. "Target is crossing the grounds with the ambassador, Abdel at their heels. Do you have a clear shot on Abdel?"

"Check," Em-Dog replied.

"Take it." When nothing happened, he spoke tersely into his mike. "Take the fucking shot. Then get out."

A moment later, Abdel slumped to the ground.

Now at the guardhouse, Batdadi grabbed the guard with his left hand and pulled him out of the structure while shielding himself with the ambassador. When Batdadi could not pull the ambassador into the guardhouse, he pushed him into the guard, revealing a pistol in his hand.

Jake leaned forward against the wrought iron railing and smiled. "Son of a bitch," he whispered.

Batdadi's eyes widened when he saw Jake. He peeked his head out of the guardhouse. "This is UAE soil. Diplomatic immunity is on my side! Do you want this fight?"

For a millisecond, the word "no" crept off Jake's lips. "I've got one more fight left in me, you piece of shit." A moment later, a bullet slammed into the middle of Batdadi's forehead. He fell sideways out of the guardhouse and thudded to the ground. "Diplomatic immunity revoked."

In the distance, sirens approached. Jake took a deep breath and then walked calmly into the gathering crowd.

40

North Carolina—two days later

Entering the pub, Jake and Alex saw the TV monitors were tuned to CNN with live feeds from the UAE embassy in Washington. They found a booth and ordered drinks. Alex pushed the file folder he was carrying to Jake's side of the table and then leaned back and pinched the bridge of his nose.

Alex waited until their waiter put their drinks on the table and walked away. "I'd like the finer details in relation to how Batdadi with Jessica help pulled off the Bronxville and Wall Street bombings and the foiled—thanks to you—plot at the Ritz-Carlton in Washington, DC. Any facts she can provide may lead to the other terrorists being caught, allowing us to tie up the loose ends, as it were." He leaned forward. "She stayed under the radar for so long. Natasha Hassan, Malik, and Abdullah Omar, the man we believe to be the Brownville terrorist, are all still at large."

Jake drank half of his beer before replying. "I'm not sure where you're going with this."

"You were brought here for a specific purpose. Mission accomplished. And thank you. I have no right to ask more, and you are free to get up, shake my hand, and walk out that door. Maybe for a few more days, we still have Jessica at Womack Army Medical Center. I want to make the most of this opportunity, but I need your help."

Jake drained the rest of his beer, stood up, and headed for the door.

Alex watched him go. "That's it? You're leaving?"

"Of course, I'm leaving. You said we don't have much time, right?"

Alex sighed, sampled his beer, and studied its dark color longingly before he stood up and followed Jake out.

41

The crew from the assault craft had watched as Jake, Em-Dog, and the three SEALs emerged chest high in the water and waded to shore. Minutes later, a boat carrying three more SEALs joined the SEAL who had stayed behind onboard Batdadi's yacht. Using an inflatable stretcher, they carried Jessica to the boat and rendezvoused with the craft.

The journey to North Carolina took just over eighty minutes. Waiting on the Fort Bragg runway was a military ambulance and a medical team. They transported Jessica to the Womack Army Medical Center.

In the hours that passed, Jessica fell in and out of consciousness. Pain throbbed in her right shoulder, deep and incised. At times, doctors and nurses surrounded her bed, regulating her IVs. Inside the room, nothing was unusual. It was a hospital environment, sparse and functional. A TV monitor hung from the ceiling next to a window that gave her a view of the world below. In the corner were two leather chairs.

In her lucid moments, she stared dejectedly at the ceiling. That was how time ticked until she observed the door was no longer open, and no bright light came from the hallway. There was no handle on the door and no way out. "This is a prison cell," she said. The fabric of her distressed, steel-blue gown irritated her skin.

There was nothing to hold her mind or her attention. Outside the room could be anything, anyone. There was nothing to mark time. Would someone come in five minutes or five hours? Would she know the difference? She had been strapped to a bed before, but the panic was no less without the straps. Trapped was trapped.

She remembered that behind the door was an FBI agent. No, he looked more like a marine. He had the standard-issue white face with the ubiquitous square shoulders and square chin, close-shaved twenty-four seven. "What does it matter? He's a serious man, the epitome of authority, a gun hanging at his hip and another on his chest," she whispered.

She touched the window with the tip of her left hand and found that it was cold. The window became torture when she did not see a new beginning. The ocean had been fluid. The fortress outside the room seemed like miles of frozen water packed across the land to trap her. "I'm trapped here, but my mind is not, and it never gets too far," she murmured.

Really? You never were the sharpest tool in the box, she heard Jess respond in her head.

"I thought you were dead," Jessica whispered.

Are you retarded? Why would you wish me dead, Jessica? You can't kill me, and I can't kill you. Why? You and I are just too much fun.

I'm tired of cursing you. It's not becoming, but you're a stupid fuck. How many times do I have to cajole you, to warn you that incarceration is not an option? No more foul language for you, babe. When I'm free, my first order of business is to find a shrink to keep you at bay.

Jess was frustrated and overpowered Jessica. In the intervening time, a doctor had entered the room, followed by a nurse wheeling a trolley. The hypodermic needle on the trolley seemed to grow as Jess focused her attention on it. The doctor had her raise her right shoulder as he examined the bullet wound and the inflamed muscles. When he pressed his fingers on that spot, the pain exploded right up to the top of her head. The nurse saw her wince and supported her.

"I'm going to inject Novocain into that inflamed muscle," the doctor said. Jess watched as he laid an extra-long hypodermic needle on a stand next to her bed.

She looked at the wall, trying not to catch the doctor's attention. Her eyes swung back to the stethoscope dangling from his chest. She grabbed it and wrapped it around his neck and then reached for the needle.

"This needle wants to be thrust into your jugular vein and tear it apart. Poor vein, it never harmed anyone." Jess sat up, brandishing the needle in one hand while she held the stethoscope around the doctor's neck with the other. The nurse backed away in horror.

When Jake entered the room, Jess thought, *There's no Jessica for you today. Time to strap in and enjoy the ride.*

Jake put his hand on his P226 pistol, which was stuck in the back of his waistband. Jess was in the corner of the room, the doctor in front, her hand yanking on the stethoscope twisted around his neck and the hypodermic needle touching his jugular vein. Jake's eyes homed in on hers.

Jess looked at the doctor, her jailer. She had planned to use him as a human shield.

"Jessica, please think about what you're doing." Jake said.

Jess fought her inner voice but momentarily gave way to Jessica. "I remember New York, staring out the window. I'd stare at the blankets of snow that lay across Central Park. I thought it was beautiful because, when I looked at the sky and saw the purity of the untouched clouds, I saw it as a new beginning. When the clouds let down their purity and painted the ground in endless piles of white, it was as if God was forgiving us for all our mistakes, so we could become pure again. I asked if you believed in God. Do you remember?"

Jake lowered his weapon slightly. He saw a dark soul in her eyes and, in those passing seconds, two identities. Though they were different in some ways, both wanted the same thing. Both were conflicted as to how to get there, blind to the paths and the destruction they had caused yet trying to see. There was no pleasure in his face, only the pain of friends lost and words spoken.

"My job isn't to judge. That's for the Lord God. I'm just here to arrange the meeting." He raised his pistol and aimed it at her.

42

S<small>AN</small> A<small>NTONIO</small> C<small>HURCH</small>, P<small>ORT</small> C<small>HARLOTTE</small>, F<small>LORIDA</small>, <small>THREE WEEKS LATER</small>

In the building that would burn in six minutes, the dog, Shorty, slept. In the rectory located directly behind San Antonio Church, Reverend Leo Logan lay on top of his duvet as he tried to sleep. He had tucked his head under the left pillow, his right hand resting adjacent to the gun under the pillow to his right. His thick, graying beard cradled his cheeks and throat and shielded him from the heat of the day, but the mosquito bite on the tip of his nose itched. The hub-mounted blades of the fan suspended from the ceiling rotated slowly. They cooled him somewhat by introducing slow movement into the otherwise hot, still air.

Father Leo, as he was known, was from Cedar Rapids, Iowa. He'd slept in his share of humid rooms but had been raised in a well-appointed house that overlooked a golf course. Still, he kept his complaints to himself. His vocation was not a career but, rather, a calling—a calling to be configured to Christ and to stand amid the world as a man after the heart of Jesus Christ.

Father Leo kept his .357 Magnum pistol, one of his only lines of defense, within reach. As he rolled onto his side, he reached out and put his hand on the pistol's plastic grip, pulling the weapon closer. He fidgeted for a minute or two and then rolled onto his back. The humidity was not what kept him awake. Following a series of recent residential break-ins by addicts, during one of which an owner was assaulted, it was the gnawing fear that the rectory was next. He flipped his body around again and finally drifted to sleep as Shorty stirred in the darkness.

Shorty's barking interrupted the transmission of the man lying in the weeds several feet away from his pickup truck. Zayan waited for the dog to settle and then put his lips back to the radio attached to chest harness. "Zayan to Abdullah. I have you in sight."

"Quora. Alhamdulillah," Abdullah replied, indicating his understanding. Aryan heard the message and approached slowly with Abdullah.

The two men, along with the sniper, were of Arabic descent. All three of them had military training, but their specialist skills were why their cells had been activated and what made them ideal for this mission. Experts in firearms, hand-to-hand combat, and explosives, they were silent movers, hardcore killers. Through the night, the men had seen nothing but animals—foxes darting in and out of gardens, snakes, and even an alligator.

They passed their sniper at the edge of San Antonio Church and then darted between the structures and the landscaped memorial prayer garden directly behind the church. As they progressed, the men eyed every corner, every road, and every window with night-vision goggles. They carried AK-47 rifles and, on the belts their holsters held, .40-caliber pistols. Their green tunics and green body armor were smeared with mud and covered with grass stains.

They found the location of their target, the rectory. Cradling their rifles, the men crawled on their elbows for two minutes before going to their hands and knees for three more minutes.

Shorty barked, but that was nothing out of the ordinary for a night in the county of Port Charlotte. The two men maneuvered to the rear of the rectory. Abdullah and Aryan peered intently at the door that their red laser aiming reticles covered.

"In position," Abdullah whispered into his radio.

"Fi almawdie," Aryan said, repeating the same words in Arabic. This was not an ordinary hit. In fact, technically, it wasn't even a hit. They had been ordered to take their target alive. The men controlled their breathing and the beating of their hearts, preparing to capture the target.

Shorty had reacted first. His continual barking ignited a chorus of other dogs in the neighborhood. Shorty was a dachshund, a scent hound. He had been bred to hunt and often trailed wild boar with Father Leo.

Father Leo leapt out of bed, moving before fully aware of what had roused him. "Shorty," he whispered. *Something is wrong,* he thought, now fully alert.

He reached under his bed and retrieved a .300 Win Mag rifle and then moved toward the back bedroom, the weapon at his shoulder. At the bedroom window, he raised the rifle and peered through the spotting scope. A masked man cradling his rifle and crawling on his elbows moved toward the caretaker's lodge. Father Leo looked up from his scope. "Son of a bitch."

He turned and left the bedroom. Hustling down the stairs, he stepped onto the cold, encaustic tiles. The hall was dark and unoccupied, so he made his way to the garage.

In the garage an overhead light flickered and pulsed like erratic arcs of lightning, but that was all. He grabbed the night-vision goggles he'd bought from a store downtown that sold police-level gear and crouched in the darkness. He slipped the googles over his eyes, and dark turned to light, fuzzy details transformed into high-def images.

Father Leo was a superbly trained marksman. His natural interest in firearms since his childhood in Iowa, coupled with his friendship with Joe, his best friend and local law enforcement officer, led to an exceptional skill level with all things related to guns. But this was not a movie where he could fantasize his way to victory. *I can take one or two quickly, but I don't know what's out there.* "Think. You don't have much time," the caretaker whispered.

He counted off a few seconds in his head. Then eight rounds slammed into the approaching men at roughly the same time, shredding their bodies. The impact of the slugs knocked them off their feet.

Two down.

He crab-walked behind the church toward the caretaker's lodge. *I'm getting too old for this shit.* There, the darkness was nearly total, someone having removed the overhead lights.

Nice tactic. But with his goggles, darkness was preferable.

In the lushly landscaped memorial prayer garden located directly behind the church, in a shadow that was deeper than the surrounding darkness, he spotted the third man.

Father Leo was crouched in a narrow alcove. He had two options. He could bull-rush and reach the man before he could react, or he could approach with stealth, take the man down quietly, and move on. He opted for the latter.

Slithering on his belly like he had through Florida swamps when he hunted, he drew within a foot of the man. Father Leo looked up as the man swiveled his gaze in an arc. When he looked away from Father Leo, the priest's rifle came up, and the man went down, blood running from his head. The accompanying headache when the man awoke would be one he would never forget.

Father Leo hurried to the caretaker's lodge. The door was slightly ajar. A partially open door was like waving a red flag and screaming, "We're in here waiting for you," so he wouldn't go in. Undaunted, he hit the door so hard it flew off its hinges. A shape was directly in front of him, slumped on the sofa.

The caretaker tried to sit up, but Father Leo put a big hand on his shoulder and held him in place. "Just chill, Matt. You took a big hit. It's a miracle you're still alive."

Matt looked down at his body, his eyes wild. "Am I here? Am I all here?"

Father Leo tightened his grip on his shoulder to calm him. "You have two arms with hands attached, two legs with feet attached, and one head with brain intact, though concussed. You have a lot of superficial cuts to your scalp, arms, and legs, and you've lost a lot of blood. But you're here, and you put up a helluva fight."

Father Leo saw tears cluster in Matt's eyes as he sank back on his pillow. "Thank you, God."

"You'll be just fine, Matt. That said, you were lucky as hell."

He had just picked up Matt's phone and dialed the number for emergency assistance when they heard an enormous explosion. He turned to see a fist of orange flame punch its way out of the church. Windows shattered, and smoke and fire rushed out as a deadly rainfall of glass and steel showered down. Alarms shrilled and erupted. A moment later, a siren started to wail.

"Shorty."

43

Naples, Florida

Jake's phone buzzed. He glanced at the screen and slid his thumb over the green icon to accept.

"Hello. Jake?"

"Hey, Nick," said Jake, his tone dulled but referring to his bother Patrick by his pet name. He put his hand to head. It was starting to ache.

"Where are you?"

"Just got back. Just put my feet up. What's going on?" Jake said irritably.

"How was your road trip? Get things figured out?"

"So-so."

"Which means you didn't and you're just blowing me off. All right, I'm not offended."

Usually, Jake looked forward to talking to his brother. Their calls and visits were infrequent. Today was different. He just wanted to lie on his sofa with his beer and think of exactly nothing. "What's going on?" he said again, more forcefully.

"Fine. I hear you loud and clear. Get the heck off the phone, you don't want to talk. I wouldn't be disturbing you except for the call I got."

Jake sat up on his sofa and put his beer down. "What call? Mom?"

The brothers' mother was now in a Florida residential care home suffering from short bouts of dementia and episodes of depression. The dementia was probably because of age. The depression was because she no longer had a social life, no longer traveled, no longer drove her red Mustang the brothers had bought years ago for her birthday. And thus, she felt she had no more reason left to live.

"Mom's nurse from Bloomingdale Park called. They couldn't reach you, so they tried me. I can't exactly get up and visit Mom. There's a lot going on at work."

"What did they call about? Is she failing mentally again? Did she fall again and crack her head?"

"No on both counts. I don't think it has to do with her health. They weren't entirely clear about what the issue was, probably because Mom wasn't entirely clear with them. I believe it involved new faces at Bloomingdale Park. I can't swear to that. But that's what it seemed to be about."

"New faces? Bloomingdale Park has turnover in residents and employees like any business, and you said her nurse called."

"Bud, I can't answer that. I thought with you being pretty much right there, you could go over and find out what's going on. They said she was really upset."

"But they didn't know why she's agitated by these people. How can that be?"

"You know how that can be," replied Patrick. "I don't care how old or out of it Mom is. If she doesn't want to cooperate, she ain't cooperating. She can be mean."

"Fine, Nick, I'll head over later today."

"Jake, all bullshit aside, you OK?"

"All bullshit aside, no, Nick. I'm not OK."

"What are you going to do about it?"

"I'm working with JSOC."

"Meaning what exactly?"

"Meaning I'm going to press on."

"You can always talk to somebody. JSOC has lots of specialists who … You went through a lot of shit on the Batdadi mission. It would mess with anybody's head. Like PTSD."

"I don't need to talk to anybody."

"Are you sure about that?"

"I'll call you back. Leo is calling." Jake ended the call.

"Lloyd." Jake used the caller's pet name as he accepted the call from his other brother, Reverend Leo Logan.

"Smoked two mutts and gave another a migraine last night."

"Come again?"

"Where are you at? It's breaking news. Turn on your flat screen."

Jake gaped at the at San Antonio Church burning on his flat screen.

Father Leo broke the pregnant pause. "Jake, you still there?"

"Leo, I'll call you back."

The line went dead. Jake grabbed his SIG Sauer P226 pistol and car keys from the table and headed out to his Ford F-150 pickup.

44

NEW YORK

As with every day in the weeks that had passed, Jessica awoke in pain. Her head hurt, a dull ache deep in her brain as well as pains on the side of her abdomen. She was grateful that the nausea had stopped. She no longer wore the cold iron cuffs that had been fastened on each wrist. Yet today, she raised her hand to see if the short chain secured to the bed rail rattled, and she had been restrained. She had limited range of movement, not because she was shackled; pain throbbed in her right shoulder. She closed her eyes and let her thoughts drift back to a recurring dream.

She was pressed against the floor of a hospital room, men shouting. *That's Jake's voice I can hear*, she realized. Something was different. Jessica was alarmed when she realized it was not a dream. What did I do? Scant memories were returning. She touched her right shoulder. It had healed. But periodically, like today, it was stiff and ached.

Batdadi's yacht—Jake shot me. And in the hospital, that was him talking to me—no pleading with me.

"OMG! What have I done?" she muttered.

Jessica snapped back to the present when a loud beep rang out in her room. After a few seconds she heard another beep.

"Good morning, Jessica." The amplified voice of a woman came from a speaker. Her eyes darted around the room and locked on a ceiling speaker.

In the Civic Center neighborhood of Lower Manhattan, New York, located on Park Row behind the Thurgood Marshall United States Courthouse at Foley Square was the first high-rise facility to be used by the Bureau of Prisons towers. Its official name was the Metropolitan Correctional Center, New York (MCC New York). MCC New York held prisoners of all security levels. Most prisoners held at MCC New York had pending cases in the United States District Court for the Southern District of New York.

Numerous high-profile individuals had been held at MCC New York during court proceedings. Among those housed at the facility at one time or another were Gambino crime family bosses John Gotti and Jackie D'Amico, drug dealer Frank Lucas, Ponzi scheme fraudster Bernard Madoff, terrorists Omar Abdel Rahman and Ramzi Yousef, financier and sex offender Jeffrey Epstein, weapons trafficker Viktor Bout, and Mexican drug lord Joaquin "El Chapo" Guzman.

Jessica was in the 10 South wing, locked inside a single-woman cell. This was her life twenty-three hours a day, and she was continuously monitored by CCTV cameras, the lights always on. She was isolated, and the only time she would be taken outside her cell would be for exercise in an indoor cage. No outdoor recreation was permitted. Prisoner 111968, as she was also known, was subject to special administrative measures, which severely restricted her communication with other prisoners and with the outside world.

Her cell, her entire world, was seventy-six square feet, seven feet by nine feet. The bed, desk and chair were firmly attached to the floor. And other than a shower, sink, and toilet, there was no other furnishing in the cell. The four-by-six-inch window with bars on the back wall of the cell emitted natural light. But without a stool, she had no a view to the outside.

Jessica's eyes moved from the speaker where the voice emanated from and focused on the automatic solid metal door—no handle, no lock, no hinges, just a window with a hatch. The door clicked open. Two men in black uniform and black body armor, heavy batons hanging on their chests at ready, entered the room.

"Jess." She slightly raised her voice. "Jess, I know you can hear me. Jess!" She screamed.

The voice that she often heard in head but that had not spoken to her in weeks did not answer.

Tears escaped from her eyes. "Jess, how did we end up here?" she whispered.

45

Dr. Zeake Lynne, a New York psychologist, had joined Dr. Anne Brody, MCC New York's psychiatrist in her office. Dr. Lynne, an Asian American, had a PhD in clinical psychology and had been practicing psychotherapy for over twenty years. She specialized in dissociative identity disorder (DID).

"Dr. Brody," he said.

"Please call me Anne."

"I'll start with what we know. Dr. Bethany Jones, Jessica's therapist treated Jessica Brooks for depression for over a decade."

"Symptoms?" said Anne.

"Mood swings, suicidal tendencies, and alcohol abuse. Over time, her conditions evolved."

"Do we have a time scale?"

Zeake found Anne's interruptions annoying but continued. "Year five. Jessica's sense of identity and reality, as well as her thoughts, sensations, perceptions, and memories had become disconnected from each other. Dr. Jones's preliminary diagnosis was DID."

"Based on what? What led her to that conclusion?"

Zeake masked his frustration. "Jessica's history of mental illness is, at best, patchy at this stage of the timeline. Dr. Jones decided that, before referring her to a specialist, she would discuss her observation with a colleague, Steve Lopez Dunhill, MD.

Anne shook her head. "And now he's dead, What was she thinking? The man had zero expertise with DID."

"We can all do better with twenty-twenty hindsight." Zeake was losing his patience with her interruptions. "Dr. Jones had witnessed the two distinct identities, and Jessica's struggle to control her behavior had increased. She was unable to recall important personal information and had memory lapses that were too extensive to be explained by ordinary forgetfulness. She admitted to Jones that she had shifts of identity as separate personalities and that she referred to the other personality as Jess. Jones's notes recorded that, during that session, Jess assumed control of Jessica's behavior and thoughts at different times."

Anne was nodding her head and looked pensive. "Yes, several employees at MCC New York have heard her calling out to this Jess. Did Jessica remember the episode?"

Here we go. She's preparing the prosecution's case. "Yes. She had complete awareness of what happened when the other identity had control. Jessica's awareness is a problem in itself. She appeared to be apprehensive of the other identity."

"Causes of dissociative identity disorder are complex," said Anne.

Really! Zeake restrained himself. "Yes, studies show that a history of trauma, usually abuse in childhood, is almost always the case for people who have severe dissociative symptoms, and that's where it gets interesting. Jones was not aware of any childhood abuse. However, the clinical notes seized from the psychiatrist, Dr. Amira Bajwa, revealed that Jessica had a sibling, Gemma. She died at aged seven. The notes indicated that the siblings were squabbling. Gemma pushed Jessica, and Jessica pushed her back, causing her fall into the adjacent lake."

"Nice … a sister."

"Please, Anne … Comments like that don't help. The incident was recorded as an accidental death. The point is Jessica blamed herself. And added to that, their father was sexually abusing the siblings—first Gemma and then Jessica." He let that settle on her. "We have a few minutes before we meet Ms. Brooks." He looked at that section of his notes that was headed DID specifics and said, "Jessica's and Jess' 'alters' are different identities. Alters in these cases can have their own age, sex, or race. Each also has his or her own posture, gestures, and distinct way of talking. You should also be aware that, as each personality reveals itself, it controls the individual's behavior and thoughts by 'switching,' and the switching can take anywhere from seconds to days."

The deputy warden, Norman Gilbert, a short man with a close-cropped head escorted Dr. Lynne and Dr. Brody to the area in 10 South that had been modified to create a room that enclosed the facade of Jessica's cell.

"Dr. Brody, your conversation with Prisoner 111968 will be private, but CCTV cameras will monitor you, Dr. Lynne, and Prisoner 111968."

"Thank you, Norm," said Dr. Brody as the deputy warden turned and left the room.

Dr. Brody and then Dr. Lynne seated themselves at the table that gave them a full view into the cell. On the table was a telephone. Jessica was seated at the window with a telephone in her hand. She appeared disheveled. Her face was expressionless. She sat motionless and did not speak to her guests.

"Good afternoon, Jessica. I'm Dr. Anne Brody, and this is Dr. Zeake Lynne." She explained that she was a psychiatrist and that Dr. Lynne was a psychologist.

"Hello, Jessica. If it's OK, we would like to talk to you," said Dr. Lynne.

Jessica remained silent and stared at them. She fidgeted with her hands. Dr. Brody was about to open her mouth to speak when Jessica said, "Please don't be offended, but I don't know you very well yet. Later, sure. But Jess, I don't know if Jess wants to work with you, and I want her to forgive me and be my friend."

Dr. Brody's face beamed. She had heard about DID but had never experienced it. She scribbled on her notepad, "Research DID, FDA-approved and/or experimental drugs."

The switch of identities was instant. Dr. Brody did not appear to detect it initially.

"Is there some aspect of this that pleases you?" Jess asked.

Dr. Brody's eyes met with Dr. Lynne's eyes. Her face displayed a startled expression.

"You, yes, Dr. Brody, I'm talking to you. Your grin looks almost sickly.

Caught off guard Dr. Brody said, "Me?"

"Yes, you. At first you were excited. Did career recognition explode in your pea brain? Oh, I get it. You're thinking I might drive you crazy. Why? Reality has set in, hmm. Jessica and me switching was not part of the plan. Plans! No plan means you'll go crazy. Hmm … well, I won't lie to you. That's what it means for some people, but only if they aren't with me. I can work without a plan."

Dr. Brody's eyes searched the table for a panic button.

"Anyway, once you have some kind of nervous breakdown, your brain is weakened. And you don't want that. Trust me. Plus, you could go off on almost any tangent. It can ruin your life for years, and sometimes you don't really recover. Your career, what would happen to your career? I don't recommend it, not for anyone, least of all you."

Jess tried to pull her chair closer to the window. It was locked down. "You're so nice! I think you're adorable! "Those big blue eyes and blond locks." Jess leaned back in her chair and crossed her legs. We need some ground rules. You need your 'plans.' Asyd Batdadi had 'plans.' Look where that got him. I heard Jake shot his fucking brains out." Jess laughed hysterically. "Don't fuck with me."

"Jessica—or is it Jess?" said Dr. Lynne.

Jess snapped her response. "You think I'm angry with you? Oh no, not at all. I didn't like that rapid changing thing with Jessica at first, not cool. Glad to see you're looking composed again, Dr. Brody. Or should I call you Anne?" Jess stood and walked back to her bed.

46

Fifty-two-year-old Elle Cohen approached the entrance to MCC New York. The guards recognized her by sight. But still they looked over her documents and identification carefully before letting her pass. She was aware how difficult it was for an attorney to see a client at MCC New York and that it was nigh on impossible to see a client housed in 10 South. She carried a purse with nothing of value in it, and she did not bring her laptop or cell phone. After she passed through x-Ray machines and full-body scanners, she went south and through more remote gates. She observed the guard tower, German shepherd dogs, and endless security cameras.

Elle Cohen was met at the security door to 10 South by a female guard, and together they walked through a series of secure doors and hallways. There was no conversation between the two. She was cognizant of the rumors that most of the guards at MCC New York did not think much of attorneys who defended criminals and often set them free. Cohen did not care; she was on the extreme of the left. Her progressive democratic view was that prison guards were like the police, who were like federal agents; they metered out justice with lies and guns. They were all evil and beneath her.

After graduating and passing the New York Bar, Cohen had pursued a career as a civil rights attorney. She' worked for the American Civil Liberties Union, the ACLU, for twenty years and had then gone into private practice and worked several high-profile cases. When Khalil Hassan had retained her to represent Jessica Brooks, she had been thrilled to take the case. The government had shown no sympathy for the fact Jessica was afflicted with a mental illness. But more importantly, she believed a witch hunt by the American government was brewing, Christians against Muslims, following the Bronxville and Wall Street bombings. Khalil Hassan and Cohen had had a close relationship in college. It had not led to anything more than emotional closeness, and their recent discussion regarding Jessica had clarified that was all it would ever be. Still, she relished and look forward to meeting her new client. Cohen was divorced. She had two adult children. So now, her work was her life.

Cohen and the guard entered the warden's office, where the warden, a tall black man shook her hand. He said, "We planned to have you meet with Jessica Brooks via Zoom visiting like our other 10 South inmates. You have connections, Ms. Cohen. The AG said you refused that arrangement."

"Yes, you've got that right. Jessica has been accused of heinous crimes. Let's not forget she's diagnosed with a mental condition. I need to build rapport with her to do my job."

"Yes, I understand. She had a visit with MCC New York's psychiatrist, and we have scheduled psychological services."

"So, you'll understand I can't communicate with her by a computer monitor."

"You'll communicate at the prisoner's cell via a direct phone line. It's not monitored."

"OK." Cohen rolled her eyes.

"We have a desk for you outside the cell. There is a partition of bulletproof glass, and it will remain closed."

Together she and the female guard left the warden's office and walked to Jessica's cell.

Cohen passed through several more security doors and eventually arrived in the area that housed Jessica's cell. She entered the makeshift room that surrounded the front of the cell. She was handed a legal pad and a single soft-tip pen.

As the guard left the room, she reminded Cohen that her conversation would be private but that CCTV cameras were monitoring both her and the prisoner. Cohen nodded. *I bet you vote Republican—extreme right of the party. Lock them up—the mentally ill, minorities, undocumented immigrants—and throw away the keys.* She hated these people—the Justice Department and its so-called network of law enforcement. Cohen was professional and said, "Thank you."

She turned away from the guard and looked around the room. She saw the window that gave her a view into the cell, and in front was a desk that had been put there for her benefit. On the table was a telephone. Cohen pivoted quickly. "Madam guard, there should be a pass-through slot in the plexiglass. I may need to pass my client—"

"Pass her what?!" the guard shot back.

"Documents to sign."

The guard said, "No. Sorry. You'll have to take that up with the warden." The guard walked out, closing the door.

Cohen sat at the desk and glared into the cell. Jessica was sitting on her bed. She appeared timid, and her hair was unkempt. Cohen was startled by her complexion; she bloomed—not what she had expected. Though she did not doubt the mountain of evidence against her, she found it hard to believe that this woman was responsible for the deaths of Alice Francis and Dr. Steve Dunhill and was a coconspirator in the Wall Street bombings.

Jessica stood and moved over to the chair that had been placed next to the phone on the floor. She bent down, picked up the phone and seated herself on the chair. Her face was expressionless. She did not speak.

"Good afternoon, Ms. Brooks. My name is Elle Cohen, Elle if you prefer. Can I call you Jessica?"

Jessica remained silent.

"I'm an attorney with Cohen and Goldman. US Attorney William Becker has decided that your case will be handled in the US States District Court for the Southern District of New York. The AG's office will be preparing the prosecution against you, and my law firm has been retained to provide you with a defense. Are you OK with that? Do you have any questions?"

Jessica remained silent and stared at her.

"Khalil Hassan is anxious to help you. He's concerned about your health." Elle noticed a change in Jessica's otherwise expressionless face when she mentioned Khalil. "Are the guards treating you well?"

"Yes." Her lips quivered when she replied.

"We expect the lead-up to your trial to be a lengthy process—possibly up to two years. We need to assess the conditions of your confinement, so you're afforded proper care and treatment."

Jessica dropped the phone and screamed, "Jess! I don't have two years." Tears formed in her eyes.

Jessica, where are your goddam manners! Pick the phone up. I've got this.

Relieved that she had heard Jess's voice, and she was not alone, Jessica did not fight the voice in her head. She gave way.

"I understand how you must feel."

"Cut the crap. I know your playbook. You're here on behalf of Khalil Hassan and need my help to impress him."

Elle appeared shocked by the sudden change in Jessica's demeanor.

"My ... my what? I'm sorry. You misunderstand me."

"Don't think I do. I'll listen to what you have to say." She stared at the heavy-built woman with short blond hair. She looked to Jess like a man. *I'll bet she bats for the other side. Don't really care so long as she breaks us out of here.* She smiled at Elle slowly.

"You can speak freely and with confidence that our conversations will go no further than this room."

Jess thought Elle naive but replied, "Are you saying there is no one listening to what we say?" She smiled. "What would you like to talk about?" *Fool.* She did not let the word slip from her mouth.

"To start, the conditions of your confinement. Tell me about your treatment here."

"There's no reason for you to be interested in my treatment here. Jessica is not staying here. I want to know what you will do about her trial."

Elle had a facial expression that indicated she was thrown off guard by Jessica's reference to herself. If she thought it was odd she did not respond. It did not slip Jess's attention, but she thought as she continued to observe her it was obvious that all the woman was interested in was building rapport with Jessica.

Jess looked at her face. It was sincere. She would play along for now. "I would like soap, shampoo, and a hairbrush."

"I will speak to the warden. That's a reasonable request. I'll be back in a couple of days."

Jess watched as she grabbed her legal pad and said, "You'll talk to Khalil. Jessica can't stay here."

47

Naples, Florida

Police Chief James Howard pulled out his cell phone. The stout, balding police chief texted his wife. They were supposed to meet for lunch. That was impossible now. He told her not to expect him for dinner either. "It's going to be a late night. Love you," he added to the message before hitting the send icon. He turned and again looked over at the crime scene. Howard had seen plenty of dead bodies over his career. But this one was up there with the most grotesque.

Bloomindale Residential Home was in Naples, a city in Collier County, Florida. The city was mostly known for its high-priced homes, white-sand beaches, and numerous golf courses. Naples was the self-titled "Golf Capital of the World" because it had the second most holes per capita out of all communities and the most holes in any city in Florida. The city was also known for appealing to retirees, and a large percentage of the population was made up of them. *A brutally murdered retiree and her nurse in a residential home is not good*, he thought.

Returning the phone to his duty belt, he focused on the bodies—one female, one male. The man had been shot in the head; the woman had taken shots to her knees and a knife to her jugular. Judging from a quick scan of the walls and windows, no bullets had missed their target; that told him the shooter was skilled.

The ID badge on the man's uniform confirmed he was an employee of the residential home. The woman had credentials in her purse identifying as her as a resident of Bloomingdale residential home. Seeing her name on her driving license, Howard had recognized her. Her son had made headlines when the president had awarded him the Congressional Medal of Honor in the Rose Garden at the White House for saving countless lives prior to the White House Correspondents' Dinner, a medal was reserved for those who have made an especially meritorious contribution to the security or national interest of the United States' world peace endeavors. *What the hell?! Who killed them? Is this connected to the incident at the Ritz-Carlton in Washington, DC?*

Judging from the postmortem lividity of the bodies, they had been dead for at least six hours, maybe more. It ran through Howard's thoughts that the killer's trail would already be going cold. Howard realized the importance of doing everything by the book. He needed to secure Bloomindale and its surrounding grounds. As an extra measure, he would request marine patrol units to cover the shoreline.

Howard recognized that this could be a high-profile case. Speaking on his radio, the chief told the dispatcher to send the entire shift and call in off-duty officers. He ended that communication and called the state attorney general. He expected that, once the call had finished, the AG's office would mobilize a crime unit from the state police to come up and lead the investigation.

Though it was only midmorning, he began to feel the telltale signs of his low blood sugar level. Healthy as a horse since a child, he had made his doctor explain multi times how diabetes could have chosen him when no one in his family had ever had it. He had come to understand that there was no specific reason but that it was quite manageable, provided he took the right precautions. He decided the first rule was not to let his wife, fourteen years his junior, know about his condition. From a pocket in his uniform, he withdrew a chocolate bar and broke it into little squares, calculating how many he might need to keep his blood sugar up for the rest of the day. He laid the silver foil on the table and put a piece of the creamy milk chocolate into his mouth. He sucked on it slowly, savoring, but paused when he saw an elderly woman exit through the dining room doors and cross the pathway adjacent the perfectly manicured lawn.

"This is a goddamn crime scene. Who's that woman?" He pointed at the woman who was hobbling down the path.

The policeman who had been manning the dining room and heard the police chief shout turned to the policeman standing not far from Howard and said, "Its May. She a resident at the home."

Howard gathered up his chocolate pieces and followed her down the path.

May was slim built, small, and afflicted with curvature of the spine. Her long white hair was swept up and fastened away from her face and neck. She navigated with the aid of a walker; her frail hands clutched the top bar of the walker. May, at ninety years old, had her fair share of wrinkles and sun damage around her face. Over her shoulder was a Chanel purse. It was small and noticeable against her frail body. Her walk was steady and purposeful. She looked neither right nor left; nor did she glance back over her shoulder. She appeared to be a woman on a mission, and the slowly gathering crowds on the pavement moved out of her way. Some smiled at what they thought was a runaway Bloomingdale resident but did not intervene. Her destination appeared to be the Ford F-150 pickup just up ahead.

She ran her walker right up to it, using a free hand to balance herself against the arch above the front wheel just as a man stepped out the vehicle. He was strikingly handsome. Howard immediately recognized him as Jake Logan.

Howard stayed at a distance but close enough to hear the conversation that ensued.

"I liked your mom. She was a good woman."

"Excuse me, ma'am." Jake appeared to be taken aback. "Ma'am, what are you talking about?"

"Oh! You don't know about the man. I saw him—"

"What man?"

"I saw him. They thought your mom was a dotty old woman. She told me and I saw him at the reception—Russian. He asked for her, your mom, by her name." May did not stop for breath. "Oh, he killed your mom last night. The police are not saying …."

"Not saying what, ma'am."

"I know. He murdered her … They are moving me out to a hotel for now. Theresa was a good woman. She did not deserve that." She pointed. "Look. Police everywhere. Jake, your mom loved you. She talked about you all the time. Just a week ago—no, maybe it was two weeks ago—she showed me the photograph she had taken of you in front of this pickup."

Howard noticed the stunned look on Jake's face. And when the woman walked away, Jake climbed back into his pickup and pulled out his phone.

When Jake emerged from his truck, he was visibly ashen. Howard had walked over to the truck and was waiting for him. Howard stuck out his hand and said, "I'm Police Chief James Howard, the lead on this investigation. Please, sir, can you come with me?"

Jake stared vacantly at him, darkness searing within him. He was indignant that Howard had not mentioned the death of his mother. He took a deep breath. *Maybe he doesn't know who I am. Or he's seriously lacking in bedside manners.* He did as Howard requested and followed him back along the path Howard had taken to reach the truck.

"Sir, I thank for your service. And I'm sorry about your mother. You should prepare yourself."

Jake's conversation with Bloomindale Residential Home had now sunk in, and he also remembered his recent award of the Congressional Medal of Honor. This was the reason Howard had focused on him and why he was highlighting his service.

Looking into his mother's room he was astonished to see that her body had not been moved. Added to that, law enforcement officers were milling around viewing the host of gruesome photos taken by Bloomindale's employees that were already making the rounds of the internet. "What the fuck? You're desecrating my mother. Either you lock this shit down, or I will," Jake said.

One of Howard's officers was blocking the entrance to his mother's room. As Jake turned to Howard to ask him to call off his pit bull, a woman stepped up to the officer and flashed her FBI credentials and told him to let Jake pass. Jake thanked her as Howard moved over to the officer to exert his belated authority.

Inside the room, there were the crime-scene technicians, uniformed police officers, detectives, and FBI agents. A pair of technicians, who had apparently photographed the scene, were packing up and preparing to leave. Jake sensed the tension between the factions in the room.

Jake stared at his mother, fighting back the tears.

Howard stepped in front of him and said, "Boys, why don't you take a break and get a cup of coffee? We'll only be a few minutes."

All eyes were on Jake.

They nodded and, one by one, left the room.

Jake was relieved to be able to have a few minutes in peace. He stood still for a moment and then went back over the room and reexamined everything. *Mom, I don't know who did this. Rest in peace. Revenge I will have.* He turned around to see Howard and a woman.

"Jake. May I call you Jake? I'm FBI Agent Megan Coleman, and you've already met Police Chief James Howard.

Jake was trying to appear as if he was not staring at Coleman when, in fact, he was staring. She was an exotic-looking woman and beautiful. Jake guessed Afro Caribbean with something else. Not that it mattered. She appeared to be in her twenties, early thirties; stood five foot four and had a body that was genetically toned. She had brown eyes with tints of green and long brown hair that was streaked blond by the sun.

"The deceased—"

"Yes, your mother. I'm very sorry for your loss."

"Who found my mother?"

"An employee of Bloomindale. She was looking for your mother's carer."

"What will happen to the body now?

"The ME is waiting to take her."

Jake looked out the window to the street. "Any CCTV footage, traffic cams?"

"Yes, we have a few cameras, and we've already requested footage. But as you know, given that this appears to be a professional kill, we are not holding out much hope."

Jake was emotional and not thinking when he said, "Why?"

"You know, with that level of cunning, plus getting around the security system and the lack of signs of a forced entry into the building, the chances are slim."

"Did you find anything else unusual?'

"No. Howard can you give us a minute?"

Howard's expression displayed that he did not like being asked to leave. He paused as if he had something to add. "No problem. I need to talk to my troops."

"Thanks. I will join you in the dining room."

Once he was out of earshot, Coleman said, "I'm here because there was an incident at MCC New Yok last night ... Well, I'm here to see if there is a connection."

Jake reached into his pocket and viewed several missed call notifications from Alex.

48

New York, eighteen hours earlier

T he day had given way to night and the lights from New York's Broadway, a contemporary rainbow, all excited and chaotic, were, in effect, the only activity. The peace of night hours dissipated with a violent storm howling in from the north. Electric and cocooned within a strong black atmosphere, the clouds brought the blacktop streets a shining sheet of rain. New Yorkers were hunkering down in anticipation. Wind waved the tree branches in a raucous confrontation, with wind speeds that exceeded sixty miles per hour. Lightning sliced across the sky, and rain gushed down.

The powerlines went first, fractured, and splintered like broken bone by the falling trees. Next, the phone lines went down. Shortly thereafter, an onslaught of trees fell as if an army of loggers had occupied the city and felled trees, blocking roads.

Inside MCC New York, the guards made their rounds or chattered in the break room awaiting the end of their shifts. Only the men headed out discussed the storm outside. Even when the power failed, the guards who remained did not panic, since they were safe inside a fortress of brick and steel, and the backup generators automatically powered up. The emergency generators kicked in so quickly it caused only seconds of momentary loss on surveillance cameras and computer monitors. Still, the guards made their way down the halls, making sure all was well—confident and in a state of being that suggested they knew they were free from danger or threat.

An anxious awareness of danger crept in with the total silence of the backup generator. The engine, a symphony of perfectly choreographed switches and pistons, died. All the lights, cameras, and consoles extinguished.

The patrolling guard's flashlights powered up, and communication radios crackled. Simultaneously with the activity of the guards, there was a loud *clang* of metal, followed by clicks as the automatic black iron gates on their sleek hinges unlocked. Contrary to the system design, the doors had not automatically locked when the power failed. A system setup intended to keep New York's most dangerous criminals caged and giving no consideration to the welfare of the inmates if the incident was a fire had failed on a catastrophic level. All over the correctional center, prisoners emerged into the hallways.

Although the MCC correctional officers received training in the use of firearms because of the potential threat of prisoners overpowering an officer, there was a prohibition on guards carrying a gun on duty. Coupled with training and batons, the guards were left with their wits to maintain order. The guards were the last line of defense, and MCC's goal and training dictated that the prisoners were secured; anything else was unthinkable.

Armed with heavy batons and using limited radio communications, the guards grouped and herded the prisoners into open central areas and forced them to lie facedown. "Clear ...clear." The word was transmitted repeatedly down the line over the next seven minutes—until shots rang out.

"We've got a shooter," shouted a guard. "Source unknown. I repeat, shooter. Location—"

The communication went dead.

The guards scrambled as they attempted to ascertain the status of their fellow guard and from where and whom the shots had emanated. The guards did not state the obvious. None of the guards had guns and that the prime suspect was a prisoner. An explosion combined with tear gas flooded one of the central areas as the chaos ramped up. The guards fought a battle to restore order.

The storm had passed, debris strewn daring New York to rebuild. The cleanup was a task beyond comprehension. Surviving the violent storm had been step one. Step two played out. Five Lenco BearCat Anti-Riot vehicles swept through the boundary gate of MCC New York. Police in body armor and carrying ballistic shields disembarked the vehicles. They moved into the prison, equipped with submachine guns, assault rifles, riot shotguns, sniper rifles, riot control agents, smoke, and stun grenades. The initial team wielded entry tools, and all the SWAT teams wore thermal, night-vision devices, and motion detectors for covertly determining the positions of hostages and hostage takers inside the structure.

The guards and prisoners had lodged where they were. Any movement would bring swift retribution by the SWAT teams inside the facility. Minutes later, those inmates who had been standing reverted to their face-down position, hands behind their backs. Engineers were not far behind the SWAT teams. And thirty minutes later, the facility powered up, and the lights came back on. The crisis had been averted, and a head count loomed.

Prisoners shuffled back into their cells. Conversation was scant but centered around their missed opportunity. All missing guards were accounted for, and those who needed medical treatment were directed to waiting ambulances that had been routed to New York-Presbyterian Lower Manhattan Hospital.

After the list of prisoners was accounted for and compared to the MCC records. There was one fatality reported. A female inmate had been discovered dead in her cell, the cause of death unknown. The superintendent, Errol Brown ordered that her body be transported to the prison morgue pending an immediate postmortem. The guard who had discovered the body confirmed that the deceased inmate was Jessica Brooks.

In another life, Errol Brown, African American, midfifties, and attractive, had been a baseball star in high school. While most young men spent their high school and college years in high school and college, Errol Brown had instead spent those years dominating American League hitters. By the time Brown was twenty-three years old, he was already a grizzled MLB veteran of six years. Back troubles, however, had started to derail Brown's career. And over time, he was never close to regaining his power-hitting form of old.

Although he would always carry the swagger of a successful athlete, he had conformed and had gone on to graduate law school. Now, as the superintendent of MCC New York, a wall was building between him and what had been a successful career. Given Jessica Brooks's notoriety, alarm bells were ringing. Jeffrey Epstein, an American financier and convicted sex offender, had died in his cell. The medical examiner had ruled the death a suicide. Epstein's lawyers had disputed the ruling, and there had been significant public skepticism about the true cause of his death. *This doesn't look good*, he thought.

Turning to his deputy he said, "Keep me in the loop. We operate on a need-to-know basis." Turning back to face the window, he muttered under his breath, "Goddamn it! It's a matter of time before Brooks's death goes viral."

One news outlet had picked up the incident at MCC New York and was reporting, supported by a liberal left expert, that the number of SWAT teams had been "over-the-top." A single voice of reason had joined the debate and vehemently stated that, in all the circumstances, the options were zero.

49

Dr. Asher Hoffman, the MCC New York medical examiner, swiped his ID and popped open the metal double doors. A tall but slight man, he headed to the gurney that was draped with a light blue sheet, covering the corpse underneath, and pushed it to his work area. Dr. Hoffman had arrived at MCC New York just before 6:00 a.m. He was unshaven and dressed in blue baggy medical scrubs. A clattering echoed from the tiled floor, breaking the silence in the morgue's surgical room when he bumped the gurney into the gut bucket. He reached down, picked it up, and placed the silver bucket on the floor adjacent to the gurney. The bucket would hold all the internal organs after the autopsy.

For the last six years, Hoff, as he was known by his friends and colleagues, had worked in the surgical room, which served as a mortuary for MCC New York. On the head of the gurney, he read the name printed on the laminated bar code, Prisoner 111968, Jessica Brooks. His face expressed repulsion. She had been the American citizen turned terrorist and responsible for the death of Alice Francis and Dr. Steve Dunhill and, in part, multiple deaths on Wall Street. *Will this autopsy show she got her just dessert?*

He parked his thoughts. He was not employed to judge. On his right, on a medical cart were his tools in size order, from the largest forceps to the smallest scalpel. He rolled the sheet down to the prisoner's neck and slid eye caps in place, shutting her eyes. *Prisoner 111968, Jessica Brooks—no matter your crime, you had a name.*

The blue sheet was resting below Jessica's chest cavity. "Holy cow!" He glared at the skin covering her right collarbone. *Perfect!* He had expected keloid scarring in and around the clavicle area. He looked again. Her skin texture was smooth, not even the hint of a scar. "How could that—be?" he whispered. *That Navy SEAL shot her shortly before she was arrested*, he recalled. *I'm pretty sure I didn't imagine that.* He reached for her medical records; the records confirmed that Jessica had had surgery on her right shoulder girdle. *It makes no sense. The best of the best surgeons always leaves a fine-line scar.* Hoff lifted the sheet covering her feet and bent over the foot with the laminated bar code, rechecking to see it matched the bar code on the gurney.

Bewildered, his eyes focused on Jessica as if she could give him an explanation. "Fingerprints," he said.

Prisoners in MCC New York don't get incarcerated until their identity has been tripled-checked by DNA, which would include fingerprints. He pulled the sheet over her body, pulled off his latex gloves, and hurried out of the surgical room to his office across the hall.

From the drawer of the desk, Hoff pulled out a CMOS fingerprint scanner. He turned off the light and closed the office door. Out in the hall, he picked up his pace and headed back to Jessica's body. He removed the CMOS from his pocket and turned it on. Lining up the lasers with Jessica's fingers one at a time, Hoff scanned a full set of prints. He powered the device off and slipped it into his pocket and turned back to the body.

Hoff had not completed his visual exam of the entire body; he pulled the sheet back completely. For the second time that day, he tensed and was visibly shocked. Jessica's medical records indicated she was twenty weeks pregnant at the date of her death. Typically, a baby bump was visible in the second trimester. Hoff was aware this was not an absolute, but this woman's abdomen was flat as a pancake, and his exam of the uterus revealed that, far from being enlarged, it was normal in size.

After he had removed the neck and chest organs, he dissected the abdominal organs. Hoff also discovered traces of solid crystalline in the mouth of Jessica, Jane Doe as he now referred to her. He suspected it was cyanide salts, but that could only be confirmed by toxicologic analysis.

He had concluded that Jane Doe's death was caused by cardiac arrest. He had many unanswered questions. That said, there was nothing more he could do here. He collected his notes, exited the surgical room, and went to his office.

Hoff scanned through his phone contacts and selected Megan Coleman, her number area code 347. New York appeared on the screen. He paused a few seconds to consider whether he was doing the right thing and then let his thumb touch the screen.

"Hoff," said a softly spoken woman. "How are you? What's up?"

"Nothing," he said defensively.

"Come on, you don't call unless you want something. I'm not doing that pretend girlfriend act again. Is your mom still hassling you about grandchildren?"

"It's nothing like that. This is something for work."

"Hoff, I'm on the FBI team investigating the incident at MCC New York. Running to a meeting in five minutes. Tell me what's going on."

"I need you to run fingerprints."

"Did Brown OK it?"

"No. He asked me to do an autopsy on Jessica Brooks." He paused, debating whether to share. *I've known Meg since middle school. She is my oldest and most trusted friend.* "He told me to report my findings only to him."

"Jessica Brooks! Jesus! Hoff, you just put me in an impossible position."

"Work email or home? The prints."

"I told you. I'm investigating the MCC New York incident."

"Home it is." He moved his thumb over send and touched the screen.

"I will call you back." Megan ended the call.

An hour later when Meg called back, Hoff was writing up his preliminary autopsy report. The report would be made final after all lab tests were complete.

"What's the story with Brown and Jessica Brooks? Why is he withholding evidence from the FBI?" Megan dispensed with pleasantries.

"I don't know. He didn't share."

"And you, Hoff, why the personal interest?"

"I did an autopsy on a body identified as Jessica Brooks." He was being economical with the truth.

"And that's all you know?" Meg asked.

Hoff remained silent.

"I love you. Why are you getting in involved in this mess?"

"What are you talking about?"

"We have a problem. I ran the fingerprints. That body you did the autopsy on—whoever she is—that's not Jessica Brooks."

Hoff had finished writing his preliminary report and spent the last fifteen minutes staring at his laptop screen. Half an hour later, he was still staring at the screen. Meg had said the body he was working on was not Jessica Brooks. *If she's not Jessica Brooks, where* is *Prisoner 111968?* He picked up the receiver and pressed the redial key for Errol Brown.

When Brown answered, Hoff did not inquire about his well-being and wait for a reply. He said, "I don't know what your game is, but count me out. Jesus Christ! We could all lose our jobs."

"What the f—" Brown restrained himself before the word left his lips. "Hoff, calm down. What are you talking about?"

"Prisoner 111968. The body in the morgue isn't Jessica Brooks. Explain that to me."

"I can't."

Hoff detected the genuineness in the superintendent's voice. "I don't know. Right now, I can't explain how a dead woman ended up in Jessica Brooks's cell. I can't make sense of any of this beyond the obvious fact. Jessica Brooks has escaped from MCC New York."

"And she left behind an unknown dead woman in her place?"

"Yes, that is even more inexplicable than how she managed to break out."

Hoff heard Brown shout, "Goddamn it," as he ended the call.

50

Fort Bragg, North Carolina

When the call from Howard Brown came into Joint Special Operations Command headquarters, Senior Chief Alex Roigin was in a meeting with the director of the FBI, Collin Mulligan. Roigin put the caller on loudspeaker.

"Mr. Roigin, there's a situation—Jessica Brooks."

"Colin Mulligan and I were just discussing her death and the FBI's investigation. What about Brooks?"

Brown drew a deep breath. "Not dead, it turns out, escaped."

"What?" Alex and Mulligan said simultaneously.

"How the f—?" Alex stopped an expletive falling from his mouth.

"No one knows how. It happened last night. There's something else."

"What?" Alex snapped. His frustration and anger were displayed on his face and in the tone of his voice.

"As yet, an unidentified woman was found dead in Brooks's cell."

"An unidentified woman?" said Mulligan. He was pinching his chin with thumb and index finger. "Meaning not a prisoner, guard, or any other employee of the prison?"

"How did she escape?" repeated Alex.

Brown replied, "The storm knocked out the power, and then the backup generator failed. Lenco BearCat reinforcement from NYPD rolled in to make sure order was maintained. We thought everything was fine following a head count. We had one fatality. I ordered a postmortem on the dead body, at the time identified as Brooks. The medical examiner just informed me that 'Prisoner 111968'—Brooks—I mean the body in the morgue isn't Brooks."

Alex appeared distracted when his assistant opened the door and stood motionless in the doorway looking at him.

"Florida's AG, Sam Baptize is on line one. He said its urgent."

When Alex answered the call, Baptize relayed the details about a shootout and explosion at San Antonio Church.

"Hold up, Sam. I'm putting the call on speakerphone. The FBI director is here."

Baptize recapped what had happened at San Antonio Church and finished up with the murders at Bloomindale Residential Home. Alex, a small man of slender build, was the mirror opposite of the sinewy, close-cropped, blond-haired Mulligan. That said, what Alex lacked in physical stature, he made up in his brainpower. That intelligence, coupled with his genius for strategy, had landed him his job at JSOC. Alex was stunned by what he heard. He didn't utter the words, but skeletons were rehashed.

"AG Baptize, this is FBI Director Collin Mulligan. Who is currently in charge at the crime scenes?"

"Police Chief James Howard."

"Give Howard this cell phone number. And ask him to text photos of the bodies, any IDs, and weapons."

"You've got it," said Baptize.

Mulligan lifted the telephone receiver sitting on the table and called Jack Curtis, the FBI team leader on the MCC New York investigation.

When Jack answered, Mulligan cut out the pleasantries and said, "What's the status of our investigation?" His tone was curt. He opened his mouth, "Jessica Br—." He stopped midsentence as he stared at the photos as they poured in. "Jack, I will call you back."

Alex had moved and was viewing the photos over his shoulder.

Alex, with professional detachment, narrated who and what they were looking at right down to the body of the elderly woman found at Bloomingdale Residential Home. Mulligan looked directly at Alex.

Alex guessed what was troubling Mulligan and said, "Who wanted them dead?"

He thought, *The question is not who. It's why, and my money's on vengeance.* "We have two dead males of Middle Eastern descent found at the San Antonio Church crime scene. Reverend Leo Logan is Jake Logan's bother. Father Leo is the priest at San Antonio Church. An educated guess—this is connected to Jessica Brooks and the recent Wall Street / Bronxville bombings."

Alex, who was now seated at the table, put his elbows on the tabletop and rested his head in his hands.

"You've put the pieces together, and that makes this an FBI matter."

Alex put his hand up indicating for Mulligan to stop. "I want to look at the crime scenes."

Mulligan did not reply immediately. He picked up the desk phone and resumed his conversation with Jack Curtis. He brought Curtis up to date with the intel on the Florida incidents and instructed Curtis to have Agent Megan Coleman take the lead with the field agents in Florida. Finally, he said, "Senior Chief Alex Roigin will meet you meet you at the crime scene. I expect you boys ... and girls to play nicely with him."

"Thank you," he said, telling himself, *It's not wise to object to the FBI babysitting me at the crime scene.* Alex appreciated that, without escalating the matter, the only way he would have access to the crime scene was if the FBI joined him.

"I'll schedule a meeting in Washington tomorrow." With that communicated, the FBI director made his way out of the conference room and was joined by his security detail before leaving the building.

As Alex headed out, he checked his phone again. There was one person he could not reach. Jake had been on the road, but he was expected back today. He had tried him several times, but the calls ended in voice mail. *Does he know about his mother? Why the fuck is he not picking up?* He sent him a text.

Sitting in the back of a black Suburban, Alex drank coffee while the vehicle headed toward Pope Airfield. He checked his phone. Jake had read his text but not replied. That he had read the message was a relief. *It's OK, Jake. I'm bringing a big gun.*

Alex, along with his security detail, boarded a Gulfstream G600 business jet, destination Punta Gorda, Florida.

After they had settled into their seats, the flight attendant approached and bent over to speak to Alex, "Sir, we are ready to go. Can we close the door?"

"No!"

"Yes," ex-Navy SEAL Mike McGrath, breathless, said. "Alex."

"Mike, you made it."

Mike seated himself and fastened his belt for the flying distance between Punta Gorda, Florida, and Pope Airfield. It was approximately 576 miles, and the estimated flying time was around one hour and twenty-six minutes. After the pilot tuned off the fasten seatbelt sign, Alex handed an updated document that tracked Jake's movements over the last twenty-four hours.

"Any words of wisdom?" Mike said.

"What? Other than pissed-off, drunk, and mad as a rattlesnake. Just bring him back."

Mike closed his eyes and smiled.

When the flight landed and taxied to an area for private jets. Alex, Mike, and the security detail disembarked. SUVs were waiting to transport them to San Antonio Church, Port Charlotte. Mike did not join Alex. He headed for the third SUV and instructed the driver to take him to Jack's Bait Shack, Naples.

"Jesus." Stepping out of one the SUVs, Alex was stifled by the odor and humidity of the Port Charlotte air. The temperature had hovered in the nighties throughout the day. The spray of SUV headlights picked up swarms of mosquitos waiting for victims. In the surrounding woods, predators, it seemed, were out in force in the fading daylight. He rubbed a line of sweat off his forehead and prepared himself for the horror he was about to see.

The debris that had rained down from the sky after the explosion covered the path to the caretaker's lodge. Smoke and mist were still rising through a crater in the center of San Antonio Church, and two sides had been blown out.

Megan Coleman met Alex at the entrance to the caretaker's lodge, the makeshift command center. Inside, the nation's intelligence was on show.

The rooms were packed with Homeland Security and FBI agents—law enforcement, people willing to give everything for their country. In the center, Reverend Leo Logan was holding court with Joe, his best friend and a local law enforcement officer.

The people in the room burst into laughter when Father Logan described the dead men and said, "It's better to be judged by twelve than carried by six."

The laughter died down when the occupants of the room, one by one, turned and watched as Senior Chief Alex Roigin entered the room.

51

Jake had risen late in the morning to work out. In the intervening period between leaving Bloomingdale Residential Home and now, he had been quiet and withdrawn. He had convinced himself that darkness hovered over him wherever he went. After his workout, he skipped lunch and headed out to spend the rest of the day drinking at Jack's.

Last evening, he was cognizant his alcohol consumption had been dangerous. He did not care, the drink was the only way he could kill the pain of all that had happened. *Stop! You can't wash it away.* He ignored his inner voice. *Alice and my mother, dead. BLT, Chuck, and Dan, killed in the line of duty. I haven't been able to do a goddamn thing to stop the carnage.*

He struggled to accept it was beyond his control. The Navy SEAL training had taught him to control everything—himself, his opponent. What all the training didn't tell him was the foremost things, the ones that determine life and death, were virtually and practically outside control.

Losing the people close to him was unbearable—for him, it was worse than death. He would die here and now if it meant Alice and his mom could have gone on living. Inside, he screamed. *I'm expected to live and carry the pain of their murders, as well as knowing that their deaths were my fault.*

The only comfort he could find was when he was drunk, so drunk he was too numb to feel anything, and then he would black out. He hit the bottle after his workout. He was so far away from his elite Navy SEAL career, he was crashing down to earth.

Jake turned on his phone and scrolled through old photos, texts, and voice messages from Alice and his mom. He left the phone on "do not disturb," sending any new calls straight to voice mail.

He was settled in Jack's. The air-conditioning was cold; the bar was quiet; and the patrons were hard-core drinkers and, he guessed, just like him, wanted to be left alone. The bartender, Murphy, was old school. He and Jake went way back. He was intelligent enough to recognize when and when not to make conversation. Nobody paid Jake any attention. It was the perfect hole-in-the-wall place to aid his slow passage to meet his maker.

Jake swirled the ice in his second bourbon and readied himself to empty the glass just as the door to Jack's opened. Inbuilt in Jake was his attention to detail and a feel for Jack's customer base. So, when the front door opened and an out-of-place man walked in, Jake's ability to sense and react to danger before it happened awakened.

The man looked to be less than thirty-five years old and like that category of Russian men who were perpetually clad in sweatpants, Timberland boots, and cropped jacket and carrying an indispensable leather man purse no matter the occasion or setting. The heat outside had not encouraged him to remove his jacket, as if he were trying to hide something. *I'll lay my money on tattoos,* Jake thought as he observed.

As the newcomer passed his booth, he noticed the bulge in his man purse and thought it safe to assume he was concealing a knife and, more than likely, a firearm. Jake concluded that the man was not your run-of-the-mill Florida redneck slaking his thirst.

Several minutes later, a waitress arrived at the man's table, and he placed an order for a bottle of IPA beer. His accent was unmistakably Russian.

"Fuck. Fuck ... May, the Bloomingdale resident." What had May said? "I saw him. They thought your mom was a dotty old woman. I saw him at the reception—Russian. He asked for her, your mom, by her name." *Whatever the man is planning, it's not good.* Jake could feel it in his gut. He had always been adept at reading people. It was like a sixth sense.

Adjusting his position in the booth, Jake angled himself so he could keep a better eye on the man. As the waitress set the drink down, he tried to touch her. She swatted the man's hand away. As she walked away, he grabbed her by the waist and pulled her to him. Jake watched but was hesitant to get involved. *I can't and shouldn't let bullshit like this go.*

Jake's Navy SEAL code name was Geronimo. He had been so named because of the night when he was out with the boys, and they happened on a Native American man beating his wife. Confronting the man, he'd said, "Hey, Chief, you can't do that. Don't hit your wife."

The Native American had replied, "Who the fuck do you think you are? Geronimo? I'll treat this bitch as I see fit."

At that point, Jake had dropped him with one punch to his face.

The boys had burst into laughter and said, "Jesus! Don't fuck with Geronimo."

Jake loathed men who disrespected women and realized he would intervene.

He removed his belt from his trousers. This man had come searching for adversity. *You've found it.* Jake slipped from his booth. Holding his belt, he headed to the man's table. *This man is not going to listen to reason.* The actions to follow dictated the element of surprise. Jake did not overestimate the man. Still his advantage did not last long. The man saw him approaching.

"Let go of her," he ordered.

The man raised his hand and showed Jake his middle finger. "This is none of your goddamn business."

"Let her go," Jake repeated.

"And if I don't? What are you going to do about it?"

The rage that Jake had been nurturing—the rage he had been caging with the bottle had found its release. "Let her go, and we'll take this outside."

The man smiled. With that, Jake put his belt back in his trouser loops and smiled back. The man took a sip of his beer and let go of the waitress.

She backed away to the safety of the bar and pulled out her phone. "I'm calling the cops," she said.

Neither the man nor Jake acted as if they cared. Without turning his back on the man, Jake moved toward the door.

Yes, outside is the place to take this fight. There are no cameras. I can do whatever I want. Whoever this asshole is, it's no coincidence he's Russian. I'm going to make him pay for Mom's death and the San Antonio Church bombing. He's begging for an ass kicking.

As they assembled behind the building, the afternoon was thick with humidity. Jake assumed the stance of a man about to fight. He did a quick scan for cameras he may have missed, as well as for makeshift weapons that could be picked up and used by either man.

It did not take long for the bragging to start. "A dog—your mother was a bitch and I put her down. Now I'll squeezed the life out of her puppy." The man running his mouth made an error. Stupidly, he raised his chin.

Jake stepped left and delivered a lethal throat punch.

The man's hands instinctively grabbed his neck as he stumbled backward, struggling to breathe. His knees buckled as he fell to the ground.

"I wouldn't piss on you, haji, if you were on fire. But I will send you to your fifty virgins in the afterlife." Jake advanced toward him.

When the assailant raised his head—there was a crack of his cartilage and a spray of blood as he broke the man's nose with a punch and sent him unconscious to the ground.

Jake had thought the fight was over and was debating whether to go back to Jack's and finish his drink. *No!* In that moment, he realized, he had broken the number one rule in street fights. *Shit! I did not watch for other assailants.* Maybe it was the sweat stinging his eyes, but what he had missed was now creeping out of the shadows, and the second man now pointed a suppressed pistol at him. *I missed, a step and now I'm going to die.*

My meeting with God had been arranged. He had cheated death so often during his career in the Navy SEALs; it was hard to believe it had finally caught up with him. He prayed his sins would be forgiven and that he would be reunited with Alice on the other side. "Make this quick," he whispered. Straightening up, he faced his killer full on.

The man holding the gun appeared dispassionate and stood about six feet tall. He was athletic, with dark brown hair, brown eyes, and pale skin. But for the man Jake had just put down, he would have thought his features were indeterminable. Dressed in the same uniform, this man had only one characteristic that distinguished him from the one lying on the ground— he was a professional. He radiated a cold calm. His breathing was steady, and his weapon did not tremble. He had done this kind of work before. *There's nothing in his eyes, no rage or vengeance. This is a transaction—cold, detached, and impersonal.*

Before he died, Jake had several questions. Who had sent the man and why? *I'll not give him or his employer satisfaction. Dignity is all I have now—might as well get it over with.*

In the distance, the klaxons of the emergency vehicles could be heard. Time was ticking down. The gunman maintained his distance. He was professional and would not take the risk just to get up and in Jake's face.

From a distance, he had watched Jake fight and knew getting too close could end badly. From where he was, he could take the shot and disappear back into the fast-approaching darkness of the night before anyone identified him or the police arrived. He had sent the man to lure Jake outside. The thug had had been paid to beat him within an inch of his life and take off before the police arrived. Now he was lying on the ground dead or fighting for his life. What he did not know was that he was also the fall guy. The police would not be looking for an assassin, and he would be the target of the investigation at Bloomindale Residential Home.

Jake had foiled that plan. Still, the man on the ground was expendable. He was nothing to him if the man did not regain consciousness and escape. The killer's goal was to take Jake out. The assassin took a deep breath, looked down, and adjusted his sight line. He applied pressure to the trigger.

52

Jake maintained eye contact with the assassin. He did not look away or close his eyes. He was not afraid to die and realized that his appointed time for this meeting had arrived. He steeled for the worst—and then it came.

There was a muffled pop followed by silence. Jake's eyes were still locked on the assassin. *What? Did he miss?*

A fraction of a second passed, and blood trickled from the assassin's head, and then he slumped to the ground. Jake realized he had been shot by someone else. *Who?*

The high-pitched volume of sirens in his ears dropped. He turned around expecting to be surrounded by patrol cars. The waitress was looking toward him, hands over her ears. When Jake turned back, a man carrying a suppressed weapon walked toward him slowly. In the late afternoon heat, the light around him rippled and bent. His face was covered by a balaclava, and he donned Gatorz sunglasses. He was cognizant that time had slowed for him when the man had shoved his face in Jake's face. "What the fuck? What's—"

"Let's go," he ordered.

Jake recognized the voice. But before he could reply, the man grabbed him under the arm and directed him toward an SUV. After the SUV took off, the man removed his sunglasses and balaclava. The voice he had recognized belonged to Mike McGrath. With his square jaw, dirty blond head of hair, and six-foot-three-inches frame, ex-Navy SEAL McGrath looked like he had stepped off a fashion shoot.

"What the hell happened out there?" Jake asked.

"I saved your life," replied Mike.

"But what where you doing here? Answer my question. Mike, what the fuck is going on? What are you doing here?"

Mike paused before he said, "If you don't already know, apparently, Jessica Brooks escaped and … we got intelligence there's a bounty on your head."

Jake drew a deep breath as his mind tried to come to terms with Mike's words. *One doesn't escape from MCC New York.* "How?"

"No one knows how."

"You said 'apparently.' Is there some confusion on the point?"

"I said 'apparently' because that's what MCC New York is reporting. It happened two nights ago. I struggle with why they wouldn't have found her by now, if she were still on the premises."

"Is any other prisoner missing?"

"No. But there's something else—equally troubling."

"What?" said Jake his voice slightly raised.

"An unidentified woman was found dead in Brooks's cell."

Jake, exhausted and emotionally compromised, could barely process these words. Megan Coleman had mentioned she was at Bloomingdale because there had been an incident at MCC New Yok, but he had not stayed to discuss her investigation. The pieces fell into place.

"An unidentified woman? Are you saying not another prisoner, guard, or other person working at the prison?"

"You've got it."

"How in God's name did she escape?" asked Jake.

"A storm knocked out the generators, and then the backup generator failed. Reinforcements arrived promptly, and they thought everything was fine until they did the autopsy on the dead body. One head was missing. Brooks. And another head was added—the dead woman. That's how she foiled the head count and bought herself time."

"Jessica couldn't have gotten far."

McGrath replied, "There's an airport nearby, plus a port and interstate highways."

"That would mean she'd need a fake ID, transportation, money—and don't forget a disguise."

"My money says she had outside help. I've no way to know that. But what I do know is, by some apparent coincidence, both the main power and the backup generator failed on the same night Jessica Brooks walks out of a maximum-security facility, and a dead woman is found in her cell. Where the hell did she come from?"

"Do you have a cause of death?"

McGrath paused momentarily as the SUV turned into Punta Gorda Airport and pulled up alongside a Gulfstream G600 business jet. "The postmortem revealed traces of solid crystalline in the mouth of the dead woman. We suspect it was cyanide salts, but that can only be confirmed by the toxicologic analysis. The medical examiner concluded that the woman's death was caused by cardiac arrest."

Jake turned to exit the SUV. "Wait," said McGrath. "The medical examiner thought he was carrying out the postmortem on Jessica. The woman was not pregnant. Jessica's medical records indicated she was twenty weeks pregnant at the date of her death."

Jake had turned to face Mike McGrath, but in that moment his body slumped back in his seat. His facial features displayed shock. "How ... how the fuck did she get pregnant?"

"Didn't you get the birds and the bees memo? How the fuck would I know?"

Jake had regained his composure. "Do you think she killed the woman?"

"I've no idea, but I think Jessica had inside, as well as outside help."

Later that night, Jake stripped off his clothes and took a shower, letting the water beat down on him as he rested his forehead against the moist tile wall. His breathing was erratic and too fast. He could not accept that Jessica had escaped from prison. *I should've killed her when I had the chance and now—*

There was something he had always been unwilling to believe or accept about her. She was a traitor and would stop at nothing to get what she believed in her twisted mind was her entitlement. He turned off the water and toweled off. *How could Jessica have escaped without help?*

Several minutes later, he had just settled in front of the TV screen when his phone buzzed. It was Megan Coleman.

"I hope you don't mind if I eat while I talk," she said. "I had time today to either eat lunch or to do a five-mile run."

"And of course, you opted to run." Jake heard utensils in the background.

"So," she said, "let's talk about Jessica Brooks. Do you have a theory on what happened with her escape?"

"Hold up. I don't know all the facts."

When Megan remained silent, Jake was not sure if it was because she was chewing her food or because she knew more than she was revealing.

"It seems impossible she'd be able to escape without some help."

"So ... you are in the loop," said Megan in an accusatory tone. "And you dated Brooks."

"What the ... You are way off the mark."

"Has Jessica tried to contact you?"

"Look. I don't know where you get your info. But if you want me to assist in the investigation ..." Jake paused. "Finish your meal, and while you do, think about your approach." He hung up, cracked open an IPA, and sat back. He wasn't thinking about Jessica's escape. He was thinking about the woman who had been on the other end of that conversation.

When Jake had met Megan Coleman during her investigation at Bloomingdale Residential Home, he had been instantly attracted to her. But his job tended to get in the way of any permanent relationship. Now, he was contemplating when he might see her again. He was pleased she had called, but he was not prepared to relitigate his relationship with Jessica. He closed his eyes. He had never thought a new woman could penetrate his cold heart, but Megan Coleman had—he had a need to care about her.

Jake fell asleep on the sofa surrounded by beer bottles. The TV was still blaring when he woke up in the early hours of the morning. *That whole thing at MCC New York was staged. Jessica was not breaking out—she was kidnapped by ... by ...*

That part evaded him.

53

By the time Jake ended his call with Alex, he had been authorized to pursue his theory on Jessica's escape. Jessica was devious. She would make mistakes. Still, she had outwitted him on many occasions. *She knows how I think—how I tick. But then, I know the same about her.* She had allies, and these thoughts did not fill him with confidence. There could be something bigger at play here.

He cleared security at MCC New York and took the elevator to the visitors' room. The woman who met Jake was in her early forties, average height, Asian American. She introduced herself as Acting Superintendent Yasmin Chang. She smiled. "What can I do for you, Mr. Logan?" Her expression appeared cooperative.

"I'd like to ask you some questions about the escape of Jessica Brooks."

"Yes, I've been expecting you."

Jake followed her out of the visitors' room and to her office. She offered him a seat and asked if he would like refreshment. She held his gaze.

"A glass of water. Thank you."

She handed him a bottle of water. "Now, how can I help you?"

Jake went over the facts he had and those added by Alex and asked her for confirmation of them.

"Your summation left out the fired shots and explosion. It's unusual for two reasons. First, initially, the shots and explosion sounded just like that—they were quite distinct."

"Are you saying the shots and explosion were not really shots and an explosion?"

"Correct. We found no evidence of an explosion or shots fired."

"Hmm. Sound effects."

"Yes. Guards do not carry weapons inside the prison, the guns could not have been fired by them, and all prisoners are searched."

"Were the guards searched?"

When she did not reply he took answer as no.

If the prisoners didn't cause it, it had to be a guard. Jake kept his thought to himself. "And Errol Brown, where is he?"

Chang remained silent.

He's a fall guy for this. "Brown," he repeated.

"He's on administrative leave."

Jake observed that her response held a tinge of … maybe remorse. The role she now held was on account of his more-than-likely unjustified fall.

"Has the dead woman been identified?"

"Yes." She pressed the button on her Cisco desk phone. "Kerry, please show Agent Coleman into my office. I anticipated your question and asked her to remain on the premises because she was the one who identified the woman and is in better position to update you."

When Megan Coleman walked into the room, she smiled. "Jake," she said and seated herself in the chair next to Jake and crossed her legs. "Yasmin, if I may."

"Of course," Chang replied. "The floor is yours."

Jake was a little surprised at her confidence. *Did they set me up?* But he could not deny he welcomed her presence.

"The dead woman, Val Winthrop, was employed in the NYPD Special

Operations Bureau and a member of the SWAT team on the night of the storm," said Megan. She opened her purse and handed Jake a photograph. Winthrop was five four, the same height as Jessica Brooks.

Jake stared at the photo and the woman's below shoulder-length black hair—the same color as Jessica's hair the last time he had seen an image of her. She had a similar great smile and warm eyes. In that image, Jessica had been wearing brown contact lenses, but he assumed they would've been removed when she was processed into MCC New York. *Jessica and Winthrop were similar.*

"She was not liked by her bosses or trusted. It did not have anything to do with the relationships she had with women. It wasn't her excessive drinking. Certain people she worked with had begun to suspect that Winthrop was a dirty cop."

Jake was still looking at the photograph. *Where is she? Pregnant? What has happened to Jessica?*

"All Val Winthrop had left in the NYPD was a toehold and only that much because cops have a powerful union. The rest of her was already out the door. Internal Affairs was circulating like buzzards around fresh kill."

"So, who put her on the SWAT team?" asked Yasmin.

"Part and parcel of our investigation," replied Megan.

"Other than those guards injured on the night in question, have any prison personnel taken sick or vacation leave in the last few days?" Jake asked.

"No, all personnel have reported for duty," Yasmin said. "In the circumstances, I don't see how personnel taking leave is relevant."

Jake glanced at Megan. It was clear to him that they were on the same page when she said, "Don't take this the wrong way, but let us be the judge of what is relevant to this investigation."

"I'll need to see the surveillance cameras," Jake said.

"I'll make arrangements."

Before she could add to her sentence he said, "And speak with the crew that restored the electrical power and backup generators."

Megan said, "I thought the system was set up so that, if the power failed, the cell doors automatically locked."

Yasmin's facial features changed. She flushed. "It seems we were hacked."

"Hacked? How?" Megan said.

How? Jake looked at her. *FBI and you're asking how?*

Megan was undeterred by Jake's stare.

"A hacker caused the cell doors to open."

"How could that have happened?" Megan pursued her line of questioning.

"Against MCC New York's rules, some of our personnel bring in their personal devices, phones, iPads, and computers. There's the occasional breach of protocol when and if they log onto outside networks."

Incredulity was written all over Jake's face. "Come again?"

"Human beings are fallible."

"What the f—" He closed his mouth before the word rolled out. "So, you opened the door so a hacker could walk in and rewrite your code, enabling the doors to open when the power failed."

"I've no defense. And yes, that's about right."

"Have you formed any theories on what happened?" asked Megan.

"No, we have not," Yasmin replied.

Later that day, Jake spoke to Jed, the engineer on the team that had repaired the blown transformer. Jed was in his late fifties; he was a slim man of average height with white hair and a goatee to match.

After he confirmed that the storm had fired the transformers, he explained how a lightning bolt could carry enough volts to cause a boom.

Jake asked, "So, like an explosion?"

"Yes, much like one," replied Jed.

"Could it have been a bomb?"

Jed looked surprised but said, "Yes, a bomb in the transformers could have taken out both transfers and knocked out the power to the prison. But ... the backup generators would kick in."

Jake thought, *The backup failed.* "Thank you, Jed.

After speaking to Ted, Jake headed over to the surveillance room. He asked to see the camera feed for the night Prisoner 111968 disappeared from MCC New York. He also requested for the room be darkened to sharpen the view on the screen.

Jake viewed the feed before the power failed, corridors, doorways, Prisoner 111968's prison cell, and adjacent rooms. When power failed, there was blackout—nothing to see. The power was restored; it flickered and again failed. From the bouncing beams of flashlights, he could make out the silhouettes of figures running.

Jake jumped when the sound of the imitation shots came from the audio. The next sound was so loud he jumped again. The second sound was the imitation explosion. As far as he could decipher, that was when the guards had escorted prisoners from their cells. *What have I learned?*

He picked up the bottle of water on the table and drank, quenching his thirst and frustration. *The power had failed—possibly an explosion. The back generator failed. There were the sounds of gunshots and an explosion that cannot be explained. MCC New York was hacked—to be confirmed. A dead woman identical to Jessica was in the building. That was the opportunity. But* how? Motive? Money for the dead women if she secured Jessica's escape. The woman is dead. Is there a money trail?

"No leads and, other than a dead woman, no suspects. And Jessica is out there somewhere doing who knows what and, more than likely, with enemies of this country." Jake's thoughts had turned to muttering. "There's no way Jessica could have escaped without help from the outside and, possibly, somebody on the inside."

He turned back to view the feed again. Before the lights had gone out, Jessica had been stretched out on her bed dressed in her orange prison jumpsuit and wearing sneakers. She was cradling her stomach and looked serene notwithstanding the sounds of the storms. There was a toilet and a sink next to the bed. It was built into the wall. His eyes went to the metal table in front of the glass window that permitted a view into her cell—the table was bolted to the floor. *Out of the ordinary? No. The chair was similarly bolted to the floor.* But what was out of the ordinary was, the position where the table was bolted down. *Visitor! Did she have a visitor?*

Then the power went out, and the cell turned black. The generator kicked in. Jessica was still in her cell, not on her bed but by the door—momentarily. The generator failed.

Jake hit reverse on the feed and froze the image. He observed a confident and smiling Jessica—Jess? "Maybe," he said. And her hands were on the button of the orange jumpsuit. *The prison computer system was hacked—the cell door opened. Did Jessica and the dead woman exchange identities at that point? Megan said the dead woman entered the prison with the NYPD SWAT team.*

Jake snapped back to the present when the door opened, and Megan Coleman walked in.

"Agent Logan."

Jake was surprised by this greeting—he thought they were on a first-name basis. She stared at the frozen image of Jessica Brooks on the screen.

"Attractive woman—the orange adds to her blooming glow."

Does she know Jessica is pregnant? He let the comment fly over—he would not reveal what she did not know.

"Find any clues?"

"Not yet."

"Why are you here? I know you're authorized to be here. But why the interest? I'm sure you know her better than I do—maybe better than anyone, which might be the reason you're here."

"What are you insinuating?"

"Did I hit a raw nerve?"

"What is your interest? This sounds like more than investigating an MCC New York prison break. What is your interest in my past and Jessica?"

Megan blushed—she had overstepped the line. "I've been assigned to work with you."

"By whom?"

"Collin Mulligan. I believe you know him as the director of the FBI."

Jake made a mental note to take the matter up with Alex for not giving him the heads-up. "So, what have you bought to this party?"

"I looked into the transformers and the generator."

"And the generator?" There was nothing new he would learn about the transformers.

"It was housed in a concrete bunker below ground and had gas lines powering it."

"What was the cause of the failure?" asked Jake.

"It was a fuel problem—an electronic control module failed. The electronic control module regulates the supply of fuel to the generator. Likely, the person who hacked MCC New York's computer system also hacked into the off-site computer that controls the fuel to the backup generator."

Jake walked over to the door. "Did you go over the visitors' log yet?"

"On my to-do list."

He held the door open for her.

Jake and Megan accessed the electronically stored visitors' records huddled together in a small cubicle. They viewed records for the last three months to cover the entirety of Jessica's incarceration. When Megan's knee touched Jake's because of the small space, a sensation radiated through his body. And when she did not pull away, he reluctantly reminded himself, *Focus. This is not the time or the place.*

"The records showed she had three visitors—Zeake Lynne, psychologist, MD; Anne Brody, psychiatrist, MD; and Elle Cohen of the law firm Cohen and Goldman," said Jake. "And I'm guessing that is not news to you."

She smiled. "So, now what?"

"Of the three names, I think Elle Cohen could be of interest. The log records no calls came in from her to Jessica, but Cohen made two in-person visits."

"What can we learn from her? Cohen will assert attorney-client privilege."

"I'm not interested in her conversation with Jessica. I'm proposing we investigate her. I guarantee neither the state nor Jessica Brooks are footing the legal bill."

"I'm on it," said Megan.

Calls were made by both Jake and Megan to their respective offices with instructions to dig into the background of both Elle Cohen and the law firm Cohen and Goldman.

When Megan ended her call Jake said, "Are you hungry?"

"Yes, breakfast was a long time ago."

They walked the short distance to 1803, a restaurant inspired by the vibrant culinary scene of New Orleans. Jake observed and was attracted to the space because it evoked the saltiness of an evening in the French Quarter, complete with balconied and outdoor dining. He thought of the intimate underground jazz club, Bon Courage, and again reminded himself of the precedence of his task at hand.

Jake perused the menu. And after Megan had made her selection, the waiter took their orders. Jake had an IPA, while Megan sipped a pinot grigio. Jake exchanged polite conversation with Megan about their respective careers. When the conversation petered out, he remained silent and didn't initiate conversation as they ate their meal. When the plates were cleared, Jake came back to why they were here.

"Jessica spoke to someone on the outside," he said.

"And the computer system both on and off site were hacked—possibly inside help. Ensuring the doors would open, not lock."

"You need to have your people talk to every guard who was on duty that night."

"That's a lot of guards."

Jake put his fork down and stared at her. *Did I see something in you?* As he stared at her, he was turned off by her attitude.

"What?" She paused as if she was considering her next words carefully. "What exactly are you trying to achieve here? Capturing Brooks and returning her to prison safely is the goal—yes. But I was briefed on your history with Brooks, and I'm perplexed by your obsession with her. And … there's the child she's carrying. Kept that to yourself—any idea who's the father?"

Jake slapped the table with the base of his fist. "What the f—" He did not finish. His phone pinged.

She looked away.

He scanned the message, pushed the phone back into his pocket, pulled out his wallet, and laid down some cash for his part of the meal. "I'm sure the FBI will reimburse you for your meal." He rose.

"Where are you going?"

"Goodnight." He turned and walked away.

54

When Jake and Alex were shown into the Oval Office, President Dayle Wesley stood up and came around his desk to greet them.

He shook Alex's hand, and then as he shook hands with Jake, he said, "I'm sorry for the loss of your mother." He paused for a while. "And your brother, how is he doing?"

"Thank you, sir, for asking. My brother is well and discussing rebuilding San Antonio Church," he replied as the president directed him and Alex to one of the sofas in the oval office.

The president did not waste any time getting to the point. "Jake, I feel confident when I say the American public, like myself, is grateful for your service to this country and what you did in Washington."

"Thank you, sir." Yes, he had taken down a wanted terrorist, but the job was not finished. He remained quiet and allowed the commander in chief to continue.

"I don't want you to think I'm not grateful for all you've done. I value your service to the country. That is the reason I invited you here to thank you in person."

This is not good, thought Jake. *He's giving me my marching orders.* "Sir."

The president put his hand up. "We want to offer you a job. We want you to lead an offensive against a world that has changed."

Jake was startled. "How?"

"We can't wait for terror to come to us. America must strike first," said Alex.

How? What? Where? Jake finally asked, "Who would I work for?"

"Me," said Alex. "We'll have access to the collective intelligence of the United States with the authority to neutralize and combat terrorism."

"And my job?"

"You will do what you have been doing."

"And my current role?"

Alex walked over to where he had laid his bag. He retrieved and opened a file, handing it to Jake.

"Khalil Hassan, Batdadi's son, is bankrolling Jessica Brooks."

Jake smiled. "I accept."

President Wesley rose from his chair to signal that the meeting was over. Jake also rose and extended his hand. The president took it and covered their clasped hands with his right hand to emphasize gratitude.

Alex thanked the president and ushered Jake out of the Oval Office. As the door closed behind them, Alex said, "I have a plane waiting for you. You need to get to Joint Base Andrews ASAP."

Though it was the last days of summer, it was hot and humid as Jake stepped onto the tarmac at Joint Base Andrews where a Boeing C-40 Clipper was fueled and waiting for the 917-mile flight to MacDill Air Force Base. On boarding the aircraft, he was greeted by a familiar crew, First Officer Karen Birch and Staff Sergeant Rickson, who was functioning as the flight attendant.

When he landed two hours and eight minutes later, leaning against a black Hummer was Mike McGrath. Not only was Mike his childhood friend, but he was one of the toughest men he had ever known in his life. An ex-Navy SEAL, McGrath was code named Gonzales because of his running speed. He had been all American University of Iowa eight hundred-meter champion. He had run the first four hundred meters in forty-nine seconds and the second in fifty-one seconds. McGrath was one of the few people who could outrun Jake. They had yet to determine who was the better street fighter.

As Jake collected the gear that had been left on the Boeing C-40 Clipper for him, he thought about his childhood and his mom. She had been a kind and giving person and had been a second mom to Mike—he recalled the countless dinners Mike had eaten at his mom's house and the hours they played together. *Yes, he was speedy*, Jake recalled, smiling. Jake's family home had been on an eighteen-hole golf course. The McGrath family home had been next door.

On the day Jake was remembering, he and Mike had been camped out on the golf course. Obscured by trees and a curve in the road, they were throwing snow and ice balls at the cars. It was a favorite winter pastime prank of the fourteen-year-old boys—that was until the day one of the ice balls hit a police car in the parking lot. McGrath took off running and had soon arrived at Jake's house. From there, he'd watched as a policeman pursued Jake, who was running for his life across the golf course. Mike had told Jake his dad had looked on through the patio windows and asked him, pointing his finger, "Why is that policeman chasing Jake?"

Jake smiled. McGrath, like many of his friends back then had been a ruthless, no-holds-barred fighter in the basement of their family homes. Yet he was a man with a big heart.

As he drove, McGrath reached behind his seat, pulled a cold beer from a cooler in the back, and offered it to Jake.

"Thank you, but I will pass."

"Are you hungry? Do you want to eat now or later?"

"Later. Let's get right down to the task at hand."

They made small talk the rest of the way to the safe house.

Approaching the main gate of the eighteen thousand-square-foot Miami beach home, McGrath radioed ahead to the guardhouse that he was coming in, plus one. The Hummer came to a stop behind the property, where the intelligence center had been set up.

To the untrained eye, the small door to the right appeared to be a service entrance As Jake entered, McGrath said, "To your right."

Jake was about to ask where when he saw a sign, "Service elevator." He gave Alex credit. He had expected to be greeted by stainless-steel, pneumatically sealed door.

McGrath pressed the call button, and they stepped inside. McGrath removed a key card from his pocket, swept it through a magnetic reader, and presented his index finger and pupil for biometric verification. Once he had been authorized, the elevator began to descend. When the elevator came to a stop, the door opened to a passageway that ended in front of a heavy blast door. Again, McGrath removed a key card from his pocket, swept it through a magnetic reader, and presented his index finger and pupil for biometric verification. Inside the room, the door shut behind them, securing them inside.

The interior reminded Jake of the first generation of Apple stores—it was clinical. He was surrounded by polished granite floors and offices walled with glass. High-definition monitors graced the walls.

"Here, we operate with no congressional oversight of what we do," said Mike. "There's a downside. If an op goes south, we'll be disavowed."

"A risk I'm prepared to take," replied Jake.

He was continuing to observe his surroundings when Daniel Walker, aka the Wizard, entered the office.

"Jake," said the Wizard as he set his chai tea latte cup and his laptop down on his desk. "It's good to have you back. I'm sorry about your mom."

"Thank you," replied Jake. "Good to see you."

"Daniel, tell Jake what you've got," said Mike as they sat down.

"I've located Batdadi's sea chest."

Jake looked at him. "Come again?" Jake's facial features exuded excitement. "Batdadi's sea chest equals Khalil's sea chest. Am I right? And you have everything?"

The wizard said, "Yes, everything. Bank accounts and data deposits."

Jake was beyond impressed with the Wizard—he had been able to do what the United States wouldn't or couldn't do.

"We have Khalil, in wrestling parlance, in a chin lock," said Mike. "The only question is, what are we planning to do?"

"I want to and will choke the life out of Khalil, Jessica, and anybody who would hurt the United States."

55

Ninety minutes by air from Miami was Musha Cay and the Islands of Copperfield Bay. Musha Cay was a seven hundred-acre, privately owned island in the Exuma chain in the southern Bahamas. It was located eighty-five miles southeast of Nassau, the capital of the Bahamas, and was owned by the illusionist David Copperfield.

Musha Cay was surrounded by three smaller islands that maintained its guests' privacy. Known for its warm waters, white sandy beaches, and lush vegetation, Musha Cay was paradise—a place one could get lost in. Invisible was exactly what Khalil wanted for Jessica and his mother, Natasha.

The private island he had leased boasted a helipad, a speedboat, and accommodation that was equal to the greatest luxury properties around the world. Though it could sleep twelve, at present, there were two residents—Jessica Brooks and Natasha. Khalil jetted to the island when his schedule permitted.

Khalil's father, Batdadi, had made a substantial living for himself. Wealthy benefactors in the Persian Gulf used Batdadi for recruiting, organizing, and orchestrating the operations of the terrorist groups active on

Pakistani soil. He served as something of a liaison between ISIS leadership and the criminal and ideological groups who fought against India, the West at large, and Pakistan's secular government. Though Khalil had no interest in taking over his father's businesses, he had inherited his empire and wealth.

Khalil had a longtime friend and one of his father's financial partners—a Russian oligarch named Valentin Popov. Valentin and Khalil had been friends since their days at Oxford University, and Batdadi had been like a second father to Valentin.

Two days before Jessica's escape from MCC New York, at Khalil's request, Valentin's $95 million yacht, *Anya*, had been moored on the Hudson River. Thereafter, and once the storm had calmed, *Anya* had left for Musha Cay. Jessica was not the only asset onboard. He had instructed Valentin to deposit US$30 million of his father's fortune in a locked cabin. In the early hours of the following day, *Anya* had stopped in the open Atlantic seaboard and had been met by a private seaplane. Natasha had boarded the yacht.

Khalil was seated in the living room with ceiling timbers and their aged stonework. The villa he had leased was Tuscan styled. Natasha joined him and, shortly thereafter, Jessica. Khalil studied his mother. Like his deceased father, she had an edacious appetite for the best of everything. She held a glass of Rayas Chateauneuf-du-Pape (Reserve) in her hand as she stared through the villa's patio window and watched the sun go down.

"The woman who died in Jessica's—"

Natasha did not finish her sentence, as Khalil intervened. "Val Winthrop, she was employed in the NYPD Special Operations and was about to be fired for transporting drugs."

"And your connection to her?"

Khalil stared at his mother. *Still vetting my friends, please.*

"Don't look at me like that. We need to o assess our exposure, do damage control, and rebuild. You have responsibilities now." She glanced at Jessica, who was sipping apple juice and looked tired.

"She was bad penny that turned up when we needed her."

"What are you talking about? I'm not going to jail. I don't think I'd like the food, let alone the company."

"For years, all she did was carry dope from point A to point B, which could be anywhere in the five boroughs of New York. At first, it was mostly cocaine, but times changed because of OxyContin. 'Don't get high on your own supply.' That was her mantra. But when her husband left her, taking their terminally ill child, she started chipping a little—just to keep from being too depressed. After a while, you couldn't really call it chipping at all. She was using."

"And you know this how?" Natasha cradled her wine and raised the glass to her mouth.

"Do you remember Valentin's brother, Andrei?"

"Yes, go on."

"I would visit Valentin, and on occasion, his brother was present. Andrei's nose would randomly bleed—just trickle down that little gutter between his nose and upper lip. He would wipe it with the palm of his hand. His septum was gone. He would tell his brother, 'I'm going to fix it.'"

Jessica's eyes were focused on Khalil as he told his story. She asked, "What does a cokehead have to do with the dead woman?"

"Val Winthrop got a part-time job as security in a club to help pay for her son's medical bills. She met Andrei and made connections, got offers in the dope biz. Do you know how the dope biz works?"

Jessica and then Natasha shook their heads.

"It's a pyramid like any other big organization. You've got your junior street dealers at the bottom, and a lot of them are juveniles. Then you've got your senior dealers who service the clubs—where Val Winthrop was recruited. The senior dealers often save by buying in bulk. Go up a little, you've got suppliers, your junior executives to keep things running smoothly, your accountants' lawyers. And then there are the top boys—where Andrei found his job because of his brother's connections. It's all compartmentalized, or at least it's supposed to be."

"San Antonio Church and the assassin at Jack's Bait Shack, was he connected to these Russians?" asked Natasha.

"San Antonio Church, no—that was revenge for my father. It was a failed attempt, but I'll avenge him," replied Khalil. Jack's Bait Shack, yes. I wrongly believed, if Jake was out of the picture … I did it for Jessica, for the child she's carrying." *I did it for you, my love.* "As I was saying, the people at the bottom know who's directly above them, but that's all they know. The people in the middle know everyone below them, but still only one layer above them. Valentin Popov is different. He's outside the pyramid, outside the hierarchy but able to tap into it to get specific jobs done."

Jessica rose and walked across the room. "I'll prepare dinner. We can continue this conversation later."

When their food was prepared, Jessica set it on the dining table, uncorked another bottle of Rayas Chateauneuf-du-Pape (Reserve), and invited Khalil and Natasha to sit and eat.

Somewhere along the lines of her life, Jessica had mastered the art of cooking steak, and the steaks were perfect. Cutting into it was like slicing into a piece of ripe fruit. Khali nodded to bestow his approval after his first bite. Natasha glanced at Jessica. Her lip curved up as she washed the steak down with her wine.

"They thought I was part of the reinforcements from NYPD Special Forces," said Jessica.

Natasha's facial features were startled. She looked at Jessica. Her face was beaming, and she turned toward Khalil.

"Yes, I sent the woman to help you." He was looking at Jessica, and then he turned Natasha.

"This woman." She paused. "You exposed us?"

"No! When the cell door opened, it was dark—dark for sure. It was her, Val Winthrop. But Jess said—"

"Jess?" asked Khalil.

Natasha interrupted, "You looked tired, dear. Did you mean Elle?"

"Yes, the lawyer, Elle," she replied. Jessica looked at Khalil. "She said you would send help." *What the fuck?! Jessica, don't say my name! If Khalil finds out you're crazy, he'll dump us.*

"I ... didn't suspect anything when the power went out because of the storm. But then the backup power went down." *Jessica, Natasha has covered for you—don't fuck it up.* "Well, that was not supposed to happen. Then"—she paused and tried to remember. *Jessica, you can't remember what happened because I saved your ass again.*

"Go on," said Natasha.

"I think ..." *Fool!* Jess screamed in her head. *The woman came into your cell and pulled the screen across behind her. She took off her clothes and gave them to you.* "That's it. The woman in the cell was close to my height, build, and had the same hair color and eyes. *Bingo! Fuck, she was as close as you can get.* Jessica heard Jess in her head. "Did I kill her and take her place?" Jessica said. *Fool! No!* "I remember now leaving the cell. Yes, a guard used his flashlight and indicated the way to go. He went into the cell."

"What happened in that cell? Khalil?" Natasha asked.

"Millions of dollars were rerouted to offshore accounts for both the guard and Winthrop. The power outage, hacking MCC New York's system, the noises of guns and bombs were all part of the 'effect.'" Khalil paused. "Cause and effect. The guard excelled. The icing on the cake—he encouraged Winthrop to digest a cyanide capsule. And as we speak, I have confirmation that his pending retirement has been brought to a fatal end."

"My dear child, you've made me proud." Natasha cradled her raised her glass and saluted her son.

Jessica pushed her chair back and rushed over to the window when she heard a helicopter landing on the helipad. "Khalil?" she called.

"My dear, nothing to worry about. The doctor is here to see you. Let's go to your room."

When Jessica turned back from the window, she looked lovingly into Khalil's eyes. "Thank you," she whispered.

"Come." Natasha reached her hand out.

56

MUSHA CAY, FOUR MONTHS LATER

J ake approached Musha Cay in the moonlight. His small boat floated calmly over the clear water. When he neared the island, he slipped the anchor over the side and gently tugged at the rope until it was secured.

Moving steadily to the other side of the boat after he had given his gear a final check, he slipped over the side and swam through the warm waters of the western Atlantic Ocean. Jake, a former Navy SEAL, was no stranger to water. With a set of night-vision goggles, he navigated his way with through the darkness of the night sky. With the moon and stars behind him, his security was the compass he attached tightly to his wrist. He pushed forward, pulling the watertight bag clipped around his waist. When he reached the island, he unclipped the bag and removed his SIG Sauer P226 and a Daniel Winkler knife. Jake checked the gun and then changed out of his wet clothes. Minutes later, he buried his swim gear near a group of palm trees. He covered the spot with palm leaves and used his knife to mark a tree near to the area.

Jake surveyed the island before he journeyed into its interior. His target was the sole property on the island—a Tuscan-styled villa. He moved between trees and the abundant and extravagant vegetation.

Moving along the side of the pool house, his position gave him a strategic advantage. The lighting in the villa was soft and increased visibility to the rooms. Although the windows were open, the villa was eerily quiet. He pulled back the slide on his gun to make sure the weapon was charged and whispered, "This is for you, Alice, and for you, Mom." *Gone but not forgotten.*

Jake had readied himself to creep forward when he caught a glimpse of Jessica. It brought back the memories of their first encounter in New York. *She was fun until …* Now was not the time for a postmortem. All he needed to know was that she gravitated to darkness. He watched until she disappeared. Stepping out from behind the pool house, he moved quickly up to the villa.

As he neared the house, a woman emerged cradling a baby. She stood in the moonlight and appeared to be comforting the child she was holding. Jake ducked and, in a squatted position, moved for cover behind the lushly planted vegetation. He observed the woman as she made her way from the villa and toward the beach. "No!" he said into the warm air. *Jessica and then the woman.* He assumed, based on the intelligence his team had gathered, the woman was Natasha. He entered the house through the wide-open French doors. Halfway through the living room, he noticed a small alcove. The alcove had an upholstered lounger with a duvet thrown over it, a baby crib, and a small table. Jake pulled out his pistol and sat down.

Jessica was in the alcove facing the baby crib. She turned and came to a sudden halt. Jake studied the alarm registered on her face. He raised his gun so it was visible to her. Her demeanor switched from shock to panic as she stared at him.

"Stay where I can see you," he said. Jake fired a round into the alcove behind her to reinforce his point.

"I knew you would come for me."

"You missed your appointment with the Lord God—my bad." Jake stood and stepped toward her.

"I'm sorry. Talk? Yes?" Jessica pleaded, nodding her head. She backed deeper into the alcove. "I didn't intend to ..." Tears flowed from her eyes. "Khalil Junior. My baby. She ... Natasha cut my baby out of me. Natasha's doctor said my baby was in danger and that I needed an urgent C-section."

Jake stared at her bloodstained nightshirt. For a second, his concentration broke. He glanced at the French doors. In the distance, a *whump-whump-whump* emanated from the beach. He recognized it as the thick noise that results from a sound wave created by the repetitive rotary motion of a helicopter blade.

"Jess?" Jessica screamed. "My son. Jess? Help me."

"You rejected judgment by twelve of your peers. Negotiations are not part of my mission parameters." Jake's comportment was dispassionate. "Your meeting with the Almighty is confirmed."

Jessica's facial features contorted.

Jess's yell was a shrill. "Jessica, the table—the gun. Shoot him." The movement of Jessica's hand was swift; she reached over to the table.

Jake felt the metal around his trigger finger grow heavy with the passing seconds; his face turned grim. He drew a breath, and in a blink of an eye, his taut finger yielded with a reverberating *bang*.

Jessica stumbled back and stared down at the red blossoming on her chest before she collapsed.

The deafening thunder of heavy machine-gun fire released itself into house and forced Jake to hit the floor as all around him the walls crumbled and the furniture was chewed up. It stopped momentarily and was replaced by the roar of the helicopter as it moved over the property. Shards of broken glass covered the floor, and seconds later, the back of the villa was the target as the machine gun rampaged.

At a break in the gun's output, Jake rose from the floor, his gun at the ready and approached the shattered frame of the French doors. The ringing in his ears had numbed the sound of the helicopter as it flew away from the property. He observed as it slowed and hovered just above the water. His stomach knotted. *It's headed for the helipad.*

The Mi-28—has no secondary transport capacity, he thought and did a quick calculation. The Mi-28 could carry two to three troops. *Three, work on three men.* He had one spare magazine and had expended two rounds of ammunition. He had to assume the odds were against him. A protracted firefight was out of the question. "Fuck!" he muttered. "The only option is to take them out aboard the helicopter."

As he maneuvered out of the shattered French windows that led down to the helipad, all the lights in the villa blacked out. In that moment, it occurred to him that whoever had planned this job was not necessarily here to hill him. *Were they here to kill Jessica? Jessica or me, they're about to storm the property to make sure the job was finished.*

Jake pulled out his night-vision googles and powered them up. Lying on his stomach, he used his elbows to pull himself forward and made his way back to the vegetation surrounding the villa. Leaving the cover of the vegetation, Jake shot out and ran at speed for the palm trees and the spot where he'd buried his gear.

Jake surveyed his surroundings. His head froze at the dock at the far end of the island. He watched as Natasha, clutching a child in her arms, boarded a speedboat. Minutes later, he heard the roar as she fired the speedboat and cast away from the dock. He muttered, "Whoever was behind the attack was not here for him." He thought about what Jessica had said, "Natasha cut my baby out." *This was about kidnaping the child. Why?* When his thoughts came back to his own reality, the boat had disappeared. "Natasha, I'll get you." *The child? An innocent life but for how long?*

Jake dived beneath the water's surface and swam. He didn't come up for air until his lungs were seared by a burning thirst for oxygen. He arrived at his boat and looked back at the villa in the distance.

57

Persian Gulf, Saadiyat Island, six weeks later

From the back, Khalil's wavy black hair fell above his flushed ears. It was similar to that of the infant he jiggled in his arms in a visibly panicked manner. Inessa wasn't sure who was most fractious, him or the baby. She moved around him and discreetly observed his eyebrows as they lowered and pulled closer together. Inessa looked down when his eyes brimmed with tears and his tightly drawn lips quivered. She thought he was utterly out of his depth. She went forward and offered to take the baby, but he shook his head abruptly, his cheeks wobbling with the jarring action. "I have to be able to cope with him! I must!"

The baby's arms became faster, grasping at the air with increased speed; his shrill cries were only broken by his gasping for breaths in between. The baby's face was blotched, and his little mouth stretched wide. Inessa smiled softly at Khalil in her soothing way and held out her arms.

"Ayree feek, Natasha." He handed over his son and sank to the floor, hiding his face. "She condemned the child to grow up without a mother."

Inessa understood that he had said, "Fuck you, mother." She knew nothing of what had happened. A beautiful blond Russian woman, Inessa had been asked by Valentin to comfort Khalil and take care of the child. She held the child close, bobbing and swaying to unheard music, humming a lullaby, composed and serene. Soon the harsh cries softened to snuffles. *Now, time to help his father.*

The waters of the Persian Gulf were quiet as the Navy SWCC boat approached. Onboard was an eight-man team. Six wet suited men with rebreathers broke the surface of the shark-infested waters. Three swam forward to the bow of the *Anya*, while the remaining three boarded from the stern.

In search of his target, Jake crept quietly into the bowels of the yacht with his M4 at the ready. As he rounded the gallery, he heard a baby crying. Seconds later, the crying stopped. He ducked back as a blond woman emerged from the cabin. Jake glanced over his shoulder and signaled to McGrath that the woman was his capture.

Jake stood in the doorway of the cabin and observed as Khalil was bent over the baby, gently stroking the child's leg with the back of his hand. "Aah."

Khalil spun to see the M4 pointed directly at his forehead. Shock and disbelief were etched on his face, and his hand gripped the edge of the baby's crib. "You have no authority here; these are UAE waters," said Khalil.

Jake tightened its grip on the M4.

"There's no extradition treaty. I suggest you turn around and get off this yacht."

"You're mistaken. I didn't come here to take you back." Jake's eyes pierced Khalil. He saw the fear in the other man's face. His eyelids tensed and pulled up. His stretched mouth was drawn back, exposing his teeth.

Khali's hand let go of the crib and reached under the blanket covering the baby.

Reflectively, Jake squeezed the trigger and sent a blitz of bullets into Khalil's head. Before his body had hit the floor, he accelerated forward and grabbed the screaming baby from its crib. The baby was in his arms when he engaged his mike and spoke. "Tabby down. Mission accomplished."

He disengaged the microphone and looked at his watch while he handed the baby to one of the Navy SEALS who had entered the room. Turning to McGrath, he said, "The Wizard updated the Natasha intel. We can make the morning flight."

Ingram Content Group UK Ltd.
Milton Keynes UK
UKHW042024210723
425591UK00013B/276/J